WELL OF RAGE

A Novel
by
Lynn Hesse

WELL OF RAGE, Copyright 2016, by LYNN HESSE. All rights reserved. Printed in the United States of America. No part of this book may be used or reproduced in any manner whatsoever without written permission except in the case of brief quotations used in critical articles and reviews.

For information, address Oak Tree Press, 1700 Dairy Avenue, #49, Corcoran, CA 93212.

Oak Tree Press books may be purchased for educational, business, or sales promotional purposes. Contact Publisher for quantity discounts.

This is a work of fiction. Names, characters, places and incidents either are the product of the author's imagination or are used fictitiously. Any resemblance to actual persons living or dead, events, or locales is entirely coincidental.

First Edition, September 2016

ISBN: 978-1-61009-249-4
LCCN: 2016952374

For mom and dad, great storytellers, who never stopped imagining a better world and believing in miracles, I thank you for the gift of tenacity.

Acknowledgements

Many people have helped along the way. They read chapters, gave feedback, helped edit, and listened to my writing saga over tea and coffee as I honed my writing craft. To each of them, I thank and hold dear: Evan Guilford-Blake, Eleanor Brownfield, Marie Carrera, Bobbie Christmas, Carla Rabb De Rosa, Lesly Fredman, David Fulmer, Kathy Ellen Herndon, Dean Hesse, Andrew Holmes, and Nancy Knight. I thank Charles D. Brockett and Heather Tosteson, editors of Wising Up Press, for taking a chance and publishing my first short story.

I must acknowledge my debt to the Unitarian Universalist Congregation Women Writers Group, Sisters in Crime, the Village Writers Group, and the Atlanta Writers Club critique group participants, especially the long-standing members: Ken Allen, Lanie Damon, Ruth Gresh, Anthony Miller, Myron Kaufman, Anthony Miller, Cheryl Snapperman, and Jean Woodall. For the Mobile Carnival Museum employees' inspiring stories about Mobile, Alabama, and in memory of Wilbur Silas Pillman Jr.'s guidance, the official Court Jester for Mystic Striper Society in Mobile for over fifty years, I curtsey.

Lastly, to my sisters and brothers in blue who risk their lives to protect and serve, and to the brave risk takers and social activists in the Atlanta and Decatur, Georgia art communities, where I replenish my creativity, I give my sincere gratitude.

Prologue

March 15, 2000

The day in Mobile began as usual with a cool breeze wafting from the Gulf, but grew darker and oppressively muggy with each passing early morning hour. Edwardo met Horacio, his bilingual supervisor, at the corner near the Mexican restaurant across from the apartment complex, where Edwardo lived with nine others without papers. He worried a lot about not having a green card, the gringo police, and being cheated and robbed. The uncertainties hung on his shoulders like a yoke, waking and sleeping, but earning enough cash bothered him more. If it stormed today, the construction work might be canceled. A rained-out day meant less money to send home to his mother and sister.

Arriving at the construction site, Edwardo was given the job to bushwhack the land. The morning passed. As he came closer to the abandoned well site on the old Deeter farm, he stopped the bushhog mower to drink water. With the sun straight above his head, he saw a large wooden object with rusty metal hinges that turned out to be part of the rotten well lid lying in the grass blocking his way. As he picked up the cover, he was drawn to look down the well.

He remembered the old village grandmother's tale about the water goddess and elfin-like creatures that punished bad boys and girls if they didn't obey their parents. Through the dry Mexican winds the nocturnal spirits called to little children who disobeyed their elders and lured them into wells and lakes with a promise of adventure. They grabbed the innocent boys and girls and threw them into the bottomless underworld silencing their screams by taking away their voices and leaving them floating with their mouths open in silent boggy graves. The parents never suspected where their children were hidden until it was too late. The children simply vanished without a trace, but sometimes, human bones were found lying on top of black cold water that was taken from a well. When Edwardo was ten years old his closest amigo disappeared, and in his boyish imagination he always thought the water gods or devils took his friend.

As Edwardo peered down the well, he heard Horacio call out for a lunch break. The sunlight bounced off something blood red about ten feet down one side of the white lime walls. The well seemed to hold the blood gem of passion. Calling to his cousin to bring a pike pole, Edwardo used the hook on the end of the pole and a standup dustpan tied to a rake to lift out the object encased in a chuck of limestone. It was a ring with many letters, numbers, and a ruby in the center. Edwardo's cousin said in broken English, "It's a school ring from 1974. See. It belonged to a *hombre desfortunado*. He's probably dead." He shrugged, looking inside the well. "Look here." He pointed at the inscription on the underneath side of the ring. "This ring tells me TWW died too young."

Edwardo grew sad as he thought of returning to Mexico empty-handed while knowing the earthbound spirit of this dead man, not water gods, had lead him to the well, and expected his wishes to be followed. The men slowly cranked the rusty handle causing the rotting rope to twine around the well shaft and forcing its secrets into the light of day. If the bucket held bones, Edwardo would honor the dead, give the ring to

Horacio, and leave tonight for Mexico. Yes. A knucklebone surfaced from the dank water and seemed to whisper that the gringo police were coming.

Chapter 1

March 1, 2000

Considering the machinery he was about to put in motion, Billie Ray Cofer smiled as he drove his Dodge Ram through the last few blocks of Mobile's exclusive Spring Hill neighborhood, and then crossed under I-65. It felt good to be headed for the bay–not only to smell the salt air, but also to complete some long overdue business.

The cab windows were down and the air seemed heavier as mansions and private schools ended near the underpass giving way to shabby service stations and half-empty strip malls. His father, Robert Kendall Cofer, called this section "nigger kindling wood" and swore many times—when he was drunk—to burn it down and destroy every last jigaboo living between the interstate and North Broad Street, but he didn't. The white landlord was one of his poker buddies.

Daddy KC, as the family called him, wasn't a subtle man when he was alive. He was a card-carrying racist and partial to a torch, a rope, or a shotgun. But he was sly enough never to admit he'd been one of the instigators in the South's last known lynching. As their last hoorah, two Klan members had tortured and hanged Michael Donald on Herndon Avenue downtown in 1981; then the KKK essentially went belly up after Donald's mother sued and won.

You were one crude SOB, Daddy. The middle-aged raconteur shook his head at the thought of his father's exploits that helped to bury the Klan.

Billie Ray liked to think of himself as a thinking-man's racist, and he was glad the older generation was dead and gone or pulling portable oxygen tanks behind them while playing golf. The militia had replaced the Klan, and Billie Ray was proud to say he had spearheaded its metamorphosis in Alabama.

He kept driving on Old Shell Road and saw some boarded-up buildings as he neared downtown and crossed Herndon Avenue. *It was a damn shame to see his city deteriorate, but that's what happens when low-lifes buy businesses, and then run them into the ground.* Stupid-ass urban renewable projects. Only his people working in small groups could turn this place around.

At least Cathedral Square still held its southern charm. He always thought of the park as the central hub of town because the Basilica of Immaculate Conception, the *Tribune* newspaper building, and Heroes Bar and Grill surrounded the park along with the abandoned movie theater and the Peanut Shop—still in operation after sixty years—further down on Dauphin Street. Billie Ray loved the smell of fresh roasted peanuts, especially when it wafted from the shop to the park.

He waved to Marvin Stillwell, who was puttering through the park in his electric wheelchair. Marvin, a disabled Desert Storm veteran, lived in the government-subsidized high-rise building adjacent to the park. Billie Ray held him—as he did all veterans—in high esteem, but the modern Section Eight building was an eyesore and stuck in his craw. He was working on a new zoning code with the housing authority to eliminate the monstrosity.

As he turned on to Government Street, a man reading a map stepped off the curb. Billie Ray swerved and said, "Damn, tourist."

The downtown hotels and restaurants were full of liberal girly-men. The last thing Billie Ray and his compatriots needed were busybodies going through their museums and shaking their heads along with their hairy-armpitted women, then judging the southern culture. Sure, they brought millions into the local economy during Mardi Gras, but afterward they needed to get the hell out of town.

He laughed at what his friend Adam Hall called the "disease of Yankeeology," and wondered if any politician truly gave a rat's ass about America. Hell, even Ronald Reagan couldn't go back and save California from sliding down the proverbial shithole after decades of democratic governors. If the donkeys were left alone, there's no telling what this world would be like when his grandson, Hudson, grew up.

Thank God for the militia comprised of men who meant to reclaim control for the sake of their country, their families, and their race. This was a battle they could not afford to lose.

Government Street ended and he passed through the Bankhead Tunnel—an ugly, yellow-tiled monstrosity that reminded Billie Ray of a gymnasium shower—and came out on to Highway 98. He would see the Gulf soon. Billie Ray wanted nothing better to do than to go fishing, let the boat float on the water and let life settle.

But first he needed to talk to Derrick Grey.

A mild breeze still lingered from the morning and played with the hair on Billie Ray's arms. So focused was he on the upcoming meeting that he lost the opportunity to appreciate the Gulf running parallel to the highway. Damn ironic, he told himself, as he zeroed in on the land and wondered how the details of life made you miss its beauty, and lulled you in to believing you had time.

After signing in at the guard shack, Billie Ray circled the parking lot and stopped in front of the Korean War Memorial. He watched people cross the Victory Bridge, a walkway designed to resemble the Namji-ri Bridge, which spanned the Nam River, a site held for five days in September of 1950 by American forces. Most of tourists walked through the World War memorials without taking off their hats, others allowed their children to play around the life-size sculpture of a Vietnam soldier and the granite wall inscribed with the names of men and women who made the ultimate sacrifice.

Billie Ray's father had been in the Korean War, but he never spoke about it. After his father died, Billie Ray found the Purple Heart in a drawer. He had it mounted in a shadow box and liked to look at it while he had his morning coffee. It made him proud to be a Cofer—it was a constant reminder that duty and honor required dedication.

He would not fail the militia or his dad.

Putting the truck in reverse, he heard the radio give the bad news that the Tide basketball team had lost again. To South Carolina's Gamecocks no less. Wimp's shooting guard, Schea Cotton, needed his black ears clipped.

Best to be on a winning team, damn it, and that's what he was going to offer Derrick Grey—the opportunity to be Mobile's next mayor, to be in the arena with the big white dogs. The way Billie Ray viewed things the Holy Trinity didn't hold a candle to the visceral power of sports, money, or sex.

Money was a motivator. When rumors had indicated Derrick was strapped for cash, Billie Ray had made one phone call and had confirmed Derrick's second mortgage application at one of the banks. Everyone knew Billie Ray and his band of like-minded compatriots carried a lot of weight in Mobile, including Derrick, but the school superintendent couldn't have an inkling he was the Brotherhood's hand-picked candidate. The Victory Bridge-priority mission terms just needed to be clarified.

* * *

Once inside the Battleship Café, Billie Ray patted his stomach, and the gold letter N engraved on his ruby ring caught the light, as if signaling the intention of his arrival. The letter stood for never let white power die. Spotting his quarry, he said, "Hey, Derrick, how the hell are you?"

"Hello, Mr. Cofer. I haven't seen you in a while. Have a seat." Derrick pointed to a chair. "This must really be important because this place is certainly out of your way."

"Naw—just under ten miles from town." Billie flicked a crumb off the table with his pinkie. "I heard you threw your hat in the mayor's ring."

Derrick nodded. "Yes, I'm glad you—"

"My, my, you're coming right on up in the world from the little boy I once knew." Billie Ray pushed up his "Grandpa Rules" baseball cap, exposing a pink crease left by the rim and settled in his chair. "Damn boyee, didn't you usta wear braces and date Joe Morrison's daughter in high school. Or college?"

Billie Ray watched Derrick split his roll choosing to ignore the mention of Sue Lynn, who had been devastated when he broke their engagement and eventually married Rose.

"That was a long time ago," Derrick said, holding Cofer's steady gaze and smiling.

"What you eating there, son? Looks mighty good. Gloria won't let me eat pork chops and gravy without bitching about my high blood pressure. Truly ruins a good meal. Indigestion sets in before I leave the table."

Derrick nodded his condolences. "So why are we here? I know it wasn't because you craved to dine on so-so tourist food. I use the bay as my getaway from the calls of parents and board members, but you have the Strikers Club, or the lodge."

Billie Ray looked out the window and saw the docked USS *Alabama* and an A-12 Blackbird spy plane on display—heaven for a man like him who collected big toys. "The Mystic Societies are all right," he said, "but I have more serious fish to fry."

Derrick buttered a roll. "You want a cup of coffee or a cola?"

"That's okay. I guess I need to get down to business. I want to ask you how your campaign's going." He watched Derrick cut into a pork chop before continuing. "You know the guys at Calpes want you to win this election. We think your opponent's an idiot."

Derrick laughed, which caused a piece of pork to lodge in his throat.

Billie Ray stood up and slapped him on the back, talking over Derrick's coughing. "We think you have a level head on your shoulders…understand how to get things done."

Derrick wiped his mouth with his napkin, and then replied, "Thanks. I appreciate your confidence in me, but it will take more than your cronies at the billiard parlor." He looked up at Billie Ray and smothered a belch with the back of his hand. "Anyhow, I hope I can help the city grow in a positive direction."

Billie Ray leaned forward. "Which positive direction we talking about, son?"

"Southern point of view, of course."

As Billie Ray sat, he said, "There you go. It's no secret I'm not crazy about some folk. As my granddad used to say, 'An uppity nigger's only good for causing trouble.' Get my drift?"

"Yes, but please keep your voice down." Derrick put down his fork. "The days are gone…even out here somebody might be listening."

Derrick looked around. Only a Hispanic maintenance guy poked at a paper cup and dropped it in a plastic bag.

Billie Ray shrugged and said, "Hell, there ain't nobody can understand English within a five-mile radius, but you and me."

Derrick finished his tea. "Don't get me wrong. I'm glad you're here, Billie Ray. I could use your help."

One corner of Cofer's mouth tilted and a throaty chuckle lingered as he leaned back in his chair and interlaced his fingers over his stomach. "Oh, so now I'm Billie Ray. Changed the subject and got to your point all in one breath. Damn, you're good. You're smart. How much you need?"

Derrick leaned on his elbows. "Honestly, I need enough to win without dipping into my sons' college fund. Money will help, but I know I'll also need your clout with some majority party members. For instance, Gerald Compton has a bruised ego over the district's affirmative action hiring policy of teachers. I couldn't help that one. Federal regulations."

"Yep, I can understand that one." He kept nodding as if in deep contemplation before he added, "You understand there's no turning back, right?"

Derrick didn't hesitate. "No problem," he said. "I want this."

Billie Ray twirled his pinkie ring and tapped it on the table before he shook hands. "Get your face out there some. Smile. We'll make it happen behind the scenes."

* * *

Derrick reviewed the conversation with Cofer as he rode home that evening. His married-man barometer—not his conscience—told him that his wife wouldn't be pleased about Billie Ray, but Rose wouldn't need to know. After all Derrick had skirted a second mortgage and had partially bankrolled his campaign. It was a twofer: a win-win situation on the homefront and for his political career.

Derrick relived the no-bullshit handshake before Billie Ray had left. It was a sealed deal. Both men knew the unspoken terms. Securing the election meant the militia constituency and Billie Ray expected Derrick's compliance with any of their future requests.

The contract was nonnegotiable, more binding than any marriage—"Until death do us part."

Chapter 2

Carly Remund needed a break from thinking about her upcoming field training at the Warner County Police Department. According to the an article in the *Tribune*, it had taken twenty years for the first woman captain to be promoted in the department in February of this year. This news made Carly wonder how difficult it would be for her to make rank, but she pushed such dreary thoughts from her mind. Entering the park at Cathedral Square, she focused on the odors of salt and seaweed wafting down Dauphin Street, and her spirits lifted. The buzz of lighthearted conversation drifted out into the park from the doorway of Heroes Bar and Grill. Although she planned on eating lunch at a local B & B, smells of frying beef and potatoes lured her closer to her favorite comfort foods inside Heroes. She watched the sundry crowd inside and browsed the posted menu in the display case. The family-friendly dining atmosphere appealed to her.

Carly noticed the building across the street with a faded Calpes sign wasn't renovated and looked abandoned until she saw someone moving around in the shadows. When she stepped off the curb to investigate, a linebacker-size guy, dressed in holey sweats, plowed into her and spun her around. Blindsided, she stepped back with an expletive.

"Sorry, lady," he said. "I'm an ox."

Carly barely looked at the fellow. "Right," she said, as she sprinted toward Calpes storefront windows. As if the bump from the encounter with the stranger had jogged a peg in a hole, she had realized every restaurant and billiard parlor on the street was packed except this joint. Walking closer, she peered through the glass storefront spying ancient billiard tables and some old white geezers with their backs to the door. Smoke filled the air surrounding the U-shaped bar and several wooden 1950s style tables and chairs. Curious, she strolled by the rundown place a couple of times and imagined if she opened the door and broke the no-female taboo that the reception would be cold stares. On her last pass, a tiny guy with thick glasses behind the bar said something to the laughing men and lumbered to the entryway and shut the blinds.

Being excluded or the brunt of the joke wasn't a new experience for the police recruit, being one of three females out of a class of thirty males, but these men gave Carly the creeps.

Obviously, the locals knew to stay out. She envisioned hooded robes hidden underneath the bar counter. Was this the place for the men whose fathers and grandfathers wielded power in the Ku Klux Klan?

Carly wondered if Harold, her downstairs neighbor, knew these men. No doubt, even in the beginning of the twenty-first century, old, white money in Mobile still discreetly elected the proper candidate who could be bought and sold.

* * *

So far this year was like the rest for Mary Williams, waiting for the white authorities to catch her son's killer. The teenager had vanished twenty-six years ago and his body was never found. The grieving mother shoved open the window and pounded the sill, releasing a loud moan. A stabbing pain raced across Mary's chest. "God help me," she said, kissing an image of her son, who had been frozen in time with the keys to his first car suspended in the air when the shutter clicked.

"Let this be the year you're returned to me. Each day, not just your birthday, I will make them remember your face, Terence—your name. I promise."

She rubbed between her pelvic bones marking where Terence's fetus was cradled so many years ago. Without her son, a dark void pulled at her soul. Most days, keeping the emptiness at bay took all her strength. Breaking her reverie, Chef Cato knocked on the door calling Mary's name. He paused for a moment, and then added, "Mrs. Williams, I know you asked for few minutes alone, but people are arriving for the noon buffet to honor Terence's birthday."

* * *

Outside Mary's house, the March winds whipped at Carly's curly hair and olive green T-shirt. The budded branches swished in a nearby maple as she crossed Francis Street and stepped in front of The Painted Lady, a Victorian mansion turned into a bed and breakfast. She had heard the B & B had the best brunch in town because Mary Williams operated the place with finesse. Since it was almost noon, she decided to venture inside, but a howling sound stopped her. Maybe it was the wind playing tricks on her, but she could have sworn she heard a cry coming from the second story. Cocking her head, she closed her eyes and concentrated. Nothing. She mumbled to herself, "It's probably my imagination," as she surveyed the area making sure she was alone. "I wouldn't want the patrol guys to see me poking around here because I heard a crazy sound. No harm in checking out the backyard. Right, Aunt Linda?"

When Carly felt stressed, she spoke, though not usually out loud, to her benefactor, as if she were there for counsel. Counting to eight, repetitively, until her mind cleared, was another option that worked.

Passing a willow tree, she spotted a meditation garden with an ivied archway in the backyard. To Carly it seemed the tree stood guard over the path to the garden. A bright-colored cardinal flicked its wings and dipped its beak in a birdbath eyeing the interloper. "Just passing through," Carly said, as she noticed the small parking lot in the rear of the location was full. She theorized a rambunctious guest probably had made the earlier noise.

The smell of greens and homemade bread made Carly's mouth water. On an impulse she knocked on the back door and entered a hallway off the kitchen.

A stunning black woman seemed to be giving last-minute instructions to a man wearing a chef's hat. She looked up at Carly and smiled. Mary Williams, the owner of The Painted Lady, asked Carly if she had a reservation.

"No. I'm afraid I don't. But I've heard your brunch is terrific."

Mary nodded and her blue silk blouse shimmered against her mahogany skin. "Of course, please stay, Miss…?"

"Carly Redmund."

Mary welcomed Carly and escorted her toward the main dining room where the background chatter of the guests beckoned. Carly estimated Mary to be six feet without her heels. Being five feet and nine inches, Carly appreciated statuesque women. When her hostess started to excuse herself, Carly stopped her. "By the way, did you hear a sound like a scream about ten minutes ago?"

Mary's eyes narrowed measuring her guest. "No. All is well." Fingering her pearl necklace, she smiled. "You know Chef Cato can handle the finishing touches without me. Let's go sit down."

She ushered Carly into the dining room, where a crystal chandelier caught the afternoon light like a prism. "We should join the others," Mary said, but Carly didn't move. She admired the white lace tablecloths and vases of pink roses decorating each of the tables.

Mary continued, "You can see a few house guests and locals have dropped by for our gourmet brunch. They're a hungry, impatient bunch." She touched Carly's shoulder. "Would you like a tour of the inn after we eat?"

"Thank you. I'd like that." Carly counted about twenty people milling around the tables as Mary nodded a hello to a patron across the room.

As if on cue, the wiry man dressed in a chef's hat materialized and seated Mary. She thanked him and took her place at the head of the table. While a waiter began serving, the chef announced the menu—asparagus, baked pears and chilled poached grouper with white wine.

The room was filled with a diverse mixture of adults and children, dressed as if attending an international conference for the artistic and chic. One woman wore a red and gold sari, and another couple wore matching African prints of royal blue and mustard yellow.

"I'm not dressed appropriately," Carly said.

"Nonsense," Mary insisted, "all of this is for you and my other guests." She swept her hands toward the deep velvet curtains and the glistening purple glassware. "I want people to be comfortable. Come."

Carly walked toward the fireplace and caught sight of the Steinway near the window. "Do you play?" Carly asked her hostess.

"Yes, a little."

"My mother plays," Carly said turning. "Whoa, is the fireplace cast iron?"

Interlacing her fingers, Mary said, "Yes, I think the black against the white tile inserts ground the room."

Carly couldn't help gushing. "I can't get over how elegant your home is."

Mary flashed a smile over her shoulder at Carly. "She is a beautiful old lady."

"That's an understatement."

Mary swept the top of the chair. "Dear, sit down and tell me about yourself. By the way, Madeline Teasler, a board member of the ACLU, is to your left, and George Paulk, the man across from you, is an aging charmer with questionable skills. Beware." Everyone laughed and greeted Carly.

She told Mary and the other guests about moving from Charleston to Mobile and described the mishaps of furnishing her loft, and then the conversation between Mary and Carly became more intimate. Monopolizing her hostess, Carly mentioned the police academy and every pent-up emotion about the experience came pouring out. Mary listened without interruption, and Carly ended with a war story about the boxing matches held the last day of the academy, dubbed 'fight day' by the instructors.

"In the final practical exercise, Sergeant Dillion or "Testosterone Man," as I called him, had his last chance to try and wash me out. I was determined to win. The sergeant disliked me. I'm guessing because I scored the highest academically. Anyway, the sarge whispered last-minute advice to my male sparring partner, and then during the fight, my challenger used an unauthorized chokehold on me. I knew blood restriction to the brain would make me pass out. The incident was meant to embarrass me...scare me, but my survival instinct kicked in. With blind luck, I landed a backward palm jab that connected with the other recruit's nose, stunned him, and gave me time to flip and pin him to the mat. The match was called, but I think the adrenaline got to my opponent. He grabbed at my legs as I stepped away. I landed on top of an ankle."

Carly pushed her unruly hair away from her forehead as she said, "'Everything is fair in love and the macho playing field, Missy Beaucoup,' as my Aunt Linda would say. I flattened that guy. It cost me a bruised ankle and hand, but so what?"

"I see you're very brave. It's better that you don't fully understand what you're up against...living in Mobile. The isms of life, here, require patience and strength." For an instant sadness morphed Mary's ageless face into a tired woman in her sixties. "Please excuse my tendency for philosophic ramblings." She cupped Carly's elbow and said, "Not a matter for today, Artemis. We will talk later while touring the mansion. Have another glass of wine, my young warrior."

* * *

Officer J.C. Grey ducked into the Central Precinct men's room wondering what was happening. The captain had jumped the chain of command and called him in to the precinct; it meant big trouble or a big favor. As he came out of the restroom, J.C. passed a beat officer talking on the telephone. He pointed at Grey, mimicked a hangman's noose and stuck his tongue out the side of his mouth.

The administration officer poked his head out of the break room and nodded toward the carpeted partitions. "Grey, you're wanted in the captain's office."

"What gives, Joel? Where are my sergeant and lieutenant and the frick'n chain of command procedure?"

The admin officer pushed his glasses up on his nose and shrugged.

As a veteran officer with more years of service than Joel, J.C. said, "Okay, never mind, dickhead. I'm going."

While trying to end a conversation on the phone with an irate citizen, Captain Forrester motioned J.C. inside the cubicle that substituted for an office. The captain responded to the citizen on the phone, "Yes, Ma'am, I assure you the officers do patrol your neighborhood in Spring Hill, but—" He listened shaking his head before interjecting, "I've been trying to explain, you've called the wrong precinct. I'll contact the captain in the precinct covering your neighborhood and have him call you. Yes. Today." He dropped the phone in the cradle.

"She hung up on me. Can you believe the bullshit, Grey?"

"No, Sir."

Looking up at J.C., the captain said, "Lady told me she pays my salary with her taxes yada, yada."

The twenty-two-year veteran of the department stood at parade rest with his uniform and face respectively worn and weary. He had heard it all. There was no need to reply.

"Officer Grey," said Forrester as his starched sleeve patch crackled, stretching across his bicep, "we—the Major and I—have been reviewing your precinct file this morning. It's impressive: five commendations in the last three months."

"Thank you, Sir." J.C. noticed he wasn't asked to sit down. He shifted the gun belt cutting into his ribs and refused to give in to the urge to brush off the front of his faded shirt.

"I want to recommend you for a Field Training Officer position. We need good FTOs."

There it was: the favor coupled with a little namedropping. Hell, both the major and Forrester knew J.C. didn't want a so-called promotion to FTO.

"We need a seasoned veteran to train a specific recruit. This will require someone with discretion because this could be a sensitive situation. As you know, there's no pay increase for field training officers. But the detective division, huh, the Criminal Investigation Division supervisors consider these types of voluntary assignments when they're reviewing applications. I would approve any request for transfer that came my way."

J.C. forced back a smile, knowing the captain was blowing smoke up his stuck-in-patrol ass. He had pissed off the wrong precinct commander as a rookie and his opportunities to go to the CID had been and were a long-gone ambition, but he kept his face blank. They both knew he had no choice.

"Sir, I understand the new academy class is coming out in a few days. Who do you want me to train?"

"A female recruit," Forrester said, opening a file. "Her name's Carly Redmund."

J.C. shifted his feet to a wider stance and waited while Forrester killed time moving a paperweight to the corner of his desk.

"She's smart, this Redmund," Forrester said. "Has a degree from Duke. The problem: she gave Sergeant Dillon hell." The captain frowned and looked at the paper on his desk. "No street experience. No military or family in law enforcement. Not a good beginning."

The captain swept his thick comb-over back into place. J.C. thought the hairdo made the captain resemble a Yorkie dog with a crooked crown.

Forrester continued, "I just hope she doesn't get herself or a fellow officer hurt before she understands what's necessary out there. Can you work with me on this?"

J.C. held Forrester's gaze for a moment before he answered. "Sir. I'm not thrilled about the idea of training a woman, let alone one who's considered a problem. But I'll do my best."

Forrester smiled. "Hell, I knew you were a team player. We'll take care of you somewhere down the line."

The captain swiveled in his chair toward his computer giving J.C. the impression he was dismissed. He started to leave, but the captain continued, "Of course, should the recruit fail to measure up to Police Officer Standard Training, we would be forced to terminate her."

J.C. almost laughed at Forrester's habit of qualifying police acronyms, but caught himself. The veteran nodded. "Yes, Sir. You'll need documentation for POST. I understand, but before I go level with me? What aren't you saying?"

"She doesn't understand there's no I in the word team. Just a couple of years as a campus cop. Can you believe that? She's a libber for sure." The captain eyes darted sideways at his full inbox.

J.C. decided to venture asking one more question. "Sir, is she a dyke?"

"No, don't think so, but it would be less trouble if she was. Just watch your back. I wouldn't trust her in a tight corner." The captain preened his mustache before closing the file. "We'll see if her high-class education helps her when some puke is kicking her brains out."

J.C. exited the captain's cubicle with his mind racing. If the brass in the hierarchy were right, J.C. would have to deal with a woman nobody liked, and of course, his wife, Noreen, would pitch a fit about a woman partner riding twelve hours a night in his patrol car. God, he hoped Redmund was dirt ugly. He already hated her guts. He popped his neck trying to work out the kinks and thought about his brother. Taking out his cellphone, J.C. flipped it open, and then shut it as he unlocked the Crown Vic, stepped in, and cleared his computer. His brother, Derrick, was busy these days.

Chapter 3

Before J.C. could put the patrol car in reverse, a message popped up on the computer screen mounted on his central console from his buddy, Don Thomas, who was already busting his chops about Redmund. His message read: "I heard the new recruit is a knock-out. You lucky dog."

J.C. wrote back, "Meet at Subway, Highway 10 & Government in an hour." Sometimes radio spot checked for unauthorized personal conversations on the terminals and sent a hard copy to the lieutenants for review. When that happened, some officer always paid. Ten years ago, J.C. had sent such a message via his computer, sharing his disgust with a fellow officer about a lazy sergeant who hadn't bothered to show up on a double homicide scene. At Christmas time with money already short, the sergeant had suspended him for three days without pay. Now that particular sergeant was the assistant chief.

J.C. parked in the middle of the unused portion of the Subway parking lot and ran several plates until Thomas showed. Thomas pulled his new Chrysler unit alongside J.C.'s raggedy one so close that the vehicles' driver-side mirrors kissed.

J.C. watched the heat rays radiating from his car hood, and then said, "You know these cars go twenty-four seven, about all this one's good for is burning a perpetrator when ya slap him up against the hood."

Thomas lifted an eyebrow. "No kidding. I'm crying for the misunderstood scumbags I arrest every day. I bet your motor pool reject is gonna sit under a shade tree most of your shift."

"Yeah, you know it." J.C. said, starting to work on an accident report with his clipboard propped against the steering wheel. "Today, I couldn't deal with the hassle over who gets what car to drive."

"Did you see I nearly decked Cantrel in the bullpen for trying to grab a new vehicle?" Thomas grunted. "What's up with these rookies?" he said, laying a forearm on the edge of his open window while the air conditioner, on full blast, gushed cold air into the parking lot.

"Different breed. Veterans should pick first, but if you don't want to stand around with your finger up your ass, wait on a car to come in when calls are pending, you take a piece of shit."

Thomas cleared his throat loud enough to drown out their idling engines and radio assigning calls. "But the more interesting thing is...." He grinned.

"What?" J.C. said, exhaling smoke from his cigarette.

"Nothing, except, you get to ride with a chick that'll keep your dick hard all shift."

"She can't be that good looking." Using a triangle, he flipped the square angle and finished drawing a diagram on the back of the report. "Anyway, I was told she has an attitude problem. A feminist."

"Yeah. I heard she got furious when they took away her whip."

The laughter faded into awkward silence as Thomas lit a cigarette, while J.C. flipped his cigarette butt out the window. "I don't know, man," he said. "This assignment sucks."

A beep sounded from J.C.'s center console computer. "Wait. Just got a message on my screen from Boyd. He says she did her campus cop thing in Charleston before moving here. Great, huh?"

Thomas scratched the top of his shaved head as he said, "A wanna-be cop trying to make the grade in the real world. Her chances are slim to none. Where'd Boyd get his information?"

"Who knows? I think his family is from Charleston." J.C. put the report away in his territory folder, and then folded his arms. "This whole thing could cause problems at home, but it's not like I have a choice."

"I suggest you introduce Noreen real quick to Miss Cutesy Pie, and let the wife set the record straight herself."

J.C. agreed, and then both men stared in silence out their front windshields. A domestic violence call was assigned to an officer two territories north of their location. They listened until backup was assigned.

J.C. gripped the steering wheel before he said, "A heads-up. Got a call over at Lukin Hall's place on Sycamore last night. Wife had some scratches. I strongly suggested he leave for a while."

Thomas nodded. "Yeah. There's a no-win situation. How many times we been over there in the last six months?"

"Too many. Lukin's an asshole, a fuckin' hothead in high school and hasn't changed a bit." He scanned the storefronts in the direction of a pawnshop. "I really hate domestics."

"Can't win crawling into a husband and wife's business. Fuck arresting the guy. Half the time the wife's beating on your back, yelling for you to let the guy go before you get the husband inside the unit and take off." Thomas rubbed his chin. "Anyway, isn't Lukin's uncle one of the chief's fishing buddies?"

"Yep, Adam Hall is also Billie Ray Cofer's amigo." The men exchanged a knowing look before J.C. added, "Both militia hardliners. But I know how to CYA. I called the uncle ASAP. He should talk to numbnuts and calm him down. Anyway, enough said."

J.C. typed a message and hit the send button as he added, "The brass and their friends gripe my ass." He tugged at the bottom of his bulletproof vest and pulled it down from his armpits. "Boy, it's hot. Let's go get some grub at Trucker Café before all hell breaks loose from the lunch crowd playing bumper cars in the intersections."

J.C. watched Thomas pull himself forward over the steering wheel, letting the cold air from the air conditioner vents stream down his chest between his vest and his sweaty T-shirt.

Shifting the heap into drive and hitting the brakes hard, J.C. said, "Thomas, you hear Fenn on I-65 asking for an ETA on the Department of Transportation?"

"Yeah, third time. DOT knows units have been out there for over three hours working traffic. Roofing tiles and body parts everywhere." Thomas continued. "You'd think civilians could learn to drive without killing each other. Working traffic around a fatality is the worst job in the department, and that's saying something."

"You could always kiss ass and get a desk job."

"Not likely. No suit and tie for me. I will stay buff and beautiful." He stuck his head out the window as he said, "Don't hate me 'cause I'm beautiful." Before J.C. could drive away, Thomas added, "By the way, I bet Redmund has long-ass legs. You're gonna likey big time. Noreen gonna make your life a living hell."

* * *

"Momma, I brought you something."

Little Terence had come into Mary's bedroom, a grin plastered from ear to ear on his impish face. Swinging an arm from behind his back, he presented a hand filled with invisible flowers.

"It's pretend for now, but someday they'll be for real. When I get a job and have money, I'll take good care of you. I promise."

The boy held the flowers forward as Mary pretended to smell the bouquet.

Thankful that her dead husband's blood ran through her son's veins, she studied the nine-year-old face. "Such beautiful irises you've given me," she said. "Purple ones, too. My favorite."

She took hold of the flowers and added, "Thank you, my sweet little man."

Terence glowed with happiness as Mary wrapped her arms around her son and held him fast. "I'll be sure to get well soon," she said. "I love you. You're the best part of my world."

Mary released him with a light squeeze, and settled back into the pillows. She watched him dart from the room, and then blessed the air behind him, her world balanced and whole.

But no more. Mary's daydream ended with a bird tweeting outside the open window. How could there be contentment? Even seeing her daughter, Evie, earn her doctorate in English literature and teach at Harvard gave Mary little joy. She set her jaw before she moved away from the window. Terence would have been forty-three years old today and probably a retired professional athlete. Now, the upcoming graduating class at Robert E. Lee High School passed a trophy case void of Terence's name, and at the 1974 high school class

WELL OF RAGE

reunions, he was referred to as "that first black football player," who disappeared without a trace. Mary held on to her rage as she turned the pages of her scrapbook full of Terence's life mementos. When his bones were finally found, the ones responsible would pay. They would acknowledge her son.

* * *

Carly bounded up the stairs to her loft apartment and stuck the key in the lock when her downstairs neighbor shouted from the corner of the building.

"Hello, Carly. May I speak with you?" Harold said.

"Hi, there." She waved at him. "Yes, but I'm in a hurry. It's my first day at the precinct." The keys on the ring dangled from the lock making a clinking noise. "I just took a quick run before the big day."

Harold Decker, the retired song-and-dance man turned museum guide, gingerly climbed the stairs, clutching at the railing. "Yes, I remember. I'll be brief. I need a favor. Can you check on Rickey this weekend? I'm going to Chicago to see my sister." He gasped and leaned his rotund body on the stair railing.

"Absolutely, Rickey and I are tight. Give us some playtime. Leave the dog food out where I can see it. Okay? Should I walk him?"

"Yes, thank you. Once a day will do. If I survive my trip into Yankee territory, I'll repay your kindness. Say, a fine dining experience when I return. We can finish our discussion about my vaudeville days over a bottle of Chianti."

"Sounds good. I won't turn down one of your delicious meals. It's a date."

Harold's pale face reddened as he brushed her comment aside. "One of these days," he handed her a key, "some young Don Juan is going to snatch you away from me."

He blew her a kiss. "But until that dreadful day, I am—"

"My main man. You suave thing." Carly touched her chest over her heart.

He turned and executed a beauty queen wave, "Au revoir."

Harold and his food were in the top ten best things that had happened in the last four months since Carly's arrival in December. Thinking about her neighbor's Spanish potato omelet made her mouth water.

In the loft entryway, Carly dropped her keys in a tiny Oriental bowl with carved dragon handles, a recent flea market find. She pulled off her running shoes and placed them under the table. Ready for her first day of patrolling the streets with a training officer, Carly felt strong and fit. Today started her new life.

She showered and towel-dried her shoulder-length hair, and then twisted it in a bun; part of her plan to minimize her sexual appeal along with a plain gold band on her left hand to dissuade advances. She meant to keep her personal life separate from work. She kissed her Duke University ring for luck and laid out her uniform, already ironed, with the shiny insignia in place.

Walking barefoot down the hallway to the kitchen, she admired the open feel of the loft. The bookcases with her treasured books blocked off her sleeping area from the kitchen and provided all the privacy she needed. Books were almost holy objects, safe havens of knowledge. Secondhand copies of *The Inferno* and *The Republic of Plato* sat next to T.S. Eliot's poems, Toni Morrison's *Jazz*, and a book of Mark Twain's short stories. This was home.

As she finished a banana and dropped the peel in the trash, the radio alarm clock went off in her bedroom, her signal that it was noon, time to get dressed. She wanted to be early for roll call. Since she would be a probationary employee for six months, small things mattered.

From the bedside radio came the local news reporter interviewing the democratic mayoral candidate, who kept repeating in a southern drawl almost the same answer to each sequential question, "My opponent, Derrick Grey, The Superintendent of Schools, has no experience in state government unless you count the PTA."

Carly hit the radio off button.

Picking up her belt, she smiled, reliving the encounter with the surly supply officer. He had thrown the belt on the counter, had leaned in with his onion breath toward Carly, and had said; "Searched for three days to find a goddamn Sam Browne small enough." He glared at her. As Carly walked away, the officer added, "Special-ordered shit wastes my time, rookie. You got that?"

Not ordering female uniforms and equipment was just another way of saying that females didn't belong and weren't expected to stay. Thinking how the women in her family tended to be stubborn, Carly buckled the belt and pushed the holster and handcuff case in place around her waist. With these simple movements, she committed herself to a career in law enforcement.

"It will work," she said. She knew no matter what she wouldn't quit. Leaving would be on her terms.

Saving her place in a book about the KKK lying open atop the bed, she placed it on the end table. The old white guys at Calpes had made her interested enough to do a little research.

The phone rang as she flipped the deadbolt open on the front door, and she heard her aunt leave a message. "Carly, this is Aunt Linda. How's my policewoman today? You're going to knock 'em dead. I mean...you know what I mean. You're a winner. Remember, Missy Beaucoup, they're lucky to have you. Lizzie, says she loves you."

Carly hadn't answered the phone because she'd felt some first-day butterflies in her stomach and hadn't wanted to worry her aunt, or her mother. Aunt Linda always passed on any news about Carly to her mother while circumventing Carly's intolerant father.

Carly listened twice to the message, finding comfort in Aunt Linda's reassuring voice, a soft, clear voice like all the Carver women. This included her younger sister, Lizzie. She had married a local boy last year, and she was living the traditional life in St. Joseph, Missouri. Too busy to call. She missed being sisters.

Carly grabbed her handbag looped over a hook mounted near the entryway. Her parents had given her the handmade leather purse when she had graduated college. Before they knew... .

Although it had been two years ago, she could still see her father's thin lips. His angry eyes had filled with disgust, as he had said, "You've ruined your life. Nothing you can do to fix it. It'll follow you wherever you go." He shoved away from the kitchen table, pulling down his flannel shirtsleeves as he said, "You killed my grandchild with your abortion."

Dropping her bag, Carly walked to the sink. "No. I won't wallow in what-ifs." Using both hands to steady the glass, she drank some water. She searched the wall until she found her favorite quote by Ralph Waldo Emerson. She repeated the mantra printed on the index card taped near the wall phone. "'Do the thing you are afraid to do and the death of fear is certain.' Focus and breathe." The nausea in her stomach abated as she washed the glass and wiped the counter. She found herself humming—maybe Chopin—from an old tape Harold played when they'd dined together. She only knew she liked how calm it made her feel.

Ten minutes later, Carly glanced in her Honda's rearview mirror and laughed. Harold was flapping his arms and directing her down the narrow driveway. The sunlight filtered through the tree canopy over her car marking the hood with a muted leafy design. A tiny yellow butterfly flitted across the windshield.

"Let's do it, woman," she said, feeling an adrenaline rush as she shooed Harold to the side and shifted into reverse. She executed a perfect three-point turnaround and headed toward her first day with Mobile's finest, the Warner County Police Department.

Chapter 4

Entering the precinct, Carly thought the bland building resembled a warehouse with partitions, and the uniformed people wore blank expressions except for a couple of guys who ogled the "new meat." She decided not to ask for directions and wove her way to the front of the building, thinking this colorless environment reminded her of watching her grandfather's black and white television set. Finding the administration officer, she asked to speak to her training officer.

"Not here yet," was the officer's answer. He hid his bandaged forearm behind the desk. Carly surmised the officer was on light duty for an injury and wasn't happy about it.

Using the downtime, she familiarized herself with the precinct. Utility shelves lined the hallway with over thirty different report forms upon them. As Carly finished stacking the forms associated with the daily activity log next to her metal clipboard, a uniformed woman with an authoritative air walked toward the recruit and extended a hand in greeting.

"Hello, I'm Lieutenant Hutchinson." She glanced at Carly's nametag. "Welcome to South Precinct, Recruit Redmund."

"Thank you, Ma'am."

"I believe you're assigned to Officer J.C. Grey for field training. He's an experienced officer. You'll learn a lot from him."

"Yes, Ma'am."

"If you have any questions or problems that your FTO or a sergeant can't help you with, come to me."

Carly liked her style: supportive without losing the aura of leadership. "Thank you, Ma'am. I'll remember that."

The middle-aged lieutenant checked her watch and said, "Recruit Redmund, excuse me. I need to check my mailbox and a mountain of paperwork." As the lieutenant turned, she pointed to rows of chairs facing a whiteboard in the next room, "I'll see you later in roll call."

Carly thought roll call began at two o'clock, but nobody was assembling in the designated spot. She didn't see any women in uniform besides the lieutenant. Carly bought a can of diet cola and walked by two women. One was obviously a secretary and the other young woman was entering data from traffic tickets into a computer while munching on a cookie. A photograph of a little boy about kindergarten age displayed on the second desk caught Carly's attention.

"Is this your child?" Carly studied the boy's cute features, ignoring a growing tightness in her chest.

The woman nodded and flipped over a ticket.

"He's so darling."

"Thanks. Joey's almost six, now." She wiped her mouth with a paper towel. "Do you have any children?"

Carly looked down, "No, no children," she said, tracing the outside edge of the photograph's metal frame. She regretted Mitch hadn't been the right guy and ending the resulting pregnancy. "You look too young to have a child that age."

"Not really. I'll be thirty soon." The fake smile relayed the woman wasn't pleased about her age.

"Fooled me," Carly said. "Hey, can you tell me how many uniformed women work in this precinct?"

"There are three other female officers, besides Sergeant Pitts and myself."

"Jeez, I thought-—

"You thought there were more female officers on the street. Right?"

Carly nodded.

"There are about thirty females out of seven hundred and fifty officers, but we're scattered throughout four precincts in detective and uniform divisions."

"I guess I won't be working with another woman too often." Carly leaned over the desk offering her hand and added, "By the way, I'm Recruit Carly Redmund."

As they shook hands, the woman laughed. "I know. Your name tag." She stood and brushed some crumbs from her khaki pants. "I'm Master Patrol Officer Jody Carter. Since I'm working administrative duty, I'm not required to wear a uniform."

Carly smiled, lying. "Oh, I see."

"I was injured on duty, and then I had Joey. It's a long story." Jody kneaded her neck and studied the pile of tickets.

"Well, I'm glad to meet you." The sound of chairs scraping the floor in the roll-call room alerted Carly. "I better go. You have a nice day, MPO Carter."

"You too, Redmund. Watch your back."

"Thanks. Will do. "It was time. The guys were sitting down in the rows of chairs. Carly

It was the only female face in the room. A short white male, Sergeant Griffin, entered the room holding a clipboard and a green file folder. Covering her mouth, Carly watched the sergeant swell up like a bantam rooster as he stepped up on to the platform and spoke to the troops.

"Guys, listen up." The group grew quiet. "We have a lot of things to cover today, and Recruit Redmund and Recruit Bengal are joining our merry band of public servants today.

Their first day with their FTOs should be an eye-opening experience."

The sergeant pointed to a potbellied officer in the front row. "Do you remember your first day on the streets? I know you don't, Harvey. You're so old your mind has rebooted and reset."

The group laughed, and the butt of the joke grinned and hung his head down, dramatizing his sorry state before he straightened up in the chair. Carly could see the side of the man's face and his blotchy red nose, a sign of a boozer.

"Anyway, we welcome you to the best precinct and the best watch in Warner County, Alabama."

The officers initiated a group round of hoorahs and grunts. Carly was amazed that they got away with breaking protocol and interrupting the sergeant—big change from the academy.

The sergeant shuffled papers. "The major wanted me to pass along his appreciation for the recent participation in the Snap and Strap last weekend. Everyone worked together, and we out-produced all the other precincts in stats. Not to mention the lives you saved by making sure the citizens buckled up."

Carly perused the room. Some of the veteran officers reacted with scornful faces, but most of the guys looked pleased to be stroked for their efforts.

"Needless to say—we—the little people, made the brass look good, again."

Carly straightened in her seat when Lieutenant Hutchinson walked into the room. The recruit wondered if she would ever be that powerful.

The sergeant nodded at the lieutenant finishing his regurgitation of memorandums and suspect-description flyers or BOLOs—be-on-the-lookout information sheets. Then Griffin asked, "Do you have anything to add, Lieutenant?"

She responded by stepping forward near the roll-call podium. "Nothing to add to help catch the bad guys, but look for another department manual change. It'll be in your mailboxes. Please read."

Carly took notes as the lieutenant finished summarizing the new vehicle chase policy and a recent staff meeting. "Are there any questions?"

The most vocal officers groaned their frustration over the third change in the chase policy this year. One of the officers asked which officer screwed up this time. The lieutenant explained, "The powers-that-be are sweating a civil suit involving Officer Milton. As you know, Milton lost control of his vehicle and hit a civilian's car head on. The bad guy got away…."

Carly couldn't believe an officer had killed a civilian, even by accident. The responsibility of her job stunned her, and her head pounded, making it hard to hear. She missed the last part of what the lieutenant said.

The lieutenant handed a neighborhood patrol request to a territory officer. "I'll need the patrol log back on my desk within thirty days. We'll discuss what needs to be done for follow-up then, Officer Brown."

In a respectful tone, Officer Brown took the sheet and said, "Ten-four, LT."

Brown scooted his large rear end into a folding chair on the end of the row and tipped his bald head toward Carly.

She returned the greeting, feeling uncomfortable as the veterans in the last row examined the new female recruit. She looked away hoping for support. On the opposite side of her, a black male, who appeared to be a rookie because of his

WELL OF RAGE

shiny badge and stiff unused gear, sat next to the wall avoiding eye contact with anyone.

The veteran officers reminded Carly of the "bad boys" in high school. Their arms folded, looking tough and never speaking to anyone outside their group. Carly knew most officers weren't predisposed to speak casually to trainees and rookies, because of the paramilitary structure; new folks needed to pay their dues without stepping on anyone's toes. That's one of the reasons why Carly sat in the middle of the room where nobody else apparently wanted to be.

They stood for the ending prayer. Since the abortion, Carly couldn't pray, but she bowed her head and blinked at the floor.

Officer Brown or "Rev," as the sergeant called him, finished with, "Lord, go with us and protect us as we attempt to do your will. Amen."

"Amen," the group muttered and dispersed.

Carly stood alone among the empty chairs, until the sergeant waved the recruit into the next room and interrupted a veteran officer, who was gathering BOLOs from a side table. "Officer Grey, this is Carly Redmund, your new recruit."

"Hello, Redmund."

Carly stuck out her hand, but instead of reciprocating, J.C. smashed the information sheets against the back of Carly's clipboard, causing her to grab for the papers. Grey turned, moved toward a folding chair where his yellow raingear tote rested, and lifted the bag by the strings. Stonefaced, he said, "Are you ready to roll? Bring the J-2."

"Sure," Carly said to J.C.'s back.

Carly cocked her head in the sergeant's direction. "J-2?"

"The BOLOs in your hand," the sergeant said. He covered a yawn with the back of his hand and nodded toward J.C.

"He's grumpy, but he's good." Then the sergeant shooed Carly toward J.C., who was retying his bootlaces.

Carly smiled. "Not a problem, Sir. I like someone who's all business."

J.C. spiraled around and shot Carly a searing gaze that made her take a step backward. The training officer's eyes narrowed, as he said, "We'll see about that."

The sergeant chuckled and tucked a thumb in his waistband. "Keep your sense of humor, Redmund."

"I will, Sir." Carly tightened her grip on the clipboard.

J.C. grunted and collected several abandoned vehicle stickers from a stacked storage cubicle. His head down, he passed Carly and the sergeant, and then opened the back door.

Someone called the sergeant on the radio. He pointed to the exit sign while reaching for the mike on his shoulder with his free hand. "Go. He'll leave you."

Carly pivoted and hustled to the parking lot.

Chapter 5

Starting her second week of street training, Carly, who was bent over her metal clipboard and writing with a pen on a form, still couldn't believe the computers weren't programmed for officers to type reports into the system. The GPS was nonexistent because a map cost the county almost nothing. It was halfway through their shift, nine o'clock in the evening, and Officer Grey was wired on coffee. "Can't you hurry up, Redmund? He clutched the steering wheel as if Carly would snatch it away. "I haven't got all night."

Knowing the other recruits drove their patrol vehicles in the first week of their field training, Carly kept quiet and finished a mundane report about vandalism. Stupid teenagers had taken a baseball bat to a mailbox. Right now, waiting on a priority-one 911 call to ease the tedium, Carly sympathized with the juveniles' shenanigans. She resented the training officer's treatment.

"It sure is a slow day. Not much going on." Carly shifted her gun belt and wedged herself into the passenger seat.

"Yep, that's real observant. Most of the time you're going to be bored, or scared shitless on this job. It's not a movie." Officer Grey shot Carly a sideways glance.

Carly continued to work on the report.

"By the way, why you want to be a cop?" J.C. asked.

Carly dropped the clipboard on her lap. "I wanted a job where I could drive fast. That's why I'm lovin' this sitting in the parking lot and making out report thing."

Officer Grey focused on the tree line. "Well, you're gonna do more report writing than you ever dreamed possible. Might as well fall in love with that seat, Recruit. It's gonna be a while before you take over the wheel of my patrol car."

Carly met her training officer's hard eyes.

When radio assigned them a call, he grabbed the radio mike away from Carly.

Clenching her jaw, she stared outside the window. They rode in silence for the rest of the shift.

* * *

The next day J.C. mellowed out a bit. They stopped by his house while on duty, and Carly met his wife. "Noreen, this is Recruit Carly Redmund. We're not busy today, but since we're out of our assigned territory you gals only got a minute to chat while I make a pit stop. No cat fights."

J.C. passed his wife standing near a gaudy maroon and gold couch holding a calico cat.

"Really, J.C. what an introduction!"

Noreen turned toward Carly. "I wanted to meet you and say hello. How's the training going?"

"Pretty good. Some days Officer Grey doesn't say much."

Noreen smiled knowingly.

Carly pointed at the glass front of a display case and continued, "You have a beautiful home, and your dolls are gorgeous."

"Thank you. Yes, the doll collection is my hobby, my expensive hobby according to J.C."

"Everyone needs a hobby." Carly fabricated a boyfriend as she said, "My fiancé and I like kayaking."

While Carly smoothed the fur back on the cat's head, she saw Noreen sight her ring finger with the gold band. "Yeah, we haven't set a date. He's still in Charleston, but someday he'll give me an engagement ring."

"How did you meet your boyfriend?" Noreen shuffled her backless high heels toward the display case containing about twenty-five vintage dolls.

"We met in college." Continuing the lie, Carly told her part of the truth about the ring. "I just wear this thing so men won't bother me."

Noreen folded her arms studying the recruit. "So you're not interested in dating officers. Still, you're awful pretty."

Before Carly could comment, J.C. reentered the room.

Noreen threw words at him, "It seems like you have a bright college gal riding with you. She has your number already. Told me you have days you hardly speak. 'A real joy to be with,' I'd say."

Noreen laughed and turned to Carly. "You'll have to come to dinner some Sunday."

J.C. cut in, "I don't give a rat's ass what either of you like as long as you quit bitching about her riding with me. Obviously, you've declared a truce. She passed your test. Great. Now can we go?"

"For heaven's sake, J.C., no call to be rude." She took a couple of steps toward him and lowered her voice, "Before you go, I need some money. Shelsy needs new ballet shoes, and Devon's swim competition is Thursday night. He lost his goggles."

Carly noticed that Grey barely listened to his wife. He darted toward the door.

"I gotta go. A call." He pointed to the radio mike hustling Carly to the door.

"But the money—" Noreen shouted.

Slamming the door in Noreen's face, Officer Grey rolled his eyes as the crackling portable radio static became audible, and he and Carly received an emergency call, "Bones found at the Deeter farm."

Carly cleared on the call trying to keep her voice level.

Grey drove and said nothing. Double checking the address on the computer screen, Carly took out the atlas and tracked the best route to the Deeter farm. Her mind whirled with possible scenarios. Adrenaline rushed through her body and a metallic taste flooded her mouth. Her fascination grew stronger as she remembered a veteran's after-shift truism: "Job security is one of the few perks about this job. There is never a shortage of crazies and crime." Master Patrol Officer Harvey had shaken his bulbous red nose and spouted his closing remark. "You get paid to handle the things nobody wants to see in the community."

About halfway to the Deeter farm, Grey blurted out, "Probably just damn squirrel bones."

Carly hoped not.

* * *

J.C. was self-absorbed. The mention of the Deeter farm brought back lurid memories. To avoid rehashing the past, he concentrated on driving to the farm, maneuvered a turn, and squealed the tires as he sped down the interstate ramp. He checked the trainee. She wasn't rattled. He'd tried his best to tick her off by working her into the ground, compounding her stress with hard-ass comments at the end of the long days. She had made a few mistakes, but nothing big. Nothing that would've got anyone hurt. Somewhere, she learned to pick her battles. He was curious about her background, but she was closed-mouthed about her personal life.

She was a natural, a-take-charge kind of gal—no matter what Forrester thought— but J.C. found himself expecting more of Carly than other recruits. He hadn't made her life easy. J.C.'s daily and weekly evaluations were brutal. Almost too cool, she hadn't reacted. His buddy, Don, had laughed when J.C. had told him how Carly had turned her low-to-average evaluations around.

"Yeah, she signed the first evaluations without comment. But she surprised me." J.C. said.

"What happened?" Don asked.

The beginning of this week, before she'd logged on the car computer, she produced a typed, thorough self-evaluation listing her skills and knowledge. I'll be damned if she hadn't documented every major call we'd worked together that first week. She was careful. Didn't challenge my judgments. Just made her point that she kept records too. She ended the conversation by thanking me for being her training officer. It made me feel like a chicken shit."

Don took a draw from his cigarette and blew out a snort, "So you're a chicken shit. What else's new?"

Damn, she smelled good riding beside him. Like warm cinnamon bread. Wholesome. J.C. wanted to taste her, satisfy his appetite, and with brute force demolish her blind faith in goodness, in justice. Something churned in his gut. He needed to break her. He thought what a sick fucker he was, lusting after a lost fawn in the woods, a perverted version of a fairy tale he'd read many times to his children when they were small. Thinking of Shelsy and Devon made him almost repentant. *Hands off. Let the rookie be...hopeful. Shit, this call better be nothing.*

When they arrived, Grey clicked off his emotions and noticed the air had cooled after the midday warmth. It was time to work the call.

What had been old man Deeter's explanation when he closed up the well? Grey couldn't remember.

As kids they had ignored the warning not to go near it. He and other boys had ridden their bikes to the Deeter farm and had explored on many summer afternoons. He recalled a huge combination lock on a chain that secured the well cover. The chain wrapped around the roof housing posts on each side with a lock securing the jimmy-rigged arrangement, but years ago, someone cut off the lock. Was the lock still hidden in the tall grasses surrounding the well?

He remembered limestone deposits contaminated the hand-dug well as he watched Carly walk over to the foreman. An old rusty chain lay on the ground near a group of workers who stopped speaking Spanish when J.C. approached. "Fuckin' Mexicans," he said under his breath. Carly glanced his way, and he swept an arm over the area. "I'm sure nobody saw a damn thing, and they conveniently don't understand or speak English. Clear this scene of everyone except the foreman and the Mexican who found the bones."

Nodding toward J.C., Carly stopped the interview in midsentence and requested in broken Spanish, "Please tell your men to leave, everyone, except you and Edwardo."

Most of the workmen climbed into a paneled truck and left. J.C. picked up a bucket from the ground. He shook the contents in a slow circular motion, Petri-dish fashion. Several knuckle bones appeared to be scattered among the dirt and debris. He froze, feeling the blood drain from his face. Spitting, he said, "God damn it, we'll have to call the suits. I hate calling those cocky son-of-a-bitches in CID."

"So they're human bones?" Carly asked.

"You think?"

Carly pursed her lips and walked away.

From a distance J.C. studied the Mexican worker, Edwardo, and saw Carly talking with her hands. She turned and walked back toward the well. *What had they found?* J.C. clenched the handle of the bucket as Carly approached. She

WELL OF RAGE

held a shiny object, a gold high school ring with an emerald, a senior ring from Robert E. Lee High School. A facial spasm under an eye pulsed as J.C. recognized the initials T.W.W. "Who knows about this?"

"As far as I know, only the foreman and the worker who found it in the well. You ran off the other workers before I could speak to them."

"Good! Keep it that way. Give me the ring." The rookie hesitated, but she didn't argue with him. He was her training officer, God, and civilians were watching. This broke the chain of custody all to hell. No property sheet, nothing signed, but life didn't always follow the rules. The recruit obeyed and gave him the ring. He slipped it into his pocket.

"Rope off this well with a fifty-foot square perimeter, use crime scene tape, and then don't move until I get back. For Godsake, don't talk to the media. I'm gonna call CID on a landline."

Carly frowned, walked off, and slurred "ten-fourer" over her shoulder. While Carly reached into the police car for crime scene tape, a crime scene van followed by a raggedy Neon turned off the pavement onto the dirt road churning up clouds of dust.

As the dust settled, J.C. stood like a brick wall in front of Carly with his arms folded over his chest, glaring at her. He barked, "Ten-four, what?"

Color climbing up her neck, Carly shouted, "Yes, Sir!"

"That's better. Show respect, Redmund." He pushed out his chest, nodded with satisfaction, and walked away.

* * *

Carly looked at the roll of crime scene tape in her hand and mumbled, "What the hell's wrong with him? Military respect in a pig's eye."

"Probably missed his coffee break, or doesn't like reporters snooping around. I'm one of those reporters." She stuck out her hand. "Hello. Marci Eplund."

Carly reddened again and stretched the crime scene tape around a tree trunk. "Didn't mean to grumble. Unprofessional."

Again, Marci stuck out a hand. "Not where I come from. My God given right to gripe."

Carly nodded. "Sorry, my hands are full. Need to string this tape pronto." She smiled at the disheveled reporter. "Besides, Officer Grey's my field training officer. I can't talk to you. Orders."

Marci shrugged. "I'm not supposed to be here. I'm new at the *Tribune*, the local newspaper. Big time reporter, Bob Singleton, is the over there in the news van. Though I've heard of Officer Grey." The female reporter nodded in J.C.'s direction. "A real sweetheart."

Carly finished roping off the perimeter. "Officer Grey's busy right now. When he's off the phone maybe he'll speak with you. Where's your vehicle parked?"

Marci craned her neck and looked around. "The green Neon over there." She nodded. "I know a way to get the information I want."

She waved in the direction of a crime scene technician, standing near the assistant coroner, Tim Price, and followed the crime scene tape away from Carly for about three yards. Then she dove under the yellow tape and dashed toward the well.

Chapter 6

At two o'clock in the morning, Derrick Grey sat in his home office, writing the last of the checks for his monthly bills. He pulled at the corners of his blond mustache, satisfied with his fruitful day. As he closed the ledger, the telephone rang. Alarmed, he snatched up the receiver. "Grey residence, he said."

"Derrick, J.C. here. Sorry to wake you, but this is important."

Derrick addressed his brother by his nickname. "Always good to hear from you, Chester. I just closed up shop, finished some boring bookwork. What's up?"

"Look. I'm driving home. I need to talk to you. I've withheld evidence, kind of."

"You're not going to ask me about ethics? Are you, brother? I'm the politician. You're the crime stopper."

"This is serious, brother. I wanted to give you a heads up…and I need to know something."

"Okay, shoot."

"You alone?"

"Sure, I'm in my office."

"Just worked a call…out at the old Deeter place. Had the damn recruit with me; she found the ring first."

"What ring?"

"Hear me out. They found some bones out there in Deeter's boarded-up well. You remember the well?"

"Sure. We played out there with Jack…old man Deeter's son. Haven't thought about him in years. What happened to him?"

"Not important. Turns out this Mexican worker gets antsy waiting to do his construction thing, and starts poking around and pries off the well cover. Sees something shiny down there with his flashlight. Gets a grappling hook and snags a water bucket. He no speaka da English, so when he sees a few bones and a high school ring, he runs to his foreman." J.C. paused. "The thing is the ring has the initials T.W.W." With the sound of squealing tires in the background, J.C. added, "That missing black kid from your high school class, wasn't his name Terence Washington Williams?"

"Yeah, the Williams kid. We weren't exactly friends. I beat him into the ground when he made fun of Austin. That's about it."

"I still miss our baby brother." J.C. said.

"Wasn't right—Austin shouldn't have died at thirteen."

"Down syndrome is a rough way to go." Silence followed until J.C. continued, "Anyway, that's why I didn't turn the ring in to property…your fight and all. I couldn't exactly remember when Terence came up missing. Thought it was your senior year."

"Yes, you were gone when I graduated."

"Yeah, I was in country."

Derrick didn't reply, waiting for the other shoe to drop.

"I confused the reporter," J.C. said. "A dope named Bob Singleton. Told him it was animal bones and dumb ass believed me. I could've also handled the foreman and that illegal Mexican, but the recruit got in the way. Tim Price, the coroner's assistant, didn't have a clue. He was too busy cleaning mud off his ass from digging in the bottom of well."

"Has he found an entire skeleton?"

"No. Only did a quick looksee before they sealed the well. Morning watch officers relieved us. They're protecting the crime scene. Price will be hauling up bags of mud all day tomorrow. He'll dry and sift the bones at the morgue."

"I see. Then the identity of the deceased isn't known. Correct?"

"That's right."

"How long before they put a name with the bones?"

"I'd say forty eight to seventy two hours. They'd be pretty sure with the ring, but they won't want to notify the family or press until they have more forensic information, matching dental records, et cetera, and cause of death."

"Right. Well, you might have overreacted, but I appreciate you watching out for me. I'll tell you some time what really happened between Williams and me." Derrick paused, then added, "That's about the time you weren't around… missed one of Grandmama's birthday fiascos. Army bastards wouldn't give you a leave from Nam."

"Bureaucratic dickheads." J.C. said.

"Fight with Williams didn't amount to much. But for now I'm concerned that you'll be in trouble. Would it be a problem, say, if you accidentally put the ring in your pocket for safekeeping at a crime scene, and you happened to find it when you emptied your pockets on the nightstand?"

"That won't fly, but I know what will."

Relieved that his brother wasn't pressing him for information about how the fight ended with Terence, Derrick said, "Then you can submit the ring tomorrow to the evidence people with a little egg on your face but no permanent damage?"

"I can do better than that."

"J.C., too many people know about the ring. I don't need any rumors about a cover up during my campaign, and you don't need to derail your career."

"You sure you don't want this ring to disappear? I can handle it. In fact, my rookie can carry the load for me with a little creative writing."

"No, put the ring where it belongs. You do damage control on your end, and I'll have my spin doctors clean up any nasty connections to Terence from my high school days—if it comes to that. Thanks for sticking your neck out for me."

"Not a problem. You know me, loyal to the end," J.C. said.

* * *

As J.C. tucked his cell in his belt holder and pulled into the driveway, he plotted how to put the screws to the rookie. It can be handled with the swipe of a pen on a property sheet. Put the rookie's name, backdate it, and no one will be the wiser.

He hit the garage door opener. "Poor thing, not only forgot to inform the coroner's office of this vital piece of evidence, but she placed the ring in the property lock box a day late."

The damn Nam nightmares and now this mess made J.C. question whether it was all worth it. The dead wouldn't leave him alone. He thought of Derrick, the only person he loved unconditionally. Their destinies intertwined; J.C. vowed to protect his brother and himself.

* * *

Marci Eplund downed the last of her coffee, wiped her red-rimmed brown eyes, and then ransacked her black satchel for a loose cigarette. No luck. She stepped down from the stool and nodded her thanks as the clerk wished her a good day. The employees of Three Georges, always pleasant in their crisp black and white uniforms, made her cringe. But, by god, they brewed strong coffee.

Marci retracted her claws. Be nice, she told herself. *Be proud you quit smoking last week. Don't be stupid—no cigarettes, no crutches.* She needed to be fully alert when she faced Mr. Editor-In-Chief who would toss her another crappy assignment. She sighed. It was going to be one of those mornings when nothing went right. Her new Doc Martens hurt her heels, and her queasy stomach didn't help the craving—she needed a cigarette bad.

It was almost eight o'clock when Marci slowed her pace inside Cathedral Park. Her spirits brightened a bit as she approached the Cathedral Basilica of the Immaculate Conception. For the umpteenth time she vowed to go inside the church. She wanted to believe God cared as she touched the ornate black wrought-iron gate. The token blessing comforted her, but only for the moment, because between the fence posts, she read the marble headstone memorializing aborted fetuses. Tears rimmed her eyes as she wondered why her own mother gave her life, but abandoned her.

The smell of roasted peanuts was already in the air from The Peanut Shop. A squirrel chattered nearby begging for food. Marci turned, clapped her hands. "Too early. Maybe after work, later, I'll buy you some peanuts."

Then the young reporter headed for the *Tribune* facing the miniature Greek fountain in the center of the park. Entering the circular doors of the *Tribune* brownstone building, she almost bumped into Stewart.

He was standing by the doors like a doorman and ushered her to the gold-leaf decorated elevators. "Hey, Stewart. What's happening in the world of intelligentsia?"

He beamed as Marci adjusted his old-fashioned, black-rimmed glasses. "Ah...I'm fine," he said as he stepped back fingering his frayed white collar. "Sorry, my world is way beyond your comprehension."

Marci shrugged. Stewart was a genius with computers, and in the past he had tracked down obscure research information for her. Stewart knew a little about any subject you could imagine—just enough to find the data hidden in the black hole of cyberspace.

His grin faded as he said, "You look wiped out. No sleep again?"

Marci touched Stewart's forearm. "An insomniac for life. You know, Stewey, I like the odd and unusual. I don't care what other people say about you."

"Yeah, I know you like me," he said trying to cover his arousal with his hands.

His mind fascinated Marci. She realized in some ways it was unfortunate she wasn't attracted to most men. They were uncomplicated creatures.

Marci stepped off the elevator and waved. "Later, Stewart."

The door to the editor's office was open and Marci caught a glimpse of her boss, Jim Branson, venting his anger close to an unlucky reporter, who drew back from Branson's mounting fury, only to bounce his head off the wall behind the couch where he was penned.

Big Jim only cared about the bottom line.

Branson had been a hard-nosed news reporter long before Marci was born. A difficult man, but he knew how to put out his version of a decent daily paper, Mobile's *Tribune*. With his stocky build and relentless, pushing energy, Marci admired and disliked him for the same reasons. He reminded Marci of a tank.

She covered the distance across the pinkish-gray tile floor to her cubicle like a trained rat in a maze comprised of fifteen other cubicles. Waving to a co-worker, she rounded the corner of the partition and viewed her desk—a disaster with research material stacked everywhere.

Marci squeezed through the cubbyhole at the end of a narrow footpath and turned on the computer. As her computer screen flashed on, Jim Branson roared, "Get in here, Eplund."

Marci jumped up.

Branson usually waited for the morning briefing to make assignments, but now he tossed Marci a manila envelope and said, "You take the story involving the skeleton found at the old Deeter place."

Not believing her good fortune, she tucked her beige shirt inside her khakis. "The Deeter farm, sure."

"Reference can fill in the background," Branson said. "Old man Deeter died about fifteen years ago, left the farm to his son, Jack."

Marci nodded. She'd already heard of the Deeter family: the rumors of their KKK sympathies and money.

"The farm's a wilderness now. After Jack sold the property to a local corporation, construction workers pulled up a bucket from the old well—been closed for years—and found some bones. Human."

"Yes, I suspected, but Bob showed up at Deeter's place and told me to get." She stopped because Branson's neck veins looked like they were about to pop.

"Eight to ten hours after the county police became involved, those bones were identified by the local crime lab as human," Branson said. Bob screwed up—we missed the story." Branson hammered his desk. "The news hit my desk at the same time that all of Mobile heard it from WUWF. Damn imbecile."

Branson pointed at Marci, "Go. Check it out. If you have a source that's on the county's payroll, use it. Find out the cause of death, other than being dumped in a well. Put a name with that skeleton, pronto. I have an itch I can't scratch—"

"Which means the big story is out there."

"Damn right. Go find it."

* * *

Carly leaned against the side of the refrigerator and dialed a number from her address book. "Viola, this is Carly, Carly Redmund."

"God, gal, it's good to hear from you. How you like the streets in Mobile?"

"It's all right." Slipping into a chair, Carly pushed her bills aside.

"Carly, I told you it's tough out there, but you'll get used to it. How's your love life?"

The sound of V's raspy voice comforted Carly as she doodled on a piece of junk mail.

"Don't have one, don't want one right now."

"Ah huh, I hear you, but I don't believe you."

"Viola, back off. Remember, I know things. I worked with you at the university, back in the days, after your second divorce." Carly sighed. "But the assistant coroner is mighty tempting."

"And?"

"And nothing. I've looked from afar. Never spoken to him."

"Hum…changing the subject. How's the training going?"

"That's what I wanted to talk to you about, but…not in-depth over the phone. In short, my training officer pulled a big no-no on chain of custody. No paperwork. Maybe I'm paranoid, but it didn't set right with me."

"Sh-it, girl. You better cover your backside."

"It's a "catch-22" situation," Carly said, as the full weight of the possible repercussions hit her. Thoughts whirled: *If it gets ugly, my word is worthless. I should've refused. Stood up to him. Right. In a public place at a crime scene, I should've challenged my training officer without proof he intended to do anything wrong, except help me.*

"Hello, you all right?" Viola asked.

"Yes, need to get my head together, V. Can't seem to concentrate." Carly fingered an electric bill and dropped it. "In a few days, I'm off for two. Thinking of taking a little road trip. Can you meet halfway between Charleston and Mobile—say, Atlanta?"

"Sure, when and where? My Harley awaits the feel of my leather chaps and my ever-growing, but I must say, fine black ass upon its quilted seat."

Carly laughed. "Viola you're a trip. You familiar with Manuel's Tavern on North Highland?"

"Sure am. Went to a bike rally in Atlanta last spring. Had me some kinda fun."

"I bet. You still have Thursdays off?"

"Sure do."

"How about noon Thursday at Manuel's. We'll eat red meat and burger out."

"Sounds good. After you leave, maybe I can pick up one of those friendly Atlanta bikers."

Carly felt better when she hung up. She nibbled on some yogurt as she gathered her bills and threw them in a pile next to her computer. Grabbing her running shoes, she looked forward to the physical exertion and clearing her mind. Remaining positive, Officer Grey might've placed the ring in property. Carly would check.

Chapter 7

Tim Price took one look at his boss, Coroner Gordon Davis, propped against the side of the crime scene van, yawning, and realized it was going to take all day to dig out the remaining bones without help. He pulled out a pair of coveralls and some rubber boots from the trunk. A long day lay ahead.

Tim spoke to Officer Grey and nodded at a female rookie, who Grey didn't bother to introduce. Surprised that Grey had been assigned the guard detail two days in row, and stranger still, Tim noted, the officer had called the morgue yesterday to check on their progress in identifying the bones. Usually, Grey did just enough to get by. Tim thought the training officer must want the rookie to experience the mundane world of police work, first and foremost. Grey could be a prick.

The assistant coroner armed himself with a flashlight, a few plastic bags, a marker, and plastic gloves as he watched the scene play out between Grey's sergeant, Officer Grey, and the rookie.

The sergeant motioned Grey over to him, and the uniformed female officer followed. Their supervisor rattled off instructions and finished by saying, "Grey, I'm out of here. Keep me informed if anything important happens."

"Will do, Sarge," J.C. said. Both men had excluded the female during the conversation as if she were invisible.

After the sergeant drove away, the recruit glanced at her watch. She seemed bored, bent under the crime scene tape, and spoke to her FTO. "Are we going to be here all afternoon?"

"Yep, if we're lucky," Grey said. "In a few more years you'll be looking forward to the no-action details. Like Yogi Bear said, 'You can learn a lot by observing the scene.'"

Tim wondered if Grey's quote was his attempt at humor.

Just to pull Gordie's chain, Tim used the county radio, instead of walking a few feet to the van. "When you get a chance, Coroner, I'll need a small shovel and some more medium plastic bags." The items weren't in the kit bag because the coroner refused to keep supplies on hand. The cheap SOB acted like he paid for supplies out of his own pocket. Waddling away, the coroner tucked his double chin and mumbled in to the radio.

Wondering why Gordie bothered to get up in the mornings, Tim descended into the well via a thick rope slung over the well roof's interior housing.

While Tim was taking a water break, the coroner returned an hour later with most of the supplies and started to walk toward his unappreciated associate, but the recruit stepped between them asking if she might assist Tim. "I'm just curious," she said. "Okay?"

"Knock yourself out, rookie," the coroner garbled.

Introducing herself first, Carly brought the items to Tim.

Tim thanked the attractive recruit. For a moment he was tongue tied, and then his words tumbled out. "Would you mind directing this floodlight into the well for me...until I can get set up again?"

Grabbing the floodlight, she said, "Sure, got it."

After Tim propelled down a few feet, he waved at Carly and said, "That's it. Thanks."

Focusing on the job, Tim forgot about his pretty helper. The scooping of the muddy contents from the bottom of the well proved to be a formidable task. His small, athletic frame barely fit into the four-foot wide well. As he lowered himself down the fifty-foot shaft, he acknowledged his body's assets. Even so, bracing himself on the walls with his feet and inching his way down, his expletives echoed upward as he descended.

* * *

Tim's shoulders were inches away from the walls. With just enough room to stoop and dig sample mud into a bag, he marked his starting point on the wall using a fluorescent marker, and then scooped a handful of soggy dirt into a bag. Identifying the dirt's quadrant on the bag, he stepped in a counterclockwise motion to the next section. A flashlight secured under an armpit, he lifted the mud and dirt into a series of bags. After surfacing several times to rest and drink copious amounts of water, Tim stood close to Carly. Aware that his sweat must be filling the air with an earthy tomb smell, he wondered how to make conversation.

"You don't need to keep the light on," Tim said, "after I get to the bottom…unless you just want to."

"I don't mind. If it's helpful." The training officer was hovering beside the rookie—appraising her.

Reading Carly's nametag, Tim smiled. "Thanks, C. Redmund. I appreciate it."

J.C. looped his fingers in his belt and directed his orders at Carly, "Just don't bother the man with questions. What you don't know you won't have to testify to in court."

He paused to make sure Carly understood, and then turned to Tim adding, "Don't discuss the case with the rookie. I'll be handling the report."

Tim tried to suppress his amusement before he answered Grey, "No problem."

He nodded at Carly. "Well, I better get back to work. I need to find the coroner."

As Tim walked toward his boss, the press fluctuated between their frenzy for the story and turning away from his smelly presence. Some actually held their noses. Most of the reporters, except the *Tribune*'s Marci Eplund, chose to keep their distance and shout questions. Tim chuckled to himself. His old friend, Marci, wasn't afraid of man or beast, but now wasn't the time for an interview. He ignored her.

Huddled, the coroner and Tim talked with their heads down until Marci careened over the police crime scene as the coroner confirmed the obvious forensic information. "At least the heart-shaped pelvic bone confirms the sex as male."

* * *

J.C. appeared, told Carly to hold the press at bay, and walked off for a smoke.

She asked the news media to be patient because the coroner would make a statement soon.

The reporter, Marci Eplund, shouted to a colleague, "That should be real informative, the twerp."

Carly wasn't sure whether "the twerp" reference was directed toward her—in uniform—or the coroner, but she asked all of the reporters to stand back.

The afternoon dragged on and Carly's training officer kept leaving for longer and longer breaks. The site was a mass of swirling dust and bugs. The mosquitoes and gnats ate at their skins, but by dusk an almost complete set of male skeletal bones had been lifted from the bottom of the well.

As the last black garbage bag filled with mud and bones passed by Carly, she realized how sad it was to see the remains of a living human being in evidence bags and stuck in a van.

Anger flooded Carly giving her courage. As she faced her training officer, Carly said loud enough for Tim Price to hear, "Sir, could I have a copy of the property sheet from the bones-found call from yesterday to staple to my copy of your report?"

J.C. barked, "I took care of it. Don't worry about it."

Carly stood her ground holding her training officer's gaze. There wasn't any property sheet or ring logged in to evidence until today, a day late. Carly had called the property room before starting her shift. She was determined to find out what was the problem and protect her job and reputation.

* * *

Meanwhile, Marci Eplund left the Deeter farm. Her old friend, Tim Price, wouldn't talk to her, and Officer Grey was as helpful as a brick. The officer had made sure the rookie cop didn't talk to anyone, including the coroner or his assistant. That left the foreman, who was at another job site in Mobile County, for Marci to interview.

When she arrived, Horacio was in front of the construction trailer. His crew was gone for the day. In short order, Horacio verified that his former employee, Edwardo Hernandez, was an undocumented worker. He had found the bones in the Deeter well, and then the police had been called. Marci wasn't surprised to hear Edwardo had quit yesterday and returned to Mexico.

Marci pulled her note pad from her shirt pocket and finished the interview sitting on the back bumper of her Neon. "Who owns this land now?"

"Not sure." The foreman checked his clipboard for the building permit application. "Huh, it's missing. But I think Jack Deeter owned the hacienda...before."

"Yeah, I know about Jack."

Horacio nodded, lapsed into Spanish, and then continued in English, "I heard when Jack Deeter's padre died, big shots hired someone to track Jack down. He was in another country, retired from the Air Force."

"That's weird. Not close family ties, huh?" Marci rapped the notebook with her pen.

"Si. These guys, they pay twice what the land is worth." Horacio took off his hard hat and wiped his forehead.

"How do you know?"

"My cousin, he surveys the land, makes specs...in 1999."

Marci grinned. "You're the guy to know. What's your cousin's name?"

"Felipe, I mean Phillip Cordez." The foreman borrowed Marci's pen and gave the reporter Cordez's phone number.

"Thanks, you've been a big help."

"*De nada.*"

Marci opened the side door of the car and turned back toward Horacio. "Thanks for being honest...talking to me about Edwardo and finding the bones. Can you think of anything else that seemed unusual?"

The foreman studied the orange light streaking the sky above the horizon. "Nothing, really. Did you see the ruby ring?"

Chapter 8

On his way to having a good day, J.C. was out of the courtroom by ten o'clock with a few hours to waste before going on duty at two in the afternoon. He was pleased that his cases either plead guilty or the traffic court judge fined the violators. Strolling, he could see the Board of Education building where Derrick worked a few blocks further down Forsyth Street. A man in a business suit, a defense attorney, spoke as he passed in a crosswalk. J.C. made eye contact and let his silence speak volumes. He didn't speak to the enemy. For a moment, the cacophony of sidewalk conversations, honking horns, and engines revving overwhelmed J.C. Panic set in like in Nam during a firefight. He felt like he couldn't breathe and sat down on a bench. He focused on the people hurrying from the parking deck to a red brick administration building where he'd taken his test for Master Patrol Officer. His adrenaline subsided. He needed to see a friendly face, Derrick's face.

Lately, his brother's busy schedule and life got in the way. Derrick's priorities had changed. He was running for mayor and seemed consumed by attending soirees of the rich parents and donors while directing the educations of the bright youth of Mobile. J.C. never broadcast it, but he ran into most of those upstanding juveniles messing up on the streets.

Feeling better, J.C. resumed his walk. A low income high-rise apartment building dominated the street and stretched from the corner to a recreational center for disadvantaged youth next to a storage-unit sized Mobile City Police

Precinct at the end of the block. He was glad to be a county officer. Policing downtown during Mardi Gras was a nightmare he didn't need.

J.C.'s lower back hurt. He hated court, even when he won. After twenty two years testifying still upset his bowels. His mind flickered to a recent memo he wrote to defend himself against a bogus complaint. Then there was Noreen.

Noreen could put pressure on a guy. She wanted more attention, "quality time," but she expected him to work as many extra jobs as possible. The living room furniture, the dolls, and her SUV payments on top of a home-equity loan required more than he cleared at the police department. His extra security job at Garrison's Jewelry added twenty or thirty hours of pay each week, but he was flat out exhausted. He needed a break. Although not big on "self-awareness," another Noreen criticism, J.C. admitted without reservation that he loved Derrick more than anyone else on earth.

It would be good to see Derrick.

J.C. crossed the street approaching the pansy flowerbeds adorning the front of a renovated eighteenth century two-story house. White. Derrick's office building was like his life, neat and tidy. Once inside J.C. followed the tongue and groove wooden flooring to Derrick's office door signed Superintendent of Schools.

J.C. spoke to Derrick's spinster secretary, Miss Mildred Stalch, and grinned his best howdy smile. "You look spiffy today, Miss Mildred."

"Spiffy, how quaint. Thank you, Officer Grey." Miss Stalch glanced down at her schedule calendar on her desk before she waved J.C. toward Derrick's office. The secretary shook her head like a disapproving schoolmarm and flicked the end of her nose as she peered over the top of her half-glasses.

J.C. barged into his brother's office banging the door against the wall. He scratched his head like a monkey as he said, "You educated dog, how's it going? Reaching across the desk, he popped Derrick's doughnut in his mouth. "I knew you didn't want this stale doughnut." J.C.'s smacked his lips and chewed.

Derrick leaned back in his leather chair and pulled down on an earlobe letting J.C. swallow. "That's okay." He looked at the open door. "You called her Miss Mildred, again, didn't you?"

J.C. closed the door and walked back toward Derrick, "You bet. I always make her day."

"By the way, I'd just picked that doughnut off the floor before you came in."

"That right?"

Derrick stood up unfolding his lanky body as J.C. shook his hand and said, "I thought I tasted bullshit."

Derrick tapped the paperwork lying in the middle of his desk and said, "Talk about bullshit. How about this one? A mom just hit a crossing guard in front of Hudson Elementary and I quote, 'At first, I didn't see the grandmother and small child in the crosswalk so I swerved causing the school-crossing guard to fall as she jumped back.'"

"Anyone hurt bad?"

"A few scratches," Derrick said, as J.C. sat down.

"Well, damn! That's okay then. What else could she do? Maybe stop? He stretched and stuck his fingers in his pockets before he added, "Although…if the grandmother had been anything like our dear grandmama, she would've survived the hit."

Derrick nodded and tossed a softball he kept on his desk up in the air. "Damn straight. Tough old bird."

"Yeah, I guess she tried to help dad out after mom died. She did her best to educate me in the social graces. Never stuck though." He pointed at his bother. "Now you, she liked."

"You mean I've conned more money out of her through the years than you."

J.C. propped his feet on the front of Derrick's desk and grinned. "I guess. Doesn't matter. Shrinks would say I'm not supposed to like you, younger brother. Come to think about it." He eyed the ceiling. "Can't stand you for a whole bunch of reasons."

"Right. Jealousy's an ugly thing." He threw J.C. the softball. "It's true blonds do have more fun."

J.C. grabbed the ball, and then threw it back hard.

Derrick caught it with one hand and slid forward resting against the desk. "Anyway, Chess, as I recall, you've always done okay." He looked at J.C.'s uniform. "When you came back from Nam, you were a rock-solid fighting machine."

"Two tours in Nam better make you a predator." Settling back in their chairs, the brothers fell into a comfortable silence. J.C. blocked the memories about the war and thought about their pranks and sexual exploits before Noreen, and their hunting and fishing trips afterward. The last few years those trips had probably kept him sane. The stocky country boy had become a man in the Army while his good-looking brother had finessed his way through college and into politics, but now, the brothers pulled together. Equals.

"So what's up, Chess?" Derrick still thought J.C.'s stiff stride favored Chester on the 1950s-1960s television show, *Gunsmoke*. "Why are you in my neighborhood so early? No folks available to harass?"

"Nope, I got my quota for this week. Just checking on you, little bro." He leaned an elbow on the desk. "I think I detect some stress and a need for a shitload of cash for your campaign. You know I'd do anything for you except—"

"You my hero, but it's under control," Derrick said, lifting his cup. "Some coffee to wash down my doughnut?"

"No thanks, just left court earlier than expected. Was wondering if you need any help with a juvenile delinquent or two? I'm sorry, 'disadvantaged youth.'" J.C. rubbed the ends of his red mustache.

"I bet you want to help. Save your strength, Officer Grey. I've got it covered." Derrick looked down at the carpet before he met his brother's eyes "How's the new deck?"

J.C. noticed the deliberate change in the conversation, but he let it slide and answered the question. "Expensive. I need to be two men with two sets of balls and one ready pecker to please Noreen. She has been online hours and hours lately. Spends my money on dolls and chats to God knows who." By the look on Derrick's face, he had read between the lines. J.C. tried to cover his slip of the tongue revealing Noreen's online affair. "I'm her sex slave, you know."

"You lying motherfucker. You wish. By the way, did you take care of your... misappropriation of evidence?"

"Done." J.C. smiled.

Derrick doodled on a scrap piece of paper. "Did you ever buy that riding mower?"

"Naw, too high. Like I said, I can't afford an extra set of nail clippers right now."

"That's rough, my brother." The phone rang and distracted Derrick. "Chess, aren't you supposed to be making America safe or something? I'm busy. Unlike some people, I work for a living."

"Yeah, I gotta get going. Need to run some errands before roll call. Besides, sergeant has had it out for me lately."

The sergeant had forced J.C. to explain his alleged rude behavior at a recent accident scene. "Wouldn't want to give the sergeant cause to write up my butt for being late. Tell your people to call my people."

As Derrick answered the phone, J.C. yelled, "Hey, you bring the babes and the beer—I'll fire up the barbecue grill."

Derrick put the person on the phone on hold. "Okay, sounds good, J.C."

The intercom blared, "Sorry to interrupt, Mr. Grey, but a Mr. Conner, is here for his eleven o'clock appointment."

"Later. This weekend, man," J.C. said, mimicking an exaggerated stiff limp, farted, and left. The old jokes, still funny, and nothing better between brothers—unless it was loyalty. Next weekend after a few beers, they could sort out whatever Derrick was holding back about that fateful night in 1974 with Terence.

* * *

Carly flopped down in the sand and watched the surf. With her mind clearer from the run from her loft to the Gulf waterfront, she enveloped her knees with her arms and let herself breathe the scent of the salt water for a couple of minutes. The sounds of the splashing waves washed over her jangled nerves. She took a deep breath and unfolded a copy of her Internal Affairs statement. Why hadn't she pointed a finger at her FTO? Was she hoping he'd 'fess up? Isolated in an interview room, she had written she thought her training officer had placed the ring in property. Now, she realized her ambiguous statement left an opening for J.C. to blame the rookie for the break in the chain of custody.

Retrieving a tissue, she blew her nose.

Grey had lied about taking the ring, and Carly had walked into a trap.

The Internal Affairs sergeant's severe face flashed in her mind. He'd slapped the statement form in front of Carly and said, "Write a statement about how the ring came up missing. Then sign it and date it. If you cross out something, initial it." The sergeant pointed at the form. "Before you start Creative Writing 101, just remember who you are and who your training officer is. You might as well tell the truth."

Apparently, she was guilty until proven innocent. The sergeant continued, "Internal Affairs has a rep. We'll get it out of you. Officer Grey has a spotless reputation, rookie."

The sergeant had left with a grunt.

Carly rubbed the sand from the tops of her thighs. What a dilemma. Defending herself further might mean continued employment, but it would leave her career in a shambles without a chance of recovery. She would be ostracized. Carly thought of her pal, Viola. What would she do?

After college Carly had worked for the Southern Charleston University Police Department, where she'd met Viola, a former city police officer. The veteran officer had shared some war stories about her ex-employer when Carly had asked for guidance about applying to Warner County PD. "You need to watch your back. Don't rattle anybody's cage," Viola had said.

Carly remembered how naïve her response had been. "I'm not confrontational. You know that, Viola. I pretty much stay to myself and do my job. If I do my job, they will accept me."

Their conversation had continued:

"Carly, I'm not talking about making trouble. I'm talking about trouble finding you, following you around because the other officers leave you out there high and dry."

"You mean they won't back me on calls?" Carly asked.

"I mean they put up major roadblocks, sabotage you. Yes. Some won't back on your calls, especially on the violent ones, if you tick them off. Sometimes you call for help, ain't nobody coming. You think a five minute fight is an eternity when you can't handcuff the perp 'cause his wrists are the size of a frickin' gorilla."

"Why would they do that if you do your job and prove yourself?"

"Oh, say, you don't play the game just right. See. You start trying to help people, and you believe that the rules apply to everybody the same, but they don't. Power breeds the same shit as the trash on the streets, but it's wrapped up all pretty with a bow. Takes money to live. Most of the big boys have several women on the side. Some women they do on duty. Some work extra jobs on PD's time."

"But surely, Viola, they're not all like that."

"No, but what are you going to do the first time your sergeant tells you to drive the chief's son home instead of booking him on a DUI?"

"I'd be diplomatic and say—"

"You'll say yes, or you'll pay big time. Believe me. All I ever did wrong was be born a black female and want to police. I walked down the halls of that precinct for four years and nobody gave me so much as a hello. No camaraderie. Nobody ate with me. Nothing. Carly, I remember one call where I checked a warehouse burglary alarm at two in the morning. Alone. Then shook in my car for a half-hour. A fuckin' Rottweiler nearly bit my leg off. Prayed I wouldn't get another call until I calmed down. It sucked!"

"It can't be that bad."

"I hope you never find out, gal. It's crazy out there in the dark with the drunks, pimps, and whores. Everybody gets lost, but you have to stay found, or get out of policing."

Right now, Carly felt excluded from both sides of the "thin blue line." The situation was her word wouldn't hold weight against the veteran's word, unless the recruit wanted to throw civilian witnesses into the mix, a police no-no. She could either rat to IA on Grey or take the fall.

Carly anticipated her training officer was going to recommend a neglect-of-duty disciplinary action, a violation that could mean termination for a probationary employee like herself. Being fired would be terrible, but this thing wasn't over until it was over.

Carly squared her shoulders and began to consider her options. She was at the bottom of the food chain, true, but what was going on? Her FTO had been unforgiving, but not spiteful during her training. He'd seemed like an honest, upright guy. She hadn't foreseen this ruthless move. Fighting paranoia, Carly wondered if the brass had decreed her demise. This debacle could do it.

No, Carly was missing something. She replayed the call to the Deeter farm, and Grey's reaction to the ring. There was something close to panic in his eyes when he'd read the initials. Then he'd become bossy and had shouted out unnecessary orders. After he'd put the ring in his pocket, he'd pretty much kept her away from everyone, including the coroner and his assistant.

As Carly made a mental checklist, she halfway blocked the sound of a dog barking somewhere on the beach until a large man with a rugged face stopped and spoke to Carly.

"Hello, beautiful evening," he said.

Carly patted the man's golden retriever. The sun was going down, and Carly almost missed the magenta streaks in the sky. "Sure is. Thanks for reminding me."

The man smiled, and Carly noticed he was handsome in a Paul Bunyan kind of way.

"Come on, Dex. Leave the pretty lady alone." The man acted like he was heading toward the parking lot, but Carly could feel the man's eyes on her backside as she walked toward the pier.

Allowing everything to fall into place on the checklist, Carly dismissed the stranger's interest. While Grey had spoken to CID investigators, Carly had been shuffled off into an anteroom at headquarters to finish paperwork. She'd been left out of the loop. Grey needed time to talk to someone else about the ring. But who? What was the connection between the ring and her training officer, or was it departmental dirty laundry? If it were a departmental cover up, then IA wouldn't protect Carly. She wasn't completely naïve. Without help she was finished.

Carly brushed the sand with a big toe. She could go to Lieutenant Hutchinson, off the record, but that would put her in a precarious position. The lieutenant would've knowledge of untruthfulness—an internal matter—that could be handled quietly, but intentionally withholding evidence from a crime scene was a criminal offense, and she'd be obliged to take action and investigate. The second option of going to the precinct sergeants, who thought Officer Grey an exemplary officer, would be useless. Carly's only untenable, but rational course of action was to bite the bullet.

Carly picked up a shell and threw it into the ocean. In the meantime she was going to talk to that assistant coroner, Price. Tim, wasn't it? He'd be able to answer a few questions. Maybe he'd keep his mouth shut, one underling to another underling. It was worth a try.

Carly recalled Tim's nerdy schoolboy demeanor and being a few inches shorter than her, but she didn't care. Carly recalled Aunt Linda's favorite quip in predicaments: "If the ship's sinking, at least have some fun on the way down."

* * *

After Carly returned home, she phoned Tim Price. "Mr. Price, this is Carly Redmund. I worked the crime scene at the old Deeter farm with Officer Grey. I'm the rookie, who … ." It dawned on Carly that Tim would've heard about the misplaced evidence through the public safety rumor mill. She faltered, "I'm still in training, but I didn't … . I promise I didn't misplace the ring. Would you be willing to meet me outside the precinct so I can explain? I need your help. I may lose my career over this craziness."

"Well, I don't see how I can help. Usually—"

"This would be off the record."

"Okay. Go on."

"I want to set the story straight and settle a few questions in my mind. I don't understand why, but Officer Grey ordered me to relinquish the ring, and then he placed it in his pocket, and kept me from talking to anyone at the crime scene. He kept the ring overnight and blamed me."

"Really," Tim said with a hint of sarcasm. "Did you tell your superiors your version?"

"No. Do you think it would've done any good?"

"You're probably right, but why do you care what I think?"

"Because, like I said, I need your help…information, to make sense of this mess and save my skin. Maybe the skeleton…the bones hold the key. I have to sort out this fiasco."

Carly took a deep breath. "I know you're directing the investigation. The man behind the curtain, so to speak. The scuttlebutt is that the coroner was appointed and not for his forensic knowledge. Correct?"

"True. The veterinarian coroner's expertise is the four-footed kind of animal." Tim paused. "Miss Redmund, this is a delicate situation. I warn you that any further conversation may drag you into more of a quagmire. I'm being pressured to close this case expeditiously."

"It's Carly, and I'll take my chances. If my life is going down the tubes, I think I deserve to know why. Don't you?"

"I can see your point and have my own reasons … . I'm afraid I've a reputation of being recalcitrant." Tim deliberated. "As my grandfather used to say, 'You help when you can and whom you can.'" Tim paused. "I guess it's possible that you and I could help each other out."

Carly wasn't sure how she could help Tim, but his tone didn't imply anything improper. She said, "Sounds good."

"I'll meet you at the old Huddle House off U.S. 10 near I-65. I think it's a café, now, the Soul Food Café. Say, seven thirty tonight. I'll be in an old yellow Volkswagen bug. If I don't show by eight, I've been called out on another dead body, so I won't be coming. Capiscie?"

"Absolutely. I got it. Thanks, Price."

"It's Tim, but don't thank me yet."

Chapter 9

Carly arrived early. Watching the blinking Soul Food Café sign, she wondered why people continued to call a business by its former establishment's name. Habit, she guessed. During her training, J.C. had informed Carly most officers liked the old names to be used on the radio because it was easier to mentally retrieve the location in a chase.

The food smelled delicious. Carly decided to risk rudeness and eat without Tim.

The buffet was open, but the prices on the signs over the grill were blank. Although renovation was in progress, the floor and booths were clean. The fatback scent made her mouth water. Carly said, "I'm starving," to a dour-faced turbaned woman coming out of the kitchen.

Carly took a deep whiff of the sweet potatoes and greens, and spied a peach cobbler in the corner of the buffet. After ordering dressing along with vegetables and cornbread, she tested the sweetened iced tea. It was just right.

She paid the impatient cashier. As Carly put her change away, Tim opened the door. He waved in her direction and flashed a prize-winning smile. She was struck by Tim's boyish face and his erect posture. He wore khaki pants and a polo shirt.

"Hey, Tim. Sorry I couldn't wait to eat. Too hungry."

"That's okay. I like a woman who takes care of herself. Be right there."

Carly chose a place in the back, away from the windows. She slid into a vinyl booth and watched Tim across the rows of black and pink-flecked tables. He'd picked a good place to meet. It was unlikely anyone would know them.

When Tim ordered a hamburger and fries, the waitress looked at him as if he had two heads.

Carly smirked behind her jumbo-sized, red plastic tea glass.

"Wat you say? You can't read," she said pointing to sign over the grill that read, NOT OPEN.

Tim hesitated.

"The sun will be a-setting soon," the waitress said in a thick African accent.

Finally, Tim leaned forward close to the buffet's glass hood. "Country fried steak with mashed potatoes and gravy," he said.

The waitress slopped the food on a plate and slid it to him.

"Love the accent," he said as he sat down. "What do you think, maybe, from Uganda?"

Carly shrugged. "I played it safe and pointed to the food I wanted."

"Smart gal."

Carly fidgeted in her seat, reacting to the gleam in Tim's eyes.

He looked back over his shoulder. "No sense of humor, either. I was just messing with her. I didn't mean to make her mad."

Carly noticed Tim's hands as he took his food off the melamine tray. His nails were clean and his hands looked strong. The scent of his aftershave reminded her of Mitch. For an instant, she couldn't think of anything but her ex-lover; she poked at her greens.

Tim began with small talk. "You're not from around here. You're accent isn't exactly southern, is it?"

"No, I grew up in the Midwest. Joplin, Missouri."

"A trucking town?"

"Yes, very small."

"Could we talk about your findings on the skeleton?" Carly blurted out. Her tolerance for chit chat exhausted.

A smirk edged its way to a corner of his mouth. "Of course," he said. "You must keep in mind it's still preliminary findings, because my knowledge is limited. I have asked an expert to verify my opinions."

Carly thought about the rapid flow of information that traveled through the grapevine from the coroner's office to the department heads. "Who?" she asked.

"Dr. Taylor White, my archeology professor from college days."

"Good. He's from outside the department. Do the police brass know about this?"

"No, the coroner isn't aware either. There are more than enough roadblocks already in this investigation, and I'd like to do it right."

"Roadblocks?" Carly questioned.

"Yes, the coroner, or Gordie as I like to call the pompous ass, has no forensic training, as you astutely gathered. He relies on the police brass to tell him what opinion to report about the mechanics, manner, and cause of death. About the only thing he's good for is determining the time of death based on the insects on a body." Tim drew a square in the air. "He has a chart for that one. Wait until you hear him drone on about the insects found on the corpses during autopsy in press interviews."

He stirred sweetener in his drink. "Think about it. Insects are his only contribution in a pitiful existence."

Carly laughed.

Tim quipped, "Knows nothing about bones. It's a brain drain working for him, but my smattering of forensics experience involving cold cases won't be adequate on this political hot potato."

"What have I missed here?"

"The brass wants this one to go away. This so-called *suicide,* if properly investigated, would embarrass some folks and make others very unhappy."

"Why, exactly?" Carly asked.

"Because it's a murder that was never investigated."

"Seriously?" Carly tried to read Tim's face.

"Yes."

"Do they think a suicide ruling will fly?"

Tim shrugged.

"Questions," Carly said. "What does this have to do with Grey? And why did he jeopardize my career, and potentially his, by withholding evidence? Why did he replace the ring the next day and blame me to cover his tracks?"

"Is that what happened?"

"That's pretty much the whole mess in a nutshell."

"Guess you didn't know J.C.'s brother is Derrick Grey, the republican candidate for mayor of our fair city."

Carly felt like she had been gut punched.

"Brothers? Isn't Derrick blond and suave while J.C. is—"

"An uncouth, red-headed redneck."

A quiver of uneasiness wrenched through Carly's body. What was she mixed up in? "Tim, what's Derrick's connection to the skeleton?"

"I'd rather not speculate, right now," Tim said, "But can I see scapegoat and your name in the same sentence."

"Look." Carly spread her fingers on the table. "I'm probably being written up as we speak, getting reprimanded for improper handling of evidence, and neglect of duty—both, firing offenses. I'm losing my butt on this one. So tell me why this crazy shit is happening to me."

Tim took his designer glasses off and laid them on the table before he answered. "Okay, I'll level with you. But my butt is on the line here too. Understand?"

"I'm listening."

"The bones have been matched to a missing black kid, a Terence Washington Williams. I wasn't forthright with you about Dr. White. We've already conferred." Tim looked up sheepishly.

Carly was about to speak when she realized Terence had to be related to Mary Williams of The Painted Lady. *Oh, God ... .*

* * *

"Listen, Carly. I'm sorry I didn't tell you about Dr. White." Tim said.

"No. It's okay. I just realized I must have met Terence's mother, Mary, at a brunch. Anyway, go on."

"Interesting, considering." He paused. "I eavesdropped on a conversation at Jenny's restaurant yesterday from my usual vantage point, a lunch counter stool. I couldn't see the employees, probably the hostess and the cook in the kitchen, but the swinging door gave them a false sense of privacy. Anyway, they talked about Derrick and Terence being students in the early 1970s at Robert E. Lee, one of the first high schools to integrate in Mobile."

"And."

"The male cook was in Derrick's class. He remembered a fight between Derrick and Terence when he read the newspaper articles about the bones being found at the Deeter's farm. Apparently, Jack Deeter and Derrick Grey were thick as thieves back when.

"So."

"This guy tells the female hostess that Derrick beat Terence to a bloody pulp because the black kid threatened Derrick's younger brother, Austin. I gathered Austin was slow."

"You mean mentally disabled?"

"Down syndrome." Tim nodded. "Apparently, Terence had pushed Austin up against a locker and called him a freak for groping Evangeline, Terence's baby sister. She was about age eight. I can visualize Evangeline's big brother exploding at a member of the Grey family, a white boy, and Derrick's reaction. According to the cook, things got out of hand. Afterward Terence came up missing."

"So, everyone figured Derrick made Terence disappear. But nobody cared because Terence was black," Carly said.

"Right," Tim nodded.

Using a fork Carly flattened the dressing on her plate, and then added, "The people who were running the show, the school officials and police, let the missing person slip into a bureaucratic river of red tape."

"Exactly."

"I can see how this could blow up in their faces—not to mention Mary's wrath," Carly said.

"Mary, she lives in Mobile?" Tim asked.

"Owns a bed and breakfast on Francis Street close to where I live. Downtown." Carly took a sip of her tea. "Talk about bad press. The NAACP would love this one, exploring the department's lack of enthusiasm in solving Terence's murder? Or for that matter, The Southern Poverty Law Center."

"NAACP, Jesus," Tim said, making the cashier stare at him. He lowered his voice, as he said, "It was a hate crime before there was one officially on the books."

"Murder is murder, no statute of limitations for prosecution. But how do we prove it?" Carly asked, pushing her plate away.

"What's this 'we' stuff?"

"I wonder if any kids from the school were interviewed."

"I seriously doubt it." Tim rubbed his temples.

"Now Derrick's a big time politician and his brother, the cop, protects him. I bet they talked after we left the crime scene that first night. Derrick probably told him to place the ring in property." For a moment, Carly stared out the window. "Too many people saw the ring...like me. Besides, it wouldn't squelch the rumors from resurfacing once the identity of the victim was known. What a dunce, my training officer."

She returned Tim's gaze, "No wonder J.C. turned pale when I showed him the ring. Do you think Derrick killed Williams?"

"Who knows? But I can tell you what the coroner will leave out of his report. A small caliber shot went through the cranium."

"What?'

"It has happened before. This revamping of the truth to fit whatever suits the powers that be."

"Right," Carly said. "I was referring to the caliber size."

"And to answer your next question, it would be a sophisticated hit for an enraged teenager. There's an entrance cavity, but not an exit, which indicates a small caliber bullet—probably a .22 caliber. It could've been a .38. I didn't find the wad. Several ribs, a knee, and a mandible bone were fractured, so I'd say he was severely beaten before he was shot. With Dr. White's help, we confirmed Terence's identity through dental records. Terence's diastema, his gapped front teeth, were obvious. Only occurs in about ten percent of the population."

"Meaning?"

"So that fact, plus the left tibia showed signs of an old fracture that healed funny. His medical records revealed such a fracture occurred when Terence was pre-pubescent. I have a friend who works at the hospital."

"Hum." Carly wiped her mouth with her napkin. "Where was J.C. while all this was going on with Derrick?"

"That part is fuzzy. He did a couple of tours in Vietnam, but I can't say when. I will say a .22 is an unlikely weapon of choice for a Vietnam vet. Of course, not outside the realm of possibility. If my gun magazine info is correct, assassins like the weapons because silencers are easy to come by."

"Maybe. A .22 handgun is light weight," Carly said, while watching Tim eat his last bite of gravy and mashed potatoes.

Tim checked his watch. "Sorry, I need to leave. I hate to cut this short, but the stray cat that refuses to leave me alone, isn't completely housebroken."

"I didn't realize the time. That reminds me I need to feed Rickey. A friend's dog."

Carly rummaged through her purse and wrote her phone number on a napkin. "Call me if anything new develops, or I'll call you soon."

"Guess this means I'm helping you."

"Good judgment is overrated," Carly said, as she clutched her purse straps.

He moved toward the trash bin. "Maybe. By the way, do you have a backup plan...job-wise that is?"

"Yeah, survive another day."

Tim laughed. "I have a tent and camping gear in storage, if it comes to that."

"Might want to dust it off." Their gaze held for a moment. Carly couldn't help noticing how silly the background music sounded as Cher belted out the last chords of the song "I Got You Babe."

Trying to hide her crimson cheeks, Carly shifted her purse and left Tim standing near the refuse bins.

At the door she turned around. "You've been great, thanks Tim. See you later."

Nevertheless, Tim followed Carly to the parking lot. "Allow me," he said, as he leaned in and opened the Honda door.

Carly noticed his muscular arms. Admonishing herself, she thought *you're losing it, gal. Steady.* When she stepped back, she kept her voice casual. "Thanks and goodnight. I appreciate all the information."

Tim shook her hand. "Carly, it's been a pleasure."

Her arm tingled from the handshake. She forgot to ask Tim why he had decided to help her.

* * *

Where was Derrick? Rose combed the sheets with her fingertips. Why would she be dreaming of Billie Ray Cofer? She detested the bigoted man. Shadows had swirled around her husband and Billie Ray. At the end of the dream a loud metallic sound pierced the blackness, and a female screamed.

Rose tried to clear her head. Forcing her legs over the side of the bed, she remembered in the dream running toward a sound...the sound of her children. This was silly. Her dreams were usually pleasant, but not this one.

She heard her two boys roughhousing near the staircase.

"Dad, Junior kicked me," yelled Dean.

"Did not, you liar," taunted Junior.

Rose rolled over and stretched before squashing Derrick's pillow under her chest and focusing on the bedside alarm clock. Eight o'clock on a Sunday—Rose's established day off.

She smelled bacon frying. Between banter and jabs, the children were no doubt helping Derrick drop pancake or biscuit batter on her clean kitchen counters and floor.

The sun rushed through the open Venetian blinds and warmed Rose's shoulder-length brunette hair as she stretched and tied a robe around herself. Before grabbing her toothbrush, she decided to ignore the feeling her husband was hiding something.

Chapter 10

Viola sat in a booth by the door looking through a film-covered window. She watched people pass on the sidewalk in front of Manuel's Tavern. The warm spring weather and her Harley had made the trip from Charleston a perfect ride. Feeling at home, she relaxed. An artist walked by the dusty, wooded bar wearing loose jeans with paint splatters. She liked the look and decided the Poncey-Highland neighborhood suited her weekend-bohemian ways.

She tucked her orange bandana inside her leather jacket and readjusted her platinum hoop earrings. This dark tavern was her kind of place. Old cards were stuck all over the ceiling with dollar bills underneath; the remnants of a bar trick that added to the mystique of the place.

The waiter who brought a couple of waters and her beer sported a curly red beard so thick that she wondered if it was real. Obviously, he was not a descendant of his dark-haired Lebanese employer. Sipping her beer, Viola scanned the room, musing about the paintings of presidents Kennedy and LBJ hanging behind the bar. She wished she'd been an activist in the sixties. But raising Tipper had kept her busy.

Now, her son only came around when he wanted money to run the streets, proving that maternal self-sacrifice—an iffy proposition at best—did not always foster gratitude, or respect. They loved each other, but they didn't like each other very much. She was wondering how to forge a truce with her son when Carly appeared out of nowhere.

* * *

Carly could tell Viola had been deep in thought and hugged her friend's shiny black neck.

"Thanks for meeting me, here in the Atlanta, Georgia. I know it's a long trip, even to see little ole me." She scanned Viola's black biker outfit. "Don't you look great?"

"Hey. I'm a happy camper, and my new bike hugs the road." Viola patted her leather-chapped thighs. "You look burnt out."

"V, I'm trying to keep it together, but the more I learn the weirder it gets. People never say what they mean."

"The South, what can I say?" Viola swirled a wrist wrapped in a studded-leather bracelet. She kept talking while her eyes followed a tall man to the bar. "How's it working out with your new pal? Tim?"

"Don't know exactly. Too early to tell. Now, Harold, my downstairs neighbor is—"

Viola squeezed Carly's shoulder and stood up. "Oh Lordy, there's George Dugan, the man of my dreams."

Sashaying to the bar, she kissed Dugan. After a few words at the bar, Viola nodded at Carly, stopped rubbing her body against the smiling man, and brought him back to the booth.

As Viola slid across the seat, she said, "Carly, let me introduce George Dugan, a good man to know, even if he is FBI."

They shook hands and Dugan loosened his tie from his fireplug neck as he sat down beside Viola. "Nice to meet you, Miss—"

"It's Redmund, but Carly is fine."

He flashed a crooked grin at both of them. When he rested an arm on the top of the booth behind Viola, his coat opened enough for Carly to see he was carrying a semi-automatic in a shoulder holster underneath his sports coat.

"This here is the best gal in the world," Dugan said, "except for my dear old mom, awe course."

Carly laughed at his Irish drawl, but Viola seemed to deflate, and Dugan added quickly, "Did I mention she's Hard-Rock-Café sexy too?"

Viola said, "Good save, George." She pointed to Dugan's handsome, thirty-something face. "Remember a woman reaches her sexual peak in her forties. You, me, anytime. I'll wear your white ass out."

He snickered. "You're too much," he said, before turning toward Carly.

"We know each other from way back, from her street officer days. Ran across this wild woman on a bank robbery case. How about you?"

Viola cut in and said, "Miss Thing worked with me in Charleston, and now she's a police recruit in Warner County, Alabama."

"Warner County, huh?" Dugan said.

"Doesn't your organization have a field office around Mobile?" Viola asked.

"Yes, on Royal Street. In fact I was transferred there a few weeks ago." Carly's thoughts must have showed on her face because he added, "I'm in Atlanta for a conference."

"Small world," Viola caught Carly's eye. "I guess you two will be bumping in to each other…on cases."

"Doubtful, until I—" Carly realized Viola and Dugan were in cahoots.

Dugan said, "I expect we will." He grinned. "Don't you jog, Carly?"

Carly took a long drink of her water. "So, we've met before near Cathedral Park...and on the beach with the dog." Trying to contain her temper, she said, "That was you in those raggedy sweats near Heroes. You nearly knocked me down."

"Yep. Again, sorry."

Stunned, Carly said, "What's the deal, V?" When Viola didn't answer, Carly crossed her arms and glared. "He's been following me. Why?"

"Okay, I knew he was going to be in Mobile, and I asked him to keep an eye on you." Viola fidgeted with a straw. "In the beginning I thought you two should meet...for social reasons, and then, with the evidence violation hanging over your head, I got worried. I knew you were stubborn. So the plan was for him to meet you accidentally and buy you a beer, or something, but you didn't cooperate."

"Unbelievable." She looked at Dugan. "The conference?"

"That much is true. I'm here for an FBI briefing, but I didn't just wander into Manuel's." He shrugged. "I owe Viola. It's a long story. But don't get me wrong. Following a curly-headed babe around Mobile wasn't hard work."

"Not impressed. This 'Big Brother is watching you.' stuff gives me the creeps."

Dugan met Carly's gaze as the agent settled back in his seat munching on Viola's chips and dip.

Carly deadpanned both of her companions before she started. "First, I don't need anyone to set me up, or hold my hand. Viola, I'm not happy you violated some friendship rule I can't name, but I guess your heart was in the right place." She held Dugan's gaze. "No more lurking around. We clear?"

Dugan nodded as Viola made a promise to butt out of Carly's life that fell short of convincing.

"Yes, Miss Redmund. May we eat now?" Dugan said.

Viola reached across the table. "Carly, I'm sorry, really—"

"Enough already, V," Carly said as she flagged down a waiter. "But you're buying."

* * *

Billie Ray was in the only traditional billiard parlor in Mobile. The place was named Calpes, but some people called it Birdies after the owner. It had real billiard tables, not poor substitutes, bastardized pool tables. The beautiful balance of the billiard tables and the cherry patina of the wood still pleased him when he played. The rest of the place was run down, but he didn't care—in fact, he liked that people shied away—because his guys could meet and talk freely about militia business.

He smoked a hand-rolled cigar at the empty bar and waited on his best friend, Adam Hall. For over twenty years, they had met each Wednesday for lunch and one-on-one gripe sessions at Calpes. Adjusting his butt on the bar stool, Billie Ray said, "Where in blue blazes is Adam?"

Karl Potter, "Birdie" as the old timers called him, was silent as usual.

Billie Ray wiped at the sweat rolling down his face. "Damn, it's hot, Potter. What's wrong with your air conditioner? Where's my cold beer?" He nodded toward the front door. "I'm gonna start going somewhere else if you don't fix it."

"Suit me just fine," he said, shoving a mug of beer toward Billie Ray.

The big man puffed on his cigar. "Come on, Birdie, baby, when you gonna fix the goddam air conditioner?"

Potter squinted over his short pointed nose through his thick glasses. "When the customers around here pay for their drinks, instead of talking me to death."

"Hell, ain't we touchy? I'm going to call Adam. Try and save me a barstool. Will ya?" He scanned the empty bar and walked toward the hallway.

"Fuck you," Potter mumbled.

Where the public phone and restroom signs were located, the knotty pine walls were slick from years of grease. Billie Ray placed a hand on the grimy wall, stretched his belly to one side, and checked the beeper on his belt. No messages. "'What in the Sam Hill is going on?'" Billie Ray said, as the answering machine picked up.

He shook his head returning to the U-shaped bar. As he plopped on a barstool, his cigar fell inside the peanut bucket, covering the nuts with ash.

Potter retrieved the burning cigar as he said, "Your disgusting cigar ruined the peanuts. You ever heard of an ashtray?"

Billie Ray smacked as he drank his beer and watched the bar owner as he placed the cigar in a clean ashtray, threw away the peanuts, and wiped the shiny shellacked bar.

"It's too hot to go fishing, and I don't want to go home." Billie Ray belched. "Besides, Gloria's working at city hall 'til four." Billie Ray finished his beer. "Maybe, I'll ride out to the hunting lodge. Might get lucky, sight one of those tree-huggers. Be a shame if they had themselves an accident out there in the woods."

"Billie Ray, it's your kind gives the South a bad name."

Spreading his fingers against the wooden bar, the militia leader pushed his glass aside and leaned over the bar. The codger's jowls shook as he said, "It's my kind hept build the South, and this town. Don't forget that. We protect our own."

Potter finished wiping the draft handles and threw the rag in a mop pail as he turned away to straighten the liquor bottles behind the bar.

Billie Ray shoved his glass off the bar. "You like the color of our money sure enough."

Potter glanced over his shoulder at the broken glass on the floor and kicked a piece out of his way.

"You'd go under if it weren't for the brotherhood meetings here on Thursday nights." Striking the bar with a finger, he said, "I've noticed that, all right, Birdie boy."

Potter shrugged, turning his back on Billie Ray.

Billie Ray slapped ten dollars down, then picked up his cigar and left. The plate glass rattled as he slammed the door.

* * *

The phone rang and startled Carly awake.

"Officer Redmund, this is Marci Eplund from the *Tribune*. Are you available to talk? I know it's early."

Carly couldn't speak. Her brain synapses weren't firing.

Marci kept talking. "Did I wake you? It's early."

"No, I mean, kind of. Haven't slept much lately. It's Recruit Redmund."

"Of course, sorry. The bones-found case has kept you busy I'm sure. I'm familiar. I'm the reporter investigating the case for the *Tribune*. We met at the Deeter farm."

"I remember." Carly transferred the phone to her strong hand and put a face with the Bette Davis voice on the other end of the line. "How did you get this number?"

"It's a small world. I know your landlady."

"Wonderful. Guess privacy wasn't part of the lease." Carly checked the clock radio. It was seven o'clock.

"Look, I know you've been warned not to talk to the press, but I can make you a deal. If you talk to me, I won't print a word without your authorization." Marci talked faster and enunciated. "I've been given information through a sympathetic source that you're being shafted on a certain disciplinary action. Not good."

There was a sound of papers rattling on the other end of the phone line. "With dismissal and/or criminal charges hanging over your head, can you afford to decline my help?"

The impact of Marci's statement hit home. Carly sat up and pushed her damp hair from her forehead. She was alert now.

"Look, Ms....?"

"Eplund, Marci."

"Marci, I gotta be honest. I don't know you, but what I saw at the Deeter farm didn't give me a favorable impression." Carly laughed. "But you sure know how to get a gal's attention by using her name close to the words, criminal charges."

"Sorry about that, but the threat is real. Isn't it?"

Carly hesitated. She wasn't sure how much the reporter knew. She could be winging it, based on conjecture. She calculated the risk. "I don't know who to trust right now. I'm going to check you out before I speak with you again. In person."

"Fair enough. By the way, do you know the militia carries a lot of weight in this town?"

* * *

It took ten minutes for Carly to shower, dress, and straighten her bedroom. She thought of Tim Price's impish grin. She had to trust somebody and her instincts told her that Tim was a nice guy. It seemed as good a reason as any to start a friendship. The assistant coroner would know, or know of, the reporter.

Carly paced from the kitchen to the living room until eight o'clock. She hoped Tim would be at his morgue. Carly guessed right. Tim picked up the phone on the second ring.

"Tim, I need to run something by you. Can you meet me for a cup?"

Tim chuckled. "Is this Carly Redmund?"

"Yes, it's me, but I don't want to talk on the phone."

"Hum, both amusing and paranoid." Carly remained silent until Tim said, "Perhaps, I was a bit hasty on the amusing part. Anyway, I will be happy to meet you."

"How about you meet me at the Pancake House at Government Street and North Broad?"

"Sure. I'll postpone this stack of paperwork. Loathe reports. Need a secretary, I mean assistant, so I don't have to work at home every night."

"I'll meet you in an hour," Carly said, and then disconnected the line. She wondered if this was a mistake. This guy was goofy cute, and she needed to remain true to her vow and not mix romance and work.

* * *

Even though the Pancake House wasn't packed, Carly and Tim sat in the back booth. With a cop's compulsion to observe people coming and going, Carly sat facing the door and the cash register. She didn't know everyone on the force, though nobody gave her a second look. Then Carly spied Don Thomas in civvies across the dining room. He kept checking his watch and sipping a cup of coffee. Reading the newspaper, he appeared unaware of the couple.

Tim ordered a diet cola, as Carly wolfed down some iced tea and a scrambled-egg-cheese sandwich on raisin toast. Waiting for Carly's second round of food, Tim said, "Hope this is not indicative of our flowering relationship. You call. I come running. Then you make me watch you eat an enormous amount of fatty food."

"So far, I can't see a problem. Most guys correlate eating food with foreplay." Carly checked herself. "Jeez that sounded—"

"Forward." Tim raked his fingers across his face. "What can I say? I'm a lucky guy."

Carly grinned as the waitress placed hash browns in front of her, and then inhaled a huge bite. "Sorry." She wiped some ketchup from her mouth with a napkin. "It's an occupational hazard, eating too fast."

"I see." Tim paused. "And the emergency?"

"No emergency. I prefer to talk in person and need your advice. Your opinion." Carly surveyed the room. "A reporter called, Marci Eplund, offering to help me, so—"

"I know Marci." Tim drank his cola slowly. "She's a woman of her word and a tenacious reporter."

"Why doesn't the look on your face match what you're saying?"

"Marci and I dated briefly, and we're still friends, but I find her…trying."

"You mean driven?"

Tim exhaled and tipped his head left, then right. "That would be a yes."

"I can deal with driven. Thanks."

Tim eyes sparkled as he leaned toward Carly.

Carly finished her drink and gathered her purse as she said, "I gotta go. I'm supposed to meet Harold, my neighbor with the dog. Sorry." She threw a twenty on the table and hustled outside leaving Tim with his mouth open.

Chapter 11

Heavenly aromas seemed to seep through the screen door, as Carly knocked on the downstairs apartment. Harold yelled, "I'm in the kitchen."

Concealing her amusement, Carly covered her mouth with the loaf of deli bread she'd brought. Harold was wearing a ruffled apron.

He caught on and looked down at his rounded stomach covered by an apple print. "The apron was Ruth's and perfectly good, so I use it. You can put the wine on the counter," he said, fluffing the apron. He shuffled across the kitchen and reached for a serving bowl. "A real man does not need to worry. And honey, I am."

Carly laughed.

A nostalgic smile crossed Harold's face. "Ruth, my sweet, late, wife and I had thirty wonderful years together on this earth. What a brilliant school teacher and conversationalist."

"You were lucky," Carly said.

He looked over his shoulder, as he folded dressing into the salad. "No. I was choosey. Just like you should be," he said. "Why don't you have a seat, dearie? You look tired."

She smiled at Harold's paternal concern as she walked to the connecting dining room, and lifted a photograph of a woman. Her hairdo and dress screaming the 1960s. "May I?" Carly asked, lifting the photo from a table near the piano.

"Of course, that's my Ruth."

She crossed the room and rested her elbows on the breakfast bar. "Ruth kind of looks like June Cleaver but—"

"But sexier. You got it. I was forty-two when we married."

Harold paused as he took some placemats from a drawer. "Before Ruth, I'd been dating four other women for years. When I asked her to be my lady and ride on the Striper's Mardi Gras float, I realized I loved her madly."

"How romantic. The king and queen wed and lived happily ever after," she said, replacing the photograph. "Now, what can I do to help?"

"Nothing, except pour the wine."

Carly opened the wine as Harold pointed up in the air. "Young lady, that year, 1969, the court jester and his maiden adorned the grandest float moving down Church Street. The festival king and queen's float paled in comparison to us."

"Hey, you and Ruth must have been a sight to see. A class act."

"I thought so. But there's thems—Mobile's elite, old money. Then there's us'n."

"Some snobs around, huh?"

"Some were and are "snickery," as my Ruth would say. Always looking down their noses. Too good for the common folk. But as a rule, the richest of the rich are down to earth.

"I've dealt with all kinds in my fifty years as the court jester. Honey, I can tell you one thing—money has nothing to do with class. You know that after one Mardi Gras, if you didn't know it before. On Fat Tuesday, the sky rains beads for days on the rich and the poor alike. And we all like our cocktails, or beers. It's just that some of us party at the Striker Club, and some do not."

"Striker Club?"

"The most elite club. It can be traced back to the early days of the mystic, secret societies. The Striker building sits next door to the museum. You'll see it when you come visit me for a tour."

He concentrated on garnishing the salmon with parsley sprigs before placing the platter on the dining room table. "There," he said, turning toward Carly and brushing crumbs away from his hands. "During Mardi Gras coins or doubloons will be thrown from the floats. I don't collect the beads, anymore, just the doubloons, the mystic societies' booties. Save me some, will ya?"

"Sure." Carly nodded.

"That's my girl. Thank you."

Lighting the candles, he said, "Each year the coins reflect a theme. Before each society's ball begins, the members throw the coins at their king and queen promenading around the ballroom floor."

"One year I set the theme for the Mystic Stripers float." He paused. "It was glorious. "The Time of Your Life." I suggested a couple dancing on a clock for the float design." He glanced nostalgically at the photograph Carly held. "The coins are nice reminders."

"I see why you want them."

"I'll be out there, but I won't fight off the parade's cretins to get the booty."

Carly put the photo back in its original spot, and then another photograph caught her attention. "Is this you?"

Harold grunted. "God, no. That's Frank, my younger cousin. Maybe at sixteen." He nodded at the photograph. "He still had some sense when that picture was taken."

Noticing Harold's no-cussing rule wasn't strictly applied in reference to Frank, Carly smiled and sat down at the table. "What happened?"

"Life happened, and Frankie didn't take to it." Harold cut his eyes toward Carly. "I feel a little like the main character in Eudora's story, "Why I Live at the P.O." I was doing fine until Frankie boy moved back home." He studied Carly and sat down opposite her. "You have read Miss Eudora Welty?"

Carly nodded, scratching Rickey's stomach as the collie rolled on the floor. "Yes, of course. What did your cousin do?"

"What hasn't he done? To give you a good example, he wanted spectator tickets to the Striker Ball because he knew their court jester—me."

"What did you do?"

"Nothing. I'd sooner given tickets to an alley cat than give my cousin and one of his trashy girlfriends coveted invitations to a formal function. Always looks like he has a hangover. Never worked a full day in his life."

Harold flapped his napkin in the air and placed it in his lap. "The clincher is how he has tried to take over at the Mardi Gras Museum. Thinks he helps me run the place, for Godsake. Comes in around noon. Won't leave, pestering the customers. If you'll pardon my French, he's a royal pain-in-my-ass."

Carly took a sip of wine. "Where had he been living before his visit?"

"California." Harold took a bite of steamed asparagus. "That tells you a lot, huh? People with good manners know when to go home."

Harold passed the breadbasket to Carly. "If he's not careful," Harold said, "I'll sic widow Girth on him." Carly had noticed that their landlady, Dotty Girth, seemed to be at the mailboxes every day when Harold returned from work.

"Believe me," Harold said with fire in his eyes. "She can make a man wish he weren't single. She's worse than a cat on catnip. And the endless stream of her tuna casseroles. Dreadful swill."

The dog whimpered for attention.

"Rickey won't even eat them, Harold said patting the dog's head. "Not even fit for my buddy, who eats roadkill."

The dog wandered out of the room, his paws making tapping noises on the hardwood floor.

"Yeah, Dotty gave my number out without my permission. I wasn't thrilled."

"Miss Dotty and Frank deserve each other." Harold flapped his hands. "Love to say good riddance to both."

Carly clapped at Harold's antics, and then asked the next obvious question. "Is Frank staying here?"

"Not on your life. He has rented a room on Government Street near The Ebony Methodist Church. Close to our black friends. Fits right in."

"Really. Is that—"

"Anywhos! Sometime—on duty is fine—you should drop by the museum. I'll introduce you to Jason and Sherri. We get the job done, then we party on Saturday afternoons after the last tour. We lock the doors, bring out our coolers, and have a cocktail or two." He winked and elbowed the air. "We have great fun. Who knows? Brian, our impish ghost, might be lurking around."

"You keep telling me about your teenage ghost. I'd love to meet him—the ghost that wrecks any museum display not to his liking. But let's make it off duty. I don't want to bring my field training officer."

Harold nodded. "How's that going?"

While she tore apart a roll, Carly said, "Not too well. I'm making it through the training okay, but hoping they don't fire me before I figure out what really happened at the Deeter farm."

Harold moved his fork like a mini baton dipping it slowly several times. "The missing ring?" he said.

"Right, the missing evidence." Swallowing a mouthful of food, she said, "Gosh, this blackened salmon is good."

"Isn't it? Did you find out anything?"

"A little. Tim, the assistant coroner, helped me piece together a good reason why J.C. acted so crazy. His brother, Derrick, had a fight with Terence Washington Williams just before he disappeared in the 1970s."

"So Officer Grey took the ring to protect his no-good-politicking brother, then changed his mind, put it wherever, and blamed you."

"He put it into a property box a day late and signed my name. I could go to IA, but there's a good chance the department has something to hide. Besides, Officer Grey would just say he was covering for me."

"It's a "he said, you said" situation. I see you're conflicted about how to handle it." Harold moved to the counter, offered Carly more fish, and refilled his plate. "So what you're really saying is Derrick is responsible for Terence's death?

"Right."

"But have you considered Derrick could be innocent?"

"I doubt it. Even my training officer acts like his brother's guilty. Either way, I just hope Tim and me, and maybe a reporter named Marci Eplund, can uncover the truth. My job depends on it."

"By the way, I understand the reporter's motivation, but why is this Tim fellow sticking his neck out?"

"Not sure, but I suspect he is tired of the coroner's incompetence—wants to do what's right by the victim's family, respect for the dead stuff. Carly shrugged. "And he likes me."

"Aha, love blooms."

"I wouldn't say that. He's a nice guy."

Harold's incredulous look revealed he thought there was more.

She felt her face reddened. "Okay he's cute, but that's it. I have my hands full with training and defending my own neck."

"The lady does protest too much."

"Give me a break. Right now, I just want dessert. I know you're hiding something in the fridge."

"Maybe. Deny all you want, missy. I saw you blush."

"Please, can we move on?"

"Okay, subject closed. For now," Harold said as he cleared the dishes from the table.

While he made coffee and set out a peach cream pie, Carly finished off the last of the wine.

"Now, this pie is sugar-free," Harold explained, "because of my pesky diabetes."

"That's fine with me. It looks yummy. And while we're waiting for the coffee, would you mind telling me about Terence's family? About Mary Williams?"

"I personally never had the pleasure of meeting Mary or her people. I know her late husband's descendants can be traced back to the *Clotilda,* the last known slave ship in North America. You know, it burned in the harbor?"

Carly shook her head.

Harold cut two large pieces of pie. "The men and women who survived built Africatown."

"Africatown?"

"North of the city. You understand the burning happened after slavery was declared illegal and just before the Civil War. After they were set free, they built a compound, circled it with a wooden-pole fence like an African village, then waited for the white landowners to complain. They didn't. Decided to leave well enough alone."

"Is a fence still there?"

"Don't think so. Never go up there. But an African named Cudo was known for passing along their stories and traditions. His pictures and such are in the museums around here. Free men have always lived there. Just can't buy most of the land. Majority of the land's in trust."

"You mean white families still own the land. Won't sell. But they rent it."

"Only one family really matters. The Brontes of Spring Hill. It's mostly their land. Always has been."

Carly thought about saying how unfair that sounded, but she opted for diplomacy. "Harold, I gotta tell you, Lincoln's a hero of mine. My best friend in Charleston was—"

"Is that right?" He slid a piece of pie in front of her. "Well, I won't hold that against you. But I won't change my mind about my black brothers. There's good ones and bad one. Even they don't want to mix with us."

He handed her a china cup of coffee. "Listen. I've been around a long time as the honorary court jester. The parade officials asked our black friends in the 1970s if they wanted to combine the Mardi Gras king and queen celebrations. Don't look so surprised, Missy. They have their own mystic society balls and parades headed by their prominent—and I might add—wealthy black families. Anyway, they said, 'No.'"

As Harold rambled on, Carly was stunned, wondering what else she didn't understand about the deep South.

"You know twenty-five thousand doesn't begin to touch even one costume for a king or queen." Harold said. "They have dozens. It takes loads of money, not to mention the right bloodline, to be a chosen as even a lady in waiting." Harold folded his napkin and laid it by his plate. "Yes, because of my fashion expertise and my show biz experience, most families come to me to recommend a designer for their gowns and trains. Never get a dime out of it."

"This blows my mind," Carly said. "I come from the work-hard-and-pray-you-can-pay-your-bills type people. For the love of … . How am I going to find my way and solve this case when I can't begin to imagine living a lifestyle surrounded by old money and high society?"

"You'll get used to our ways," he said, as he poured her another cup of coffee. "Until then, I can steer you in the right direction." Squeezing Carly's hand, Harold added, "Besides, like I said, I know a few people who know the right people. Designers and such." He waved his hands in the air. "It will sort out. You'll see."

* * *

The next morning, Derrick awoke with his arm around Rose's waist. "Honey, it's time to get up," he said, nibbling her ear.

Rose brushed the air in front of her face. "Stop it. I want to sleep some more."

Derrick patted her rear, then rolled out of bed and headed for the shower. "You'll feel better if you go make the coffee."

"Okay, okay," Rose said, as she stretched her lean body and remembered Junior had to be at school early for a makeup test. He had broken his arm jumping from a tree in their backyard and had missed a day of school. He was a little monkey, her Bibey. She adored him. He was Derrick in miniature.

Rose didn't do breakfast. Her morning ritual included nursing a cup of strong coffee and finishing with a cigarette on the deck after Derrick left for work. A half-hearted closet smoker, she never smoked in public. Ladies didn't smoke or curse. It was common. Neither Rose's mother or Derrick's grandmama, both deceased, ever knew about Rose's vice, and she didn't intend for the truth to be uncovered.

A few minutes later, she yawned and put the cereal and milk on the table as the children scrambled for the television remote.

As the boys ate in front of the television, Derrick kissed Rose goodbye and whispered, "You're the sexiest thing I've ever seen in your PJs."

Rose shot a Mona Lisa smile at him and reached for her cigarette and lighter before prancing toward the French doors that led to the deck. "Later, Cowboy," she said.

Starting his Mazda, Derrick visualized Rose walking across the room in her robe. Gorgeous and graceful. She always made the out-of-sync something inside him shift back in place. She was the perfect wife and mother—loyal and clueless about how the world worked outside her kitchen. He hoped he never had to tell her.

Derrick's routine, including the ten-minute drive to the office, pleased him. His workdays always began with his secretary, Miss Mildred Stalch. Today she approached like a discreet waitress, setting the pink-colored phone messages on top of his pile of mail. The first, marked "return call-urgent," was from Billie Ray Cofer.

Passing in front of Derrick's desk, Mildred coughed and waited for her boss to look up. When he did, the secretary said, "The Cofers make bad business partners."

Of course, someone had seen him and Billie Ray at the Battleship Café and the grapevine's news had reached Mildred in record time. Although not known for gossiping, she would mention any rumor that might endanger his reputation.

Out of respect to her age, Derrick always used a mild tone and a formal greeting. "Thank you, Miss Stalch," he grinned, "What would I do without you? You keep me grounded." He lost his smile. "But I know who and what I am dealing with here. Unfortunately..." He scanned Mildred's lined face. "Can I rely on you to keep me informed of any fallout?"

"Of course."

"You see, Mr. Cofer's money will be useful in my campaign."

Mildred's cool gaze held Derrick's a second longer, and then she said, "I understand."

* * *

"Do you get to see your family much in Missouri?" Marci asked, passing Carly another beer.

"No, not really." Hating small talk, Carly forged ahead—hoping their first face to face would go well. "How about your family? Any brothers or sisters?"

"Nope. I'm an only child," Marci said looking down for a spilt second. "Spoiled rotten. You?"

Carly read Marci's body language indicating she wasn't being totally truthful, though she said, "I have a younger sister. She lives in Missouri."

Carly pulled her chair closer to the table allowing a patron to pass. "I hear this place has great seafood."

"Yes, Wintzell's has the best oysters in town." Marci propped an ankle on a knee and squared her body. "If you like to read while you eat, just check out a wall."

Carly scanned the walls covered in photographs, signatures, and sayings. "The picture of Spiro Agnew in his heyday is folksy and different, but I gotta say the jokes are pretty lame."

"Yeah, and ironic, as demonstrated by the many wordy plaques about how women talk too much," Marci said with a shrug. "Apparently, the male proprietor doesn't like female input."

The waitress brought Carly her water and put pen to pad waiting for their order.

Marci said, "Oh, I'm sorry we're still waiting for a third party to return from the john."

"Really," the waitress snapped, and then walked away.

"I guess we're interrupting her day," Carly said, as she laid her menu on the table. "But it is busy in here." She looked around for Tim, but didn't see him. "Anyway, so how's the reporting biz?"

"About like PD I would imagine. Always busy. Political bull. Same stuff, just another day." Marci waved a finger in the air, adding, "Except yesterday—I had a door slammed in my face."

"Are you kidding?"

"Nope. And with my winning personality too."

Carly laughed. "Tell me about it."

"Mrs. Mary Williams doesn't like reporters. I'd guess in general. I quote, 'We did her and Terence an injustice in the 1970s.' Heck, I was barely out of diapers. It wasn't my fault the press caved to political pressure. Integration had to be a bitch for everyone."

"Good point, but it's got to be traumatic for Mary. Not knowing what happened to her son all these years." Even in Carly's alcohol-induced euphoria, her worries seemed trivial in comparison to Mary's loss.

Smiling, Tim returned from the restroom. "What did I miss, Carly? You look like someone died."

Marci interjected, "None of your business. Except we agreed you're paying the bill, because you made us wait to order."

"I think I left my wallet at home."

"Sit down, Tim." Carly pulled at his arm. "Just hate a tight wad. Don't you, Marci?"

"Bad as a wimpy guy who can't hold his beer and goes to the toilet every five minutes."

As if on cue, the waitress came back, and they ordered. Before a conversation could get underway, Tim saw a friend, a doctor from the county hospital, and excused himself. Watching his easy stride, Carly remembered Tim and Marci had been tight. Whatever passions had been between them seemed to have cooled in the last three years, but Tim had chosen a public place for them to meet. The Williams case would've had to wait until a rapport was established among the trio.

Carly turned her attention to Marci. "Tell me more about yourself."

"You first." She pointed to the band on Carly's left hand.

"Oh, this? Not married, ever. Wear it to remind myself to be more responsible. A bad relationship. A stupid mistake." Carly finished off her beer. "How about you?"

"Made a few myself. Know how that goes." She turned her face by pushing an index finger against her jaw. "Gaze upon this profile. Besides, it's hard to find someone who appreciates, or for that matter, can live with my better qualities. Too headstrong."

Carly took in Marci's no-makeup appearance complete with a prominent nose, and instantly liked her. Her gut feeling was that Marci was bisexual. She knew the cost of being driven and smart and admired Marci's laid-back style that camouflaged a no-bullshit approach. Like most guys on the force. In Carly's opinion ultra-feminine women cared about the wrong things—long nails, hair, and the labels in their clothes.

"Hey, being free and single has its compensations," Carly replied. "Right?"

"Damn straight. Couldn't take someone telling me what to do. Calling and checking-in stuff would grate on my last nerve."

"Relationships are work."

Tim returned just as the waitress served the food—fried oysters for Marci, chili for Tim, and gumbo for Carly. They ate in silence allowing Carly to think about the case. "It's strange that Jack Deeter Sr. and Billie Ray Cofer were neighbors. Couldn't be a coincidence that Terence's bones ended up in the Deeter well?"

Marci nodded. "I don't have any sources, yet, but I think Cofer—the white supremist bastard—and Deeter are key players in this whole tangled knot."

"Wait a minute, ladies. Are you saying that Cofer—granted a racist—and Jack Sr. are somehow responsible for Terence's death, because of where Terence's body was dumped?"

"Yes, Tim," Carly replied. "I'll bet Cofer is—"

Marci leaned forward and blurted out, "Part of the cover-up, if not part of the no-name dummy corporation."

Tim glanced around the room, but nobody seemed to notice Marci's out burst. "Keep it down. Will ya?" he said. "Anyone could have dumped the body."

Marci shook her head. "The foreman's cousin did the specs on the Deeter land. It sold for over twice what it was worth."

Carly tapped Marci's shoulder. "That makes sense," she said. "Probably the Cofer and Deeter families were close. Grey mentioned as a kid romping across the farm and the old hunting lodge with Jack Jr." Carly added, "How much land are we talking about?"

"From I-65 north for thirty square miles or so," Marci said.

"That's a big spread. Big enough for, say, a training compound."

"That's a bit off-track. I still contend you're stretching your so-called logic," Tim said. He raised his empty beer bottle in the waitress's direction.

Marci looked off into the distance. "That might explain the high price tag on Jack's land."

"What are you talking about?" Tim said.

Taking a sip of beer, Marci said, "Try to keep up. News flash: To keep someone like Jack quiet about an illegal training compound would cost a lot of money."

"A compound makes weird sense," Carly said. "Still...where are Cofer's boys? His sons?"

"I got this one," Tim jumped in. "Two are dead. One died in Vietnam, and the youngest wrapped his red Firebird around a tree when he was coming home from a party. Old man Cofer had given him the Firebird in high school. The old man never got over it, according to the guys at the barbershop. The third one, a kid during the time we're talking about, lives around here. But he's a professor and has little to do with the old man. I think there's a grandson. Might be in kindergarten."

"You sure know a lot about the locals," Carly said, "for a guy that spends most of his time in a morgue with dead bodies."

"I can't help it if the fairer sex likes a guy who listens."

Both women cleared their throats at the same time.

"And I can blend in, too," Tim said. "When I want."

"You mean stalk," Marci said.

"Thanks. I remember endearing things about you too," Tim said, and then grinned at Carly.

"You see why we stopped dating."

"Huh, I refuse to comment. Let's get back to the matter at hand. The point is…." Lowering her voice, she continued, "What we're really saying is that Jack Jr. and the Grey brothers have conspired to cover up, or directly participated in the killing of Terence Washington Williams."

"If that's the theory, Miss Redmund, prove it." Tim folded his arms.

"Such negativity," Marci said. "We've little to nothing to lose by trying."

"Absolutely." Carly counted off on her fingers. "We have a budding forensic scientist, a first-time hard-news reporter, and a rookie cop. I'd say this is a dangerous situation for our adversaries. They'll underestimate us."

Tim shrugged. "I hate to admit it, but you're right."

"To truth, justice, and the American way." Marci raised her mug.

"And to trust among friends," Carly said.

Tim raised his glass and toasted. "Whatever. You two are way too much."

"We know," Carly said, realizing the Grey brothers and their allies were prepped and ready for this fight.

Chapter 12

"Come on. We're going to be late," Carly called over her shoulder as she took long strides up the walkway, stopping on the stoop to wait for Marci to catch up.

"I'm coming, but I still don't know why you're dragging me along," Marci whined. "Remember, Mrs. Williams doesn't like me."

"Look. I don't want to talk to this grieving woman about her murdered son either. Especially, since the police department screwed up the initial investigation. Besides, you're versed in the historical facts. I need your expertise."

"Bull—you can't lift my mood with simple compliments. I'm determined to nurse this hangover as long as I want." Marci rubbed her temples. "God, I need aspirin and coffee."

"Bad tempered for sure."

"And your point?" asked Marci.

Carly rolled her eyes. "Hush. Let me knock on the door. Try to act professional for a few minutes. Okay?"

"If I have to, all right. Knock."

Mary answered the door wearing a maroon silk shirt over brown tailored slacks. She displayed perfect posture. Around her neck hung a silver amulet in the shape of a sphinx, glittering in the sunlight. She waved them into a room across from the dining room where weeks earlier Carly had had brunch.

"Well, come into the sitting room," Mary said, glaring at Marci.

"This is Marci Eplund, my friend and a reporter from the *Tribune*," Carly said.

Mary barley nodded and focused her attention on Carly. "I hope you're serious about investigating Terence's murder. I have no patience for reporters who sell newspapers by trivializing death. Caring nothing for the victim's family. Before the coroner called me about finding my son, I saw the *Tribune's* disrespectful headline, 'Bones Found on Deeter Farm,' without my son's name, *Terence Washington Williams*, mentioned anywhere in the paper."

Carly shot a warning look at Marci, who was letting her anger, simmer just below the surface.

Marci exhaled, and then said, "I apologize. Another reporter didn't do his homework."

Mary's face remained stern.

"Look. Carly and I have a deal. I don't write the story without her authorization. You feel you were treated unfairly. I'll do my best, not add to the injustice of the situation."

Mary said nothing.

Carly broke the tension. "I can assure you this is about catching the killer or killers. Could we sit down?"

"Of course, please sit." Mary made a point of looking at both of them when she said, "Would you like a cup of coffee?"

Sitting on a small settee, Marci scanned the room. "Beautiful piano," she said.

The Steinway sat between two windows. A breeze drifted through the room from an open window framed by ruby-red velvet drapes trimmed in gold fringe. The midday light struck the polished, hardwood floor and warmed the room.

"Thank you," Mary said, unfolding her hands. "I believe Cato, my chef, just made some coffee. Let me go and see."

Once Mary left the room, Marci and Carly exchanged glances.

"I'm glad I didn't try to tackle this by myself," Carly said. "She doesn't seem pleased to see us."

"You got that right. You take the lead. I'm saying as little as—"

Mary reentered the room carrying an African hand-carved wooden tray. Blue Willow china cups and a decanter rattled as she placed them upon an antique coffee table.

"Mrs. Williams, this is wonderful," Carly said. "It smells delicious."

Mary smiled, poured the coffee, and then leaned back in an overstuffed satin chair. Sipping her coffee, she said, "Now, young women, ask your questions."

"Okay, I'll start," Carly said as she stirred cream and sugar into her coffee. "We need to know anything, details, you know about your son's disappearance—his murder—which would help us build a case." She reached for her notepad and pen inside her jacket pocket.

Mary didn't rush her reply. In a cool tone she asked, "Aren't you in trouble over Terence's high school ring being misplaced?"

Carly hesitated, wondering if Mary would believe her. The rapport established from their previous luncheon had obviously evaporated. "Yes, but my field training officer took it."

"I heard it was J.C. Grey," Mary shrugged. "Just testing."

When Carly and Marci made eye contact, the older woman smiled at them, appearing to savor their confusion. "I did my homework. I still have a few friends in high places."

"Then you know Grey set me up?" Carly said.

"What I know is that I haven't seen J.C. since he graduated from high school. That was a few years before his brother Derrick, but I know the family all too well."

She fell silent and gazed at the cloverleaf design on the mantel's shelf. "I'm not easily fooled," she said. "It's quite simple. Hatred and jealousy killed my son. You see, desegregation grated on the nerves of the whites. They knew education would make my race prosper.

"They hated my family back then, and most—not all—hate us now. Did you know my late husband, Edgar, graduated from Howard University and owned a successful dry cleaning business? No, I didn't think so."

Again, Mary, paused and studied them before she continued. "He fought for civil rights and gave money to the cause long before any liberal whites joined the movement. Terence was so much like his father. His charisma and talent. A handsome young man, my son." Her voice softened, as she said, "Did you know he was a football star?"

"Yes," Carly said. "We heard Terence was the best."

The hardness returned to Ms. Williams's manner as she said, "That's right. They let him play on the team, but they wouldn't shower with him." For an instant, her voice had quivered. "He helped score almost every point in the last game before they murdered him. Derrick Grey, the ...." Tears welled in her eyes. "Derrick was the quarterback on the team, but everyone knew that the 'nigger' running back won that game."

Carly was shocked that Mary had used the "N word." Sticking her hair behind her ears, she put her pen down and asked, "Did Derrick have it in for Terence before the incident with Austin?"

Mary straightened in her chair. "Terence took away Derrick's thunder. The so-called revenge fight was an excuse to get rid of my son. It was common knowledge in the black community that Derrick and his racist thugs beat my Terence unmercifully. After Derrick ran away, Jack Deeter and his buddies cleaned up. Finished my son."

Carly leaned forward in her seat. "No doubt in your mind, Derrick killed Terence?"

"None. I believe Jack, and God knows who else, threw Terence in that well. I have prayed to be able to forgive the Grey and Deeter families, but I can't." Her hands shook as she placed her cup on the tray. "I just hope he wasn't alive when they dumped him in that well."

Carly suddenly realized that Mary didn't know that Terence had been shot in the head. Refocusing, Carly said, "Did Austin ever touch any other girls at the school before he touched your daughter? I understand he tried to fondle her."

"My daughter's name is Evangeline."

"I'm sorry, I should've remembered. Evangeline."

Mary nodded. "Anyway, the white school administrators knew he was a problem. Always playing with himself in public. The boy was smart enough to know messing with a black girl would be overlooked. I'm sure they saw no reason to protect a black baby factory. We black folks be sinful beasts. You knows?

"Ms. Eplund, over there, knows how we are portrayed in the media, even today. Isn't that right?"

With a tight jaw Marci looked at the rose carpet and put her cup back on the tray.

Mary continued. "They treated Austin as if he were a mischievous child who we'd have to abide. Well, Terence was proud to be black, and he loved his sister. He didn't put up with it."

"What exactly happened the day Terence confronted the Grey boy about Evangeline?"

"I wasn't there, but Terence told me that he flattened Austin against the lockers, and told him never to bother his sister again. Terence didn't hit him. He wasn't a bully. There wasn't a scratch on the child."

Carly decided to risk angering Mary. "Did Terence threaten to kill him?" she asked.

Mary gave Carly a dismissive glance. "I raised Terence right. He could defend his sister without terrorizing a disabled child. He was angry, not stupid." Terence's mother stood and began gathering the cups and spoons. "I'm sorry. You must excuse me. I have guests coming from Atlanta today."

The interview was over.

"Thank you for your time. We can show ourselves out," Marci said as she walked toward the door.

"You've been a great help," Carly said. "I promise, Mrs. Williams, we'll do our best to sort this out, find the perpetrators, and keep you updated."

Marci and Carly were silent as they drove away from Mary's house. Carly thought about how terrible it would be to outlive your child and wondered if some actions were unforgiveable. Like murder, like abortion. Twisting the gold band on her left ring finger, she relived the sterile clinic scene with her feet in stirrups and the unbelievable feeling of emptiness.

But she had made her choice. She couldn't go back.

* * *

Billie Ray loved his grandson, Hudson. Six years ago at his birth, Billie Ray had experienced the joy of becoming a grandfather and had found his mere presence made the boy happy. Billie Ray felt adored.

When he gave Hudson his first .22 rifle, the kid nearly lost his lunch. He jumped like a jack-in-the-box. All day, they had been shooting tin cans on a stump from the back deck.

Nobody in the family bothered to cross Billie Ray when it came to the subject of guns. His participation in the militia group preempted other opinions on guns and rifles. The right to bear arms was a God-given right, and any liberals who wanted to interfere, be they family or the federal government, needed to stay the hell away from Billie Ray's property.

Hudson had been chattering nonstop, while Billie Ray glued a wooden wheel on a toy cart. "Grandpa, you can fix anything."

Billie Ray smiled and handed Hudson the cart. "Almost," he said, and then picked up his Remington shotgun and sighted it in.

"The birds." Hudson pointed at several finches that flew away. "They see us?"

Billie Ray nailed a squirrel about fifty yards away as he explained. "Yes, they can see us, but if we're real quiet and don't move much, they think we're part of the trees. They think we're not a threat, something to be afraid of. Surprise helps us destroy our enemies."

Hudson grabbed the deck railing. "But Grandpa, the squirrels aren't mean? Are they?"

"No, not really." Billie Ray loaded rounds of birdshot into the Remington and snapped the action closed. "They're just practice. It's foreign and dark-skinned people who pollute the white gene pool and prevent the new world order."

Billie Ray looked at Hudson's frowning face. Realizing the child didn't understand, he laughed. "It's okay, boy. You're young yet. We have time to teach you who's the enemy. Whites are smarter, stronger than the others. You'll see the problem next year at school. As clear to you as the nose on your face."

He grabbed Hudson's nose and pretended to twist the end. The little boy giggled, and Billie Ray patted his grandson's shoulder. "The Cofers must stay pure. We won't mingle with other races who don't look like us. Talk like us. Someday, Uncle Adam can tell you the Bible story of the Tower of Babel.

"Now, try hitting that bird. That's right, stock to your shoulder, front sight, and squeeze the—"

The .22 rifle went off.

Hudson missed and lowered his rifle. Almost crying. "Jeez," he said as Billie Ray shot the bird. The small-feathered body dropped to the ground with a thud.

Pointing the barrel away from Hudson, Billy Ray said, "We all have to learn. That's why you have me." He patted Hudson's shoulder. "Don't forget God separates people by color, the strong from the weak. You come from the best. You're special, Hudson. God made you white and a Cofer."

Hudson smiled with pride.

Chapter 13

Waiting for the full name and background minutiae on the local corporation that bought the land, Marci was anxious. She had set up a two o'clock appointment with Jack Deeter, who had an hour layover at the Montgomery Regional Airport. *Where the hell was Stewart? He should have the information by now.* She needed to get going, and she wasn't looking forward to the two-hour trip in the cameraman's van to Montgomery.

She recalled the phone conversation with Jack Deeter. The obnoxious jerk. He'd made sure Carly understood his father, "Daddy Deeter," had been respected in his community and had attended college with her boss, Jim Branson.

Not that Branson would give two hoots or a good Goddamn.

It was almost eleven. Hunger pangs and the abdominal gurgling noises reminded her she had drunk enough coffee, and she hadn't eaten since somebody gave her a bagel yesterday.

This story was a treadmill you couldn't get off, but so far she had met the *Tribune's* deadlines despite Branson hounding her for more details to uphold and confirm his no bullshit, two-source confirmation policy. The endless days were wearing her down.

Putting on her last pair of clean underwear this morning, she had reconsidered her khaki pants and blue travel shirt on their third day of duty. She always wore a shell under the long sleeve travel blouse. It didn't smell good, but it didn't reek. The air sanitizer sprayed inside the armholes of the blouse would have to hold her for one more day.

Yesterday, craving a hot bath and a steak, she settled for what Laura brought back from the cantina. A bodybuilder. She liked to take the stairs on her breaks and nagged Marci about not eating right or exercising.

Laura lifted a bag as she barked, "Eat this. Turkey on rye. You look like shit."

"Thanks, pal. By the way, I love your look. It is almost as chic as my stinko-khaki combo."

Laura responded by conducting a straight-armed drop over the cubicle wall with the bag of food. It hit the desk with a wet thud.

The drink spilled. "Damn it, Lars," Marci said.

Laura smoothed her red leather skirt. "Such common vocab, from a front-page reporter no less." She shook her head. "A heart attack waiting to happen. Anyway, haven't you heard the old expression, 'Don't bite the hand that feeds you?'"

"Okay, I hear you. But for inspiration let me feel your bicep?"

Laura lifted both of her middle fingers toward Marci and walked off.

With vacuum-like efficiency, Marci stuffed a huge piece of sandwich in her mouth and tracked a shadow skim across her desk.

"Stewart, is that you?"

"Yeah, how'd you know?"

"You radiate animal magnetism."

"And you eat like an animal, Marci. Give me a break."

She smashed the paper bag and threw it in the trash as she said, "No can do, Stewy. I must point out that social graces aren't your forte—one of the reasons I like you—but a few are necessary. Like saying hello would be nice."

She twirled a pen between her fingers. "Still, I do like your just-the-facts approach to life. Anyway, what you got?"

Stewart's face revealed the rollercoaster emotions Marci's words evoked. He seemed to settle on the words, "I like you." He smiled and handed Marci a printout. "There's something strange about this MSU Corporation. My best guess is that it's a dummy Corp."

"Yes, just as we thought. Do you have a name instead of a logo for the corporation? A few shareholders' names?"

"Nope, not yet, I'm working on it. What were they really building out there in the sticks?"

"Hard to say. They were still clearing the land when the skeleton was found in the well."

Stewart gave her a confused look.

"Okay, I kind of goofed. Didn't really nail it down when I should've." Marci blinked several times. "Give me a break. Anyway, Carly and I suspect a militia training compound."

He shifted the paper close to her face. "Makes sense. It indicates here a private hunting reserve, but the finances and board members are hidden in a technical maze. It'll take me a few hours to sort this one."

"Right. Thanks, Stewart. I owe you one. Keep looking, oh great wizard of cyberspace. Gotta go. Jack Deeter is due at the Montgomery Airport at two."

"How're you going to handle it? He has got a rep for being a Neanderthal. "

"I intend to walk softly around Jackie boy and let the tribal drums beat." She tapped the desk. "We'll see what lies he tries to pass off as the truth."

* * *

Marci jotted down notes as the photographer drove his van in heavy traffic on I-65. For the benefit of the forthcoming interview, she wanted to gain Jack's trust, if not his rapport, but the rich stymied her. Her take on the wealthy was they had something to hide, either in their shady business dealings or in their raunchy personal lives. Life was messy, not perfect and comfortable, unless others took the fall, or took out the trash. Nothing stood pristine for long.

Aware of another human being in the van, she said, "Chris, what do you think? This guy is arrogant. He sounded annoyed on the initial phone call, dismissive even, but he consented to the interview fast enough. What's his angle? He knows I know he became a millionaire with the sale of his inherited property. He isn't sure if I know about the silent investors and the training compound."

"Sounds like you answered your own question."

"Yeah, privately-owned paramilitary facilities are illegal in this state. Go figure."

Chris shrugged and shot her a glance before he lit up a cigarette.

"Damn, that smells good," she said, inhaling as much the smoke as she could before reluctantly opening her window. "Thanks, man, for helping me avoid temptation."

Chris lifted one side of his mouth, an almost grin.

"Anyway, an article in *Alabama* magazine last winter listed Jack Deeter's assets as 'Mobile's Most Eligible Bachelor.'" Marci laughed. "The rugged outdoorsman in a Neiman Marcus flannel shirt."

The shirt had highlighted the blue in his powerful eyes. Even though, Marci usually preferred the softer sex, and knew the photo shot was hype—the cleft chin and square jaw above broad linebacker shoulders were almost too much to bear.

Even if, Deeter's authenticity was a pretense, he carried it off with finesse.

Marci wanted to be on top of her game. Feeling brain-dead, she climbed to the back of the van and frantically rehearsed questions. Nothing helped. She was blocked.

Chris ignored Marci and kept his eyes on the centerline. When the cameraman left I-65N, he negotiated the ramp to I-80W and yelled out orders: "Look alive. Find out where we should meet him. I'll need to park soon."

Marci punched the numbers on her cell, and then heard Jack laugh and excuse himself before he said, "Jack Deeter here. How may I help you?"

Was this the same distasteful man who'd conversed with her this morning?

"Mr. Deeter, she said. "This is Marci Eplund from the *Tribune*. I'm here at the airport. Where should I meet you?"

"Well, I'm having a delightful time at the airport bar. You can't miss it. It's just inside the main entrance, straight shot to the atrium area. Why don't you meet me here?"

"That'll be fine. Give me ten minutes or so."

"Just don't break my mood. You must celebrate with me. I made close to a hundred thou in the market this morning."

"Congratulations, you must be ecstatic. I'll be there soon."

"Thank you. I'm not going anywhere." The line went dead.

"Chris, I think he might be drunk."

Glancing over his shoulder, he said in a monotone voice, "That could be good or bad."

"Yeah, depends if Jack is a mean drunk or a nice drunk. He shouldn't be too plowed, unless he started on the plane."

Their final exit ramp landed them in an ugly industrial district east of the airport. The pell-mell of signage and traffic took on a *noir* flavor through the murky van windows.

The stress was getting to Marci. She shook her head like a wet dog.

Climbing back into the front passenger seat, she directed Chris to park in the one-hour lot, and then fidgeted while the photographer loaded his gear.

"Comb your hair or something," Chris said.

"Why, what's the matter with it?" Marci said, getting out of the van and dropping her satchel behind the rear doors. She already knew her oily, dark hair was plastered against her forehead leaving the impression of a stringy mop.

Chris motioned her out of the way. "Just step back so I can get inside the van."

As he grabbed a camera floodlight, Marci leaned against the doorframe and let a familiar tape play inside her head: "Marci, do something with that hair. Greasy, mousy hair won't help you be wanted by a loving family."

Marci answered as if Mother Superior were present inside the van, "Well, Mother, this will have to do." She turned toward Chris, "Hell, at least Jack won't want to play the distraction-by-attraction game with me."

Chris shrugged. "Ready then? Let's go."

* * *

The familiar street was deserted in Carly's dream:

She parked the borrowed green 1954 Chevrolet truck along the curb of a wooden-framed house. The simplicity of the neighborhood in the pre-dawn tranquility struck her as comforting. Rubbing her hand over the seat upholstery, she followed the blue vinyl cording and wondered if she should leave the keys inside the truck, or keep them for her next watch.

Then a light went on somewhere within the small house. A figure began to stir. A woman's silhouette came to the picture window. But she didn't wave. They acknowledged each other through the darkness. Permission granted.

Carly understood it was all right to use the truck for as long as she needed. Shutting the truck door, she tossed the keys in the air, caught them, and rolled them around in her palm.

At four in the morning, the street looked clean, and the light from the street lamps filtered through the tree canopies, making a lacy outline on the pavement. The houses were middle class starter homes from the 1950s. Somehow, Carly knew in the future they would become homes for working class residents struggling to keep their gutters repaired and the grass mowed.

Carly strode to the middle of the street and pivoted, gazing at the truck. Thankful for the sturdy vehicle, she questioned the color. The limerick green, like in her nephew's nursery, didn't fit. She must be dreaming.

Willing the dream to continue, she crossed the street, smiling as she approached the red brick columns of her porch. She visualized Mitch waiting for her inside. After climbing the three steps to the porch, reality broke through. No, he wouldn't be there. But she wanted him to be there. Needed him.

A vision of Mitch caressing her ankle woke Carly. She pulled her hand from her underpants. Trying to empty her mind, she gave up and counted the uncovered pipes in the ceiling rafters of the loft.

Mitch was good, too good. She pictured his amoral mouth and his analytical rhetoric floating out into comic-strip dialogue balloons. Nothing but lies. She hated the person she had been with him.

What had attracted Carly to Mitch was a chance moment. While on her rounds as a campus cop, she'd witnessed him saying goodbye to his children outside his office at Duke University. Gentleness flowed from him. Carly had never seen such masculine tenderness. She was immediately hooked.

When Carly registered for a psychology class with Professor Mitchell Taylor, she already knew she was attracted to him, and then he'd shown interest in her midterm essay. "Miss Redmund, with a little revising, I'd recommend your term paper for publication in a journal. You need to meet me in my office during student advisement hours."

Carly was never published, but the groundwork for their affair was laid.

When an inopportune call from Mitch's home had interrupted one of their meetings, he'd said, "My wife is a woman who devotes herself to her church and children. Marriage is a vehicle for social standing in the community. The package is what gives her life purpose, not me."

After several weeks, Mitch had touched Carly's hand and had asked as he'd given her a long searching look. "Can you stay for a cup of coffee at the student center? I need to unwind. I'd enjoy your company."

Then he'd courted her subtly. "Appreciate you, Officer," he said, as he handed her a bottle of water while Carly directed traffic in a crosswalk. On her birthday she asked Mitch to meet for a drink. He flashed her a million dollar smile, and Carly was smitten.

Weeks later, in bed with him, Carly had said, "Don't you ever feel guilty? I do. Your wife has to know."

"No, you're my soul mate." Mitch kissed her shoulder. "Besides, I know my wife. If she finds out about our affair, she'll never let on."

There had been times when Carly rationalized her questionable behavior and convinced herself Mitch's wife preferred the arrangement. After all her husband was a devoted father. Carly meant nothing. She meant nothing to their life.

By the time Carly understood the affair was a minefield, she'd fallen in love for the first time. When she tried to pull away and regain a sense of balance, Mitch spoke those three magic words, "I love you," and begged for time to work things out.

What a mess. It seemed like yesterday, not two years ago. Seeking sanctuary, returning home to Missouri before she'd moved to Mobile, had been a joke. A disaster.

Carly turned over in bed and hit the alarm button. Time to get up and get busy. No points for hindsight. Get over it, as Marci might say.

Her interview with Jack Deeter at the airport was today. Afterward, the women were supposed to meet and strategize.

A plan of action would make Carly feel better.

* * *

The airport bar was easy to find for Marci, but it wasn't much to look at. The orange and brown decor was raunchy 1970s. Based on hearsay, she knew the drinks weren't watered down, just overpriced, leaving unwary travelers who stayed too long inebriated.

Jack stood and greeted Marci with a handshake, and then waited for her to sit down. Not used to gallantry, she blushed, but concealed her face by bending down to retrieve her tape recorder. Recovering somewhat, she asked Jack if he minded a taped interview.

"Of course not," he said. "Welcome to the Dannelly Field airport bar ambience. This fellow is Jarrell, my personal assistant."

Marci introduced Chris, who was busy checking out the barmaid's huge breasts.

"Now, Miss Eplund, you have questions about my old homestead?"

Marci hesitated because she realized Jarrell was standing directly behind Jack's shoulders, giving them the appearance of a two-headed, action figure.

"Mr. Deeter—"

"Please, call me Jack."

Marci forced a smile, tried to start again. But Jack lifted his scotch glass across her view and interrupted. "Pamela, please bring me another scotch. And Miss Eplund and...Chris, whatever they would like to drink."

Marci declined the offer, but to her chagrin Chris asked for a beer.

Jack touched Pamela's forearm, obviously someone who dealt with a waitress as a personal acquaintance. Way too familiar.

Marci dove into the interview. "Okay, Jack, explain to me why your land sold for twice as much as it was worth?"

Jack placed his clear cocktail glass on the table and paused for the dramatic effect before he answered. "My, you don't waste any time. Do you, girlie?"

Marci held his gaze.

Jack smirked and circled a finger around the top of his cocktail glass, knowing he'd got to her with the 'girlie' term. "Perhaps I did bargain shrewdly with the corporation until I received a price that was somewhat high compared to the fair market value. But, as they say, there are three things that set the price in real estate deals: location, location, location."

When the waitress returned with the drinks, she gave Marci a glass of water and attempted to remove Jack's half-empty one, but he indicated he wanted a third drink, patted her hand, and slid a tip in-between her fingers, moving the money up and down.

Marci recoiled at his innuendo, but continued. "By the way, refresh my memory. What do the initials MSU stand for? The corporation name?"

"Honey, I thought you'd know. I thought reporters were big on doing their homework. I have no idea. Really."

For the second time in less than five minutes, Marci's face reddened. She deliberately squared off in Jack's direction.

He waved a white napkin in the air. "Calm down. I meant no harm."

Pretending to search for some information in her bag, Marci said, "No problem," and then flipped the sheets of paper on her notepad. This guy was pushing her buttons, and he knew it. Marci decided for fun to go fishing for information. "Were there any other factors, say political, that influenced the unusually high selling price?"

A muscle under one of Jack's eyes flinched. Marci caught it.

"Such as?" Jack said.

"Being an informed investor, I'm sure you know who owns MSU."

"No, I can't recall at the moment." He steepled his fingers adding, "I dealt exclusively with their commercial agent, Bob Weeks. He made a hefty commission, and I obtained my asking price. We were both happy. There were no complications to iron out. I never entertained the idea that I would meet the new company owners. Their lawyers handled it all."

Jack finished his drinks and waved for another one.

In her peripheral vision, Marci saw the bodyguard shift his folded arms to his side. She guessed he was reacting to his employer's loose tongue.

Marci flashed back to a deposition she had given on a civil suit. Legal counsel at the newspaper had coached her about listening carefully to every question and if possible, answering yes or no.

Since Jack was on the defensive, Marci gulped some water and forced ahead. "So you knew the company was owned by more than one person. Do you recall at least some of the parties' names listed on the paperwork?"

"Quite frankly, no, nor do I have a photographic memory. The reams of legal documents I signed were read thoroughly by my lawyers. I just signed them. Honestly, it bores me. I pay dearly for their services. My Jewish accountant keeps my high-priced Creole and Italian lawyers honest and vice versa; they don't like each other very much."

He paused, and then added, "By the way, what a classic Roman nose you have."

Even with Jack's inhibitions and judgment about gone, Marci couldn't believe the man thought she would fall for his flirtatious garbage. "Let me clarify what you're saying. You are telling me you closed a huge land deal in the dark without researching the company history?"

"Miss Eplund, I am retired Air Force, not a financier. I learn as I go. We *nouveau riche* can afford to be naïve. As long as I protect my first million, I'm okay. It's making it grow that's difficult. The wolves do surround you quickly, but Jarrell here keeps most of them at bay."

Jack tried to snap his fingers, but failed. "I simply lucked out with the sale of Dad's land," Jack said. "What can I say?"

She changed tactics. "When did your father dig the well on the farm?"

"Hum, maybe the 1950s. I remember it as always closed. Abandoned. I wasn't supposed to play around there."

He mimicked a kid's high sign for being quiet, but missed his mouth brushing his cheek instead. "Don't tell anyone. Very dangerous for children."

Marci smiled.

Jack slurred, "You have a pretty schmile."

Chris chuckled at Jack's drunken blabbering.

Marci shot the cameraman a look. Blocking her irritation, she said, "How well did you know Terence Washington Williams?"

"Only in passing, not for long. Most of my senior year, I went to North Jackson High School on the lily-white side of town. My parents and others paid mucho dinero to make sure the assigned black students were bused to other schools. It worked for a while."

"What did you hear after Terence disappeared?"

"That every white teenager within forty miles of Mobile wanted to take credit for beating that black bastard. Civil rights in a pig's eye! School desegregation and forced busing just fueled racial hatred. Privately, most of us thought the Klan had killed him."

Marci waited.

"I remember his mother's face on television." Jack shrugged. "She knew he was dead. She had signed his death warrant when she had fought to send him to a white school. Such is life," he said. "By the way—for the record—my parents were separatists, not bigots." He leaned in closer to Marci as he said, "My mother was a well-bred Georgia peach."

Marci fought the urge to hit Jack. His haughtiness trivialized Mary's anguish. "Did the authorities check your farm for Terence's body?" Marci said.

"Why would they?" His irises widened. "You must be kidding. I'm sure the police took a report, but a missing colored boy wasn't a high priority. I'd be surprised if they searched for him."

Marci went for it. "Was your father a member of the KKK?"

"Hell, no, but he was a crazy SOB. He hailed from those Arkansas folks, north of the Mason Dixon line. He rated a man by his handshake and bearing. Didn't care about the war — the Civil War."

Jack shook his head and gulped his fourth Scotch. "Forbearance wasn't my Dad's strong suit inside the family. But outside the family, anyone else—a colored boy—no way; he wouldn't have hurt a hair on his head."

Marci studied Jack. He was drunk, but not dumb.

Jack pointed to his chest, saying, "Don't look at me. I...I was too busy chasing ass, practicing football. Apthapetic, apa...didn't care. I wanted no part of any trouble."

Pushing her luck, Marci said, "Weren't you in the ROTC program at Robert E. Lee High School?"

"So?" he said and attempted to sit up straight in the chair.

"I bet you were in something like the civil air patrol in elementary, too. I expect Louis Beam had admirers up this way in Alabama. I can see a young man who joins ROTC— already knows hand-to-hand techniques, joins another like-minded military group desiring order and control. So, he goes on to a career in the armed services—"

"And your point?"

"So, before the Air Force, you would've considered violence, like beating or shooting, a necessary thing to eradicate a problem like this Terence. Just your duty as part of the white race."

"Hey, wait a minute."

"Terence, a great running back, had the audacity to go to an all-white school, and had outshone the white players. He made you itch. Yes?"

Glassy-eyed, Jack met her gaze with steely silence.

"Bitch," Jack said, pushing his drink across the table toward Marci. "Shut that damn recorder off and get that fucking camera out of my face."

Chapter 14

J.C. sat in the back of the roll call room dreading another day of babysitting the rookie. Up front the lieutenant was yapping, but the training officer wasn't listening. Yesterday had been a bad day. Angry, screaming faces flooded his brain. The cheating wife, the undeserved ticket, and the neighbor's barking dog were major crises to these civilians. J.C. thought about his last call, an accident, and the gruesome sight of a body smashed like a blown-up pancake after being ejected from a moving vehicle. Now, that was something to get upset about.

But officers didn't have that luxury. They handled it. Had to.

Twenty minutes out of the bullpen on their first call, J.C. studied Carly, who was methodically photographing Elma Hall's cuts and bruises. *Must have been a hell of a domestic.*

He flexed his fingers and barked, "Hurry up, Redmund. We don't have all day."

Officer Clay walked in, shook his head, and then radioed that the scene was under control.

"Sorry, man," J.C. said. "The damn rookie cramps my style. Has the sarge been calling me?"

"Yep, five times. He's pissed. Just hope it's only your edge that you're losing, big fella."

"Whatever, Clay. How come short guys like you always have a big mouth? Just watch the happy couple while I take the recruit outside for a chat."

As he switched to the talk-around channel on his talkie, J.C. motioned with his head for Redmund to follow. Clay had been right. The sergeant ended the conversation with J.C. by saying they'd talk later.

J.C.' felt his boots hit the sloping driveway punctuating each angry word, as he ranted at Carly. "I could lose everything if this clown kills her one day, and I didn't act," he said, as he opened the trunk of the patrol car. "Elma's as much to blame for the situation as Lukin. She stays with the asshole." J.C. checked to see if Carly was listening and continued. "Taking this idiot down to the jail won't solve a thing. Shit, Lukin will be bailed out, and they'll be back together—all lovey dovey—before you complete the paperwork."

J.C. fumbled for a domestic violence form hidden in his seat-back organizer, his usual spot for his gear, which had been thrown in the trunk to accommodate Carly riding shotgun.

Tossing items around inside the trunk, he said, "Can't find a fucking thing in here. Where's that form? Domestics prove my theory nobody wants to take responsibility for their own problems."

Carly retrieved the correct form from her clipboard storage area and handed it to J.C. "Here, Sir. Personally, I think she's scared to death of her husband."

"Yeah, so what?" He snatched the form. "Even the solicitor and DA hate these types of cases. The victim never wants to testify and always tries to drop the charges before the court date."

"But I thought the new state law allows the officer to take out the warrant, so it can't be dropped later."

As J.C. raised his voice, he said, "It's pointless prosecuting a case without the victim. It wastes my time and the prosecuting attorney's. Looks bad, losing cases. You wait 'til the defense drills you a new A-hole on the stand. You won't be so sympathetic."

Carly kept her mouth shut and followed him up the steep driveway. As they reentered through the carport doorway, Clay rushed past them. "Gotta go. A robbery-in-progress on Sutter."

J.C. felt trapped. "Great," he said to Clay's back. "Stuck on a domestic when a robbery's going down."

He paced in the kitchen and focused on Elma's blouse hanging from her skinny body. The torn pieces kept shifting from side to side as she trembled. The woman had a tiny tattoo of a bluebird on her right shoulder. She was trying to light a cigarette with a cheap lighter, but her hands were shaking.

"Here, let me get that, Ma'am," he said. J.C. surprised himself lighting Elma's cigarette.

"For Godsake, just Elma," she said. "You've known me forever." Covering herself up with a robe, she told her story, smoking like it was her first time. Disgusted by the taste.

"I came home after working at the hotel, the Holiday Inn Express, to find Lukin crazy drunk. He accused me of sleeping around, instead of working. Apparently, his drinking buddies decided because I didn't want sex three times a day, I was messing around with another guy. Believe me, another guy is the last thing I need right now." She looked around nervously and caught her husband eyeballing her. "Could I get some water to take some aspirin? My head hurts."

"Sure," J.C. said. He nodded at Carly across the room.

Elma found the pills in a cabinet, while Carly filled a glass she found in the drainer with water. "Here's something to wash them down," Carly said.

Elma thanked Carly, who began to ask the standard questions for the report. "So you work at the Holiday Inn Express. What do you do there?"

"Desk clerk."

As Elma continued to answer Carly's questions, J.C. watched Lukin squirming in a nearby chair. The man was slime.

J.C. stood, looping his thumbs inside his belt. "Elma, do you want to prosecute?"

Elma shook her head. "Just make him leave, Officer. Please, I don't know what he'll do when you go. He might kill me."

No choice. There it was; a civil suit waiting to happen.

J.C. pointed to Lukin, slumped in an Afghan chair puffing on a cigarette. "Arrest our bad guy, Redmund," he said.

Carly shot J.C. a look for alerting the perp, and then put down her clipboard positioning her feet in a wide stance as she said, "You're under arrest, Sir."

Lukin took his time. He scratched the side of his cheek before he ground the end of his cigarette in the ashtray, stood up, and turned around leaving his hands by his side. "Put your right hand behind your back," Carly said. "Now your left."

After the handcuffs clicked shut, Carly double locked the cuffs and leaned Lukin against the breakfast bar. "Spread your legs," she said. "Do you have any drugs or weapons on you?"

"Nope."

Carly patted him down and dumped his pocket debris on the counter. "Okay, let's go, Sir."

Lukin stopped short, making the rookie almost collide with him, and then nodded toward the pack of cigarettes on the counter. "Hey, I need my Salems."

J.C. answered. "I'll put them in a paper sack. You'll get them at the jail. Walk."

Near the roadway Lukin whispered to the recruit, "You get off on this, don't you, princess?"

Carly tightened her grip on the cuffs, but J.C. pushed her aside.

"I'll handle this," he said, twisting the linkage between the cuffs.

Lukin yelled, "Ouch, man."

J.C. slammed Lukin against the car door, searched him again, and placed him in the back seat of the patrol car. "Watch your head. There's not much room back there for your big mouth."

When J.C. turned around, Carly said, "Why did you do that?"

J.C. smirked. "You looked flustered."

"No, I was fine."

"You better toughen up. You're gonna hear everthing out here," J.C. said.

When they arrived at the jail, J.C. left Carly at intake with Lukin, made a beeline for the lobby phone, and called Adam Hall. "This is Officer Grey. I had to arrest your nephew again."

* * *

Elma, her eyes almost swollen shut from the beating, blindly threw clothes into a large plastic trash bag. Her neighbor, Barbara, blocked the doorway of the bedroom with her huge body. "Hey gal, why you didn't go with the ambulance mens? You needs help."

"Barbara, you know I don't have insurance. It'll be six months before I get some, and that's if Lukin doesn't make me lose this job, too."

Without looking, Barbara stuffed some clothes into the trash bag. "The sonabitch. I heard you yelling from next door and called the po-leeces."

Elma nodded. "He tried to choke me this time. He knows I'm not whoring around. Goes crazy on that shit he buys in the street."

Barbara shook her wiry hair. "Gettin' real bad. You think he's hooked on that stuff? Crack or H?"

"Who knows, but he's nuts if he thinks I'm getting pregnant on top of everything."

"He still hounding you about that?" Elma nodded. "You're right. You be strong, Miss Thing."

Elma sat on the bed, held Lukin's shirt against her face, and cried. "I still love him, Miss B-bee. I can't help it."

Barbara put a flabby arm around Elma's shoulders. "Oh honey, we womens always lov'em, but we cain't get pulled down. It be a good thing that the po-leeces took him away. A good thing."

"You're right, but the cops don't get it." Elma sniffled and wiped her nose. "Lukin, he'll bond out and be back in a couple of days. Mad at me."

Barbara bent down and made Elma look at her. "You hear me. You gotta get outta here 'fore he kill you." She held Elma at arm's length. "He mean. You know Momma B-bee's right."

As Elma hugged Barbara, the Amazon woman plunged her hand into her bra and took out a sweaty ten dollar bill from between her sagging breasts. "Here baby, you take this. I'll pray God keep you safe, but 'til He do, you gotta do fer yo'self."

* * *

J.C. put down his beer. With Noreen busy out in the kitchen doing dishes, he could call Don. He wanted a little privacy.

"Hey Don, this is J.C."

"How you doing, buddy boy? Don said. "You run out of beer or something?"

"Naw, I just missed the sound of your squeaky voice."

"Right, well, it's nice to know somebody loves me. The wife's been an "ice princess" lately." The sound of a door slamming shut reverberated in the phone.

"God, women can be a pain in the ass," J.C. said squeezing a rubber exercise ball in his free hand.

"Anyway, I thought I'd interrupt your vacation."

"Yeah. Good you did. I been meaning to clue you in on a little scene I witnessed a few days ago. By the way, thanks for asking about my new bowfinger."

"Okay. How's the new boat?"

Don sighed. "She's the most voluptuous, satisfying woman a man could have."

"What does Jody think?"

"My old lady, who cares?"

J.C. bounced the ball against the wooden paneling.

"I'm in love with another woman. You can't expect my wife to be pleased."

"Yeah, I guess Jody hates it when you swab the decks of your boat."

"Exactly," Don said. "Your rookie and Tim Price are seeing each other off duty. I saw them at the downtown the Pancake House last week. They were thick as thieves."

"Really, I didn't know she dated men." J.C. scooped the ball off the floor.

"Is that jealousy in your voice, Red?"

"Nope, she's too bitch-on-steroids for me. I'll pass."

"Okay, I hear you. How's she doing on the road? Anymore screw ups?"

"You mean evidence-wise? No, I'm watching her like a damn drill sergeant."

"Is she going to make it?"

"Who knows? She's too stubborn to resign. I'll be glad when the eight weeks are over, and I can quit watching out for her butt." There was a pause. "That Price is a Jewish dickhead. Likes to throw around big words. Acts superior."

"Yeah, so what? If college-educated boys are her thing, lets you off the hook with Noreen."

J.C. grunted. "May they climax mentally and be one."

"Didn't they both work that case at the Deeter farm?"

"So?"

"I bet your rookie is trying to redeem herself, playing detective."

"Shit. Poking her nose where it doesn't belong," J.C. said, "might just finish Redmund's career before it starts."

* * *

Eight out of fourteen militia members had shown up for the Thursday night meeting at Calpes. The small group liked to call themselves a cell of "leaderless resistance." In theory, no particular person headed the group, but everyone knew Billie Ray had the last word. Usually, they arrived around seven o'clock, ate sandwiches, and drank pitchers of beer until Birdie Potter locked the front door around nine and left them to fend for themselves.

The room, which by this time reeked of stale beer and cigarette smoke, hushed as Billie Ray spoke. "Men, I need to let you know about the efforts to block the section-eight housing on Montgomery Street. We have made contact with a commissioner who's sympathetic to our point of view. The project has been delayed through zoning complications."

The group voiced their approval.

"A temporary solution, but it's one step closer," Billie Ray said.

Adam spoke up. "Very good. Excellent, B.R. Why those Democrats think they're helping the poor with housing that will be crime-and-drug-infested in six months is beyond me. You'd never be able to put enough cops in those damn projects." He paused, and then added, "Before I forget, Billie Ray, of course, you know Officer J.C. Grey. He's a big guy. Red hair."

"J.C., not since he was a kid," Billie Ray took a draw on his cigar. "Only had dealings with his brother, Derrick, our mayor-to-be."

"He helped me out the other morning with Lukin. The idiot beat his wife half to death again, tried to strangle her. Anyway, J.C. handled the call. Lucky for Lukin they went to the same high school. I guess I should've talked to Lukin before...but I've been so busy." Adam studied his sandwich on a paper plate. "I got a break on the bond. He charged him with a misdemeanor assault instead of a felony. That's all he could do, but it still cost me close to a thousand dollars.

"I didn't want to use the house deed in lieu of cash because Virginia, my dear bride, would've had a fit." He raked a fork through the ketchup left on his plate.

"J.C. sounds like a good man," Billie Ray said. "Can we get back to business?"

"You know, I agree with the wife about Lukin. He's not reliable," Adam said. "He might take off and not show up for his arraignment date. I wasn't going to venture losing my house if he did. Lukin's a real pain in the whazoo."

Billie Ray exploded. "Yeah, he is. How many times are you gonna wipe that drug-taking pinhead's ass?"

"No cause to cuss at me. If it wasn't for Lukin's mom, patience of Job that Claire, I'd let him rot in jail."

Billie Ray wanted to make an insinuating comment about Claire and Adam, an elder in his church, but he let it go because he heard Dave Jordan's booming voice shooting out from the kitchen.

Jordan walked up behind Adam and slapped him on the back as he said, "Hey, heard your reprobate nephew was in jail again. How the hell are you otherwise?"

"Okay, I guess. Be nice if you warned us before crawling into a place by using the service entrance."

Dave was always late and liked to use the unlocked back door to make his grand entrances. He lumbered further into the room, shifting his weight from his heels to his toes. Maintaining a nonchalant attitude, Dave checked out a billiard game in progress.

"I can see you guys can't play worth a damn, so where's the Goddamn beer, anyway? You lowlifes already guzzle it down?"

Everyone laughed, and "Tee" Smith got up from his barstool and went to the draft handles to pour Dave a mug. "If I remember correctly, this brand is your poison?"

"Fantastic, my good man."

"That's what they all say—after," Tee said, making a guttural noise when he handed Dave a beer.

Dave nodded toward Billie Ray. "I thought you screened your friends? I think you let a commie homo sneak into this group. He'll be blowing me a kiss next."

Once the laughter died down, Dave circled back to Billie Ray and Adam. Drumming the bar as he sat down, he said, "So what did I miss?"

"Nothing much," Adam replied. "Billie Ray has blocked the new Section Eight housing on Montgomery and made all those illegitimate babies homeless with their welfare moms."

"Lordy, you're an insensitive redneck pecker-head, Adam." The group roared at Dave as he continued over the jeers and sniggers. "Those mud parents have a right to raise their babies on your taxes any way they see fit. They just want a new start in a quiet, clean place to have the chance to say no to drugs and violence."

"And my kinfolks needs a place to work, since affirmative action gave all thems jobs to your left-wing brothers and sisters," Tee said.

Billie Ray chimed in with his version of black dialect, "I says it's only right you gives me a job, because pappy bees white and my mammie bees black."

"I'll tell you one thing," Dave said. "If we still had occupied slave quarters, we wouldn't have all these rapes and murders in our streets. Hard work curbs all that anger."

Tee nodded. "Damn straight."

"Here's to militia cells all over America filled with dedicated men, true patriots," Dave said, patting his chest. "The men who would give up their lives for the cause."

"I second that," said Adam. "Jews, niggers, wetbacks, and chinks can be stopped by united groups like us."

"How true," Billie Ray said. "In the brotherhood and in God we trust. Amen!"

"Amen," the group repeated.

The group raised their mugs and beer bottles in a salute to the brotherhood. The sound of the final smack of their drinks on the bar rose into the smoky air and seemed to hang in a foggy cloud above the men's heads.

Chapter 15

"Tracie, give me a big bag of chocolate covered peanuts." Marci said, pointing to the sacks atop the display case. "My friend can't make up her mind."

"Now here's a good woman to know, Carly. She hears it all from behind that glass counter."

"I can imagine. This shop seems to be a hub for the locals."

"Yes. My people have been roasting peanuts and living in Mobile for a long, long time," Tracie said, standing on her tiptoes to hand Marci her order.

Carly scooted toward the antique register allowing an elderly woman with a poodle hairdo to squeeze by, and then said, "I'll keep that in mind. Could I just have a small bag of raw peanuts for my squirrel friends in the park?"

"Sure. Those squirrels help keep the doors open."

As Tracie filled the bag, she asked, "Where're you from, Carly?"

"Southwest Missouri."

"I was right. Thought the Midwest."

After Carly paid for her order, she said, "How old is that roasting machine? It reminds me of a small cement mixer with a hand crank."

An apron-clad man working the roaster whispered something in Tracie's ear while Carly continued. "That wonderful smell carries all the way to the park."

"Yes, everyone loves it," Tracie said. "Now, the machine, it's old. An original. My Dad bought it way back in the early nineteen-hundreds."

"Wow, and it still runs."

"Like a top. All we do is keep it clean and oil it once in a while. That's Henry, my husband."

Her husband smiled and cranked the bin. It began to spin.

Tracie turned her attention back to the women. "Are you two working together at the *Tribune*?"

"No way," Marci said, Carly's a soon-to-be cop with the county."

"Really, how exciting—"

"And dangerous," the poodle-haired matron added from her perch on a stool near the back wall. "Aren't you afraid?"

"Can't say yet. My scariest call has been finding some muddy bones."

"Oh, yes, the bones found at the old Deeter place...in the well," the elderly woman said. "I read about them finding that boy, the Williams boy's remains. Terrible thing." She fumbled in her purse and retrieved a tissue, and then added, "I just don't understand. Why would a star athlete want to kill himself?"

"That's the million-dollar question we'd all like to ask the coroner," Marci said.

Reading the look on Carly's face, Marci said, "Sorry. I guess you didn't know—"

"About the coroner's ruling? No, I didn't."

"I thought Tim called you."

"No, I still ... ." Carly caught Marci's eye and signaled to drop the subject in front of the matron and Tracie.

"Right, well ... ." Marci opened the door. "I need to get back to work. Walk with me. Will ya?"

"See you next time, Tracie," Carly said waving goodbye.

Just before the door swung shut, the gray-haired woman stuck her head outside the door and told them goodbye.

As they started to walk away, Carly said, "Who was that woman?"

"Carol Duboise—rich as hell—and out for her daily constitutional. She likes to haunt all the local businesses—to eavesdrop, mostly."

"You think." As they crossed the street and headed toward Cathedral Square, Carly asked, "Anyway, when did Tim talk to you?"

"Yesterday. Again, I didn't mean to blindside you back there."

"It's okay. I should keep up better. Didn't hear or see a thing. So, tell me. Did the coroner convince Tim to cave? What happened?"

Before answering Marci studied Carly for a moment. "I'd say no. He was pretty upset. He'd taken the day off for family business, and the asshole coroner took the opportunity to close the case with his suicide ruling."

"I see." Carly stuffed her peanut bag in her sweatshirt pocket and sat down on a park bench. "I guess Tim gave it his best shot. I should be grateful. The powers that be have been pressuring the coroner's office from the get go."

"Cheer up, gal. Have a little faith," Marci said. "Cases can be reopened. In fact, I think Tim is working on an angle as we speak."

Slinging her satchel on the park bench, missing Carly's hand by a fraction-of-an-inch, Marci continued. "Now, let me tell you about the interview with Jack Deeter."

* * *

"Derrick, I don't need to know the details. If you did the deed, it's not important to me. Just tell me what you need." Billie Ray tucked the phone between his shoulder and chin, uncurling the phone cord wadded atop his LaZBoy armrest.

"I appreciate your support, Billie Ray," Derrick said, "I need this thing to go away. Sooner than later. The spin doctors, along with my secretary, are weaving their magic to defuse the matter. But there are some loose ends. Can you'll oblige me a favor or two?"

"Sure. In the big picture, how sticky is this thing?"

"Depends." Derrick hesitated. "Didn't your group buy the Deeter farm from Jack?"

"Yeah, a few months back through our corporation, MSU." Billie Ray reclined in his lounge chair, and then added, "We're not directly tied to the development."

"Can you get to Jack and secure his silence? We don't need to be connected with him right now."

"That won't be a problem." Billie Ray cleared his throat thinking about what a ruthless SOB Derrick was. *This man could be useful.* Billie Ray added, "Jack owes us. How exactly is he involved?"

"After I beat the holy shit out of Terence—the black bastard—I think Jack or his pals cleaned up the mess." Derrick breathed audibly over the phone. "Damn, that was a long time ago."

"What do you mean? You think he dumped the body?"

"I'm not sure. Complicated. I never knew who or what finished Terence off...the beating or someone, something else. He disappeared from my world. That's all I cared about then." Derrick coughed, clearing his throat.

"When the bones turned up in Deeter's well, I immediately thought Jack dumped the body there. Other guys may have helped him. Jack was in the crowd during the fight. I never asked, and he never volunteered additional information."

Waiting for Derrick to finish, Billie Ray remained silent.

"Hell, I was a kid. I ran." After a pause, Derrick said, "According to J.C., the skull found in the well had a small caliber bullet hole in it."

"It's hard to believe teenagers not bragging or talking about doing such a thing," Billie Ray said.

"Well, we were scared. And ROTC buddies, smart enough to know if we kept our mouths shut it would blow over. The white police force wasn't going to investigate the disappearance of a black kid, not with integration a thorn in their side. A few months later, Jack went into the service, and I went to college. Terence Washington Williams was considered old news long before we left."

"I see. So, I'll find those loose ends and clear your way," Billie Ray said, finalizing the deal.

"Look. I don't want anyone hurt. Just remind them of their culpability in Terence's death. We all have a lot to lose."

"Don't trouble yourself." Billy Ray said, "My associates and I don't wear white sheets, or burn crosses anymore, son, but we get the job done. Everyone has family members loyal to the cause. Nowadays, my guys prefer persuasion—not violence."

Billie Ray rubbed his stomach as he said, "However, this muddy water could make your campaign a dirty mess if we're not careful."

"I agree," Derrick said.

"Listen, don't worry about it. Jack made a bundle off our property deal. He'll be willing to keep our conversations confidential."

"Thanks, I feel better. I'll keep in contact, but I...."

Billie Ray waited while Derrick groped for the right words.

Finally, he continued, "Billie Ray, you gotta keep J.C. out of this. He told me about the bullet hole in the skull and the high school ring's initials before the public knew. Otherwise, he's not in this thing."

"I hear what you're saying. You want your brother's career left unblemished."

"Yeah, I'd appreciate it."

When Billie Ray didn't assure him J.C. wouldn't be implicated, Derrick explained. "Anyway, J.C.'s rookie, a female named, Carly Redmund, knows too much along with her new friend, Marci Eplund, a *Tribune* reporter. And Tim Price, the coroner's assistant, could be a problem. He's kicking up a fuss about the coroner's suicide ruling. Can you obtain background information on Redmund, Eplund, and Price? We might need the information."

"I like the way you think, sonny boy. I have a member who's a computer geek, so no problem. Are there any more players I should know about?"

"None. Right now. Thanks, Billie Ray. You're the right man to have in the wings."

"Forget it. I'll work it out with a few phone calls. Friends help friends and things get done."

* * *

Elma finished the supper dishes as Lukin answered the wall telephone. She tried not to follow the conversation, but Lukin was shouting. She could hear him over the rattling fan beating against the rust-colored linoleum floor. He was saying something about a special job worth lots of money.

Lukin turned his back and walked to the doorway between the kitchen and living room. Lowering his voice, his eyes darted in Elma's direction.

In response, she poked her head inside the pantry and organized the canned goods. Elma thought about the terms of Lukin's probation as she moved to the kitchen sink. In lieu of six months in jail, he had promised to finish an anger management class sponsored by the State Court of Warner County. Lucky for them, because they needed whatever money Lukin bought home.

But any further violence, use of drugs or alcohol, or a no-show at his therapy would revoke his probation.

She'd moved back home from her mother's two weeks after Lukin's arrest. Her mom's place was small, and there really wasn't room for her. Besides, her moody stepfather objected.

During their reconciliatory period, Lukin had been docile and attentive—the days almost like the honeymoon they never had. Elma wanted to believe it was possible to be happy. For the first time in years, she felt on top of things. Even her boss had remarked about her reliability. In fact, the head desk clerk was quitting soon, and she might have a shot at the position.

But she wouldn't dare tell Lukin. It would hurt his pride.

With more money she could quit her second job, an aide at an old folks home. She had just started a couple of weeks ago, but she already hated it.

Lukin yelled in Elma's ear. "What the hell are you doing?" She jerked away from the sink, splashing water on her blouse.

"Jeez, nothing. I was thinking about…about my gram." Elma said, wiping at her blouse with a dishtowel. "I need to go see her next week."

"You go by too much as it is. You'll pester that old woman to death."

"Don't say that. I don't want to think about her dying."

Lukin ran his hands underneath Elma's blouse, pulled her bra above her breasts, and pinched her nipples. "We all gotta go sometime, sweetheart. You need to think about me, right now."

Elma stiffened as Lukin loosened her drawstring pants. Repulsed by his remarks and her absurd arousal, she tried to push him away.

"Okay, then do me," he said shoving Elma down to her knees. He held her shoulders as he ordered his wife to unzip his blue jeans.

"I don't want to, Lukin. I don't like—"

Lukin twisted Elma's hair. "Do it, now!"

She complied.

Lukin held the back of her head with both hands and pushed his penis deep into her mouth.

"That's it, baby. Take it all."

When Elma gagged, Lukin came and let go of her.

He stepped back, pulled up his jeans, and opened the refrigerator. Popping the tab on a can of beer, he turned and walked into the living room.

Left on all fours, Elma heaved and rolled into a ball on the floor. The evening sun streamed through the demitasse curtains, baking the center of the room as Elma edged into the shadows.

Chapter 16

Marci stood grinning down at Carly.

"I'm waiting. What did Jack tell you?" Carly said, as she propped an elbow on the back of the park bench,

Marci sat and pushed her satchel away, forcing Carly to slide across the hand-painted bench with a mural depicting the Spanish fleet docked in Mobile harbor in 1738. "It's not what he said, but what he *didn't* say."

Sighing, Carly said, "Which was?"

"He dumped the body in the well, all right. He changed schools a week after Terence's disappearance. Moved to an expensive private school, North Jackson, on the other side of town."

"But your proof of criminal activity?"

"Nada. Even drunk he didn't reveal much. I'd say Cofer already got to him."

"Jeez, we need a break," Carly said.

"But Jack didn't deny his racist attitude and that he really disliked his Arkansas-born father, a regular Joe, not part of the KKK. No connection. In fact, Stewart couldn't find any information connecting him to any political organization. Never gave a dime to the right or the left."

"Mildly interesting, but because Deeter Sr. is dead, I don't see the significance."

"I'm not finished," Marci said. "Jackie boy's batty mother, Constance, is still alive and residing at the exclusive Harrington Hills, an active senior complex. She's old money, a real southern belle, and a member of the Daughters of the Confederacy. That's all I know."

"I bet Harold or Mary could give us the lowdown on Jack's mother. I'll call them," Carly said, "if you'll call Harrington's and make sure we can get inside."

* * *

"Hate to call you at the office, but can you drive out to the hunting lodge off County Line Road late this afternoon?"

Derrick hesitated until he recognized Billie Ray's voice. "Sure. I'll see you there. Say about five thirty."

"That's fine." The line went dead.

The cloak-and-dagger stuff was unnerving. He rubbed his temples. He hadn't heard from Billie Ray in almost a week. In fact, Derrick had put the unpleasantness out of his mind hoping the problem had been fixed. This meeting wasn't a good sign.

Derrick searched his office for a distraction. Last year Rose had decorated the room with secondhand wingback leather chairs with gold rivets. Usually, he enjoyed the burgundy colors in the furniture and the Moravian rug, but nothing soothed him now. A persistent, acid pain in his stomach prompted him to open his desk drawer and shuffle through the bottles.

"Damn this ulcer," he said, choosing Tylenol instead of Maalox for the pounding pain in his head.

Miss Stalch walked into the room with a queenly air. "You look atrocious," she said. "What is troubling you?"

"I have a splitting headache and a late meeting."

"I see. You didn't have one scheduled on your calendar. Therefore, I assume Billie Ray is the man hampering your return to home and hearth."

He grinned. "You never miss a thing."

"I certainly don't. I transferred the call."

"Yes, we're meeting, informally, away from the office."

"I understand, Mr. Grey. My calendar will not document this personal meeting. Private matters shouldn't be a concern for the public."

"Exactly. As usual, you're perceptive, Miss Stalch. Are there any more people I need to see in the waiting room?"

"The waiting room is empty. If you wish, your last phone conversation for the day was Cofer."

Noticing his secretary didn't say Mr. Cofer, Derrick nodded. "You read my mind. I'll be leaving shortly. If Rose calls, tell her I'll be home by seven."

"Of course."

Derrick watched Mildred leave. Sometimes, she was too discerning. Although he'd said nothing to his secretary, she knew Rose was calling less. When she did call, Derrick was always unavailable.

He packed his briefcase and reviewed his appointments for the next day. He was scheduled for breakfast with Henry Pullman, his campaign manager, who wanted a meeting to revamp the Labor Union speech. Derrick was too tired to telephone Henry about Billie Ray tonight. Besides, it might be nothing, even though Billie Ray's tone had indicated trouble.

Derrick popped the snaps down on his briefcase and grabbed the Maalox bottle, chugging a couple of mouthfuls. He grimaced. It tasted like unadulterated chalk.

One more meeting, then homeward bound. Maybe Rose would meet him at the door smiling and stop obsessing about those damn dreams.

As he blocked his marital strife from his mind and closed the office door, high school memories of a particular date with Sue Lynn Morrison on a hot summer night replaced reality.

The local lover's lane was a rutted dirt road that ran off Route 20, near the lodge that only a few local hunters and cops ventured. The adults ignored the local teenagers' late night carousing, honoring their primal mating instinct. *Yeah, life was simple, in those days.*

Derrick laughed at himself as he drove his SUV onto U.S. 20. Following the highway for a couple of miles, he turned down a winding dirt road that ended deep in the woods at the lodge.

A long time ago, he'd ridden many times with his grandfather to the lodge, but he had hardly remembered being inside the structure. Nature always held his attention. He enjoyed its dichotomy. He'd known his greatest peace and his most violent impulses in those woods. At age twelve he killed his first deer.

Derrick swung into the gravel parking area, turned off the engine, and felt the quiet settle on him. He got out of his vehicle and stretched. Shedding the office, he shook a cramp from his right leg. The change jingling in his pocket. Feeling almost happy, he walked toward the road.

The willow trees lining the road created the illusion of a leafy tunnel. His fondest memories were of the dangling limbs brushing the top of his granddad's pickup truck, and that vision, somehow, softening the blows of the rocks and gravel that hit the belly of the truck. Windows open, everyone bouncing from side to side, while the wind blew and the lower branches scraped the door panels. The outside world had stayed at bay that fall, and he had shot a ten-point buck—a boyhood dream come true.

Derrick picked up a pebble and threw it. The last big rain had left ridges and furrows in the dried mud, as if some gigantic carver had whittled permanent grooves into a slab of petrified wood.

A dust cloud blocked his view of the horizon. With a cupped hand he shielded his eyes from the sun. A black Ford F-250 plowed through the haze of flying dirt. Billie Ray's polished truck glistened in the April sunlight. The rhino-powered truck gained dominion for a second before the back two-thirds disappeared into the brown shroud. The scene moved together, truck and shroud, a still frame advancing and hurling debris in its wake.

Derrick's shoulder muscles felt tight. On impulse, he sprinted to the wrap-around porch and leapt up. He stood still and closed his eyes. A rocking chair caught the breeze, making the chair runners work back and forth over a loose nail in a four-inch plank. The creaking sound broke his concentration, and he jerked the rocker close to his body. Derrick sat pressing his weight into the basket-weave seat. He planted his feet far apart, and faced the road.

* * *

Lukin was late. Ned Caldwell glanced at his watch. Three thirty.

He had set the meeting at a mega discount department in the middle of the afternoon. Sitting at a corner table of the snack bar, he muttered to himself, "Just a piece of white trash."

The militia had voted. Lukin had been their choice to make the hit, mainly because he knew nothing about Ned, their retired FBI agent. Ned had gotten bored after six months of his golden years, had moved from Georgia recently, and had joined the brotherhood cell in Mobile. Alabama was a change, but he liked it.

WELL OF RAGE

He sipped his coffee slowly. *This dope-head lowlife is about to receive a wake-up call.*

Lukin ambled into the store bobbing his head from side to side like a toy dog with a spring neck. He grabbed two hotdogs and a muffin at the snack bar before plopping down at the old man's table.

"Dig the *Hawaii Five-O* beard. What's up, dude?" Lukin said.

Watching Lukin, Ned unzipped his blue sweatshirt and scooted back in his chair.

Lukin gobbled his food like a stray dog and started talking with his mouth full. "Man, I'm starving. Some nut tried to cut in my lane. I never budged an inch. Made him back off. What a fucker."

The old man stared at Lukin's back-street tattoo of an American eagle with the stars and stripes in the background. The thug smelled sweet, a sure sign he'd been smoking a joint before the meet.

Lukin flexed his skinny biceps and kept rambling on. "So I said, 'Hit me. I need the insurance money.'" He laughed.

Ned said nothing.

Wiping his hands on his pants, Lukin looked around the empty snack area. "If you're the right guy, you don't have much to say. Huh?" he said.

The old man eyed Lukin, who shrugged. "I'll be back, man," he said, and then shuffled to the trash bin with his faded olive pants dragging the floor, his sneakers untied.

When Lukin returned, Ned pushed a note toward Lukin. "Shut up and read," the old man said.

Lukin bought a candy bar and read the note with his lips moving; "'Wait five minutes. Come to the men's bathroom.'"

Ned shook his head and left.

As Lukin entered the bathroom, the old man handed him an out-of-service orange cone, and ordered him to place it outside. Lukin threw the cone outside the door, fiddled with the lock, and then turned to see the octogenarian's metamorphosis.

The man now appeared demonic. Bluish-purple veins bulged in his neck and his thin lips snarled as he brandished a .357 with a four-inch barrel into Lukin's gut.

"Hey, wait! I don't even have a dollar left on me." Lukin raised his hands over his head.

"I told you to shut up. Listen very closely. If you screw up, you're dead." Ned pushed Lukin's scrawny body against the dingy tile wall.

As the old man wheeled Lukin around, the fluorescent light made Lukin squint and emphasized his dark circles and ruddy complexion, making his skin look like it had bug juice splattered on it.

"You're an ugly motherfucker," Ned said. "I hate dope heads."

"Lighten up, dude. I feel sick. Listen, I'm straight 'cept—" Lukin broke free by elbowing the old man, who used Lukin's momentum to spin him around, then jabbed his gun into Lukin's temple.

"Damn it, man," Lukin sputtered. "You made your point. What the hell do you want?"

"I want your complete attention. Now that I have it, here's the assignment." Ned let go of Lukin. "Your benefactors need you to stage a burglary, then take out a bothersome female."

"Okay, no big deal." Lukin rubbed his cut lip.

"Can you handle a female that isn't a dimwitted flake?" The old man asked, digging in his pants pocket for a wad of cash.

"I can handle any cunt that walks the earth."

Ned laughed. "We'll see, Mr. Chuckles. Underestimating your opponent can be dangerous. By the way, the agreed upon amount of fifteen hundred dollars will be given to you after the job is completed. Here's a couple hundred for expenses," he added, tossing the money to Lukin, who immediately counted the cash.

"My, my, they're getting exactly what they're paying for—a greedy loser. At least try not to be a total fool. Don't undertake this job stoned like you are now."

"I thought I was getting half the money now and half after."

"Because I don't trust you, dickhead. New rules."

Ned retrieved an envelope from his sweatshirt pocket and slapped it into Lukin's hand. "Inside is a name, address, and photo. Destroy the envelope and contents once you ID the target. Remember, if you botch this, I will personally take you out."

"Okay, "G-Man," I got it." Lukin straightened his stretched-out muscle shirt and glanced at the photo. "This is going to be fun," he said.

The man pushed Lukin back like he smelled bad and issued his order: "Wait a couple of minutes. Go out into the store and buy something. I don't want security to get suspicious."

Throwing a disposable cellphone at Lukin, Ned said, "I'll call you." Then the harmless-looking senior disappeared.

* * *

Rose and Derrick were arguing again—this time in their bedroom.

As Rose pulled the covers around her waist, she said, "Damn it, Derrick, stop being evasive. I need you to tell me about the campaign. What's going on?"

Derrick put his newspaper in his lap. "Nothing much; it's so-so. I'll be glad when it's over."

"Have you prepared your acceptance speech?"

"No, it's a little early," he said continuing to glance at the headlines. He caught Rosie's disapproving look from the corner of his eye.

"I read that story about the skeleton of that poor teenager being found on the Deeter property. It made me sick to think about how horrible it would be...the loss of a child."

"Good God, Rose. How can you personalize and moon over every somber event on the planet?"

"I don't see why sympathy for his poor mother is wrong."

"You're impossible, sometimes. I'm getting up." With that, Derrick threw the newspaper on the bed and retreated into the bathroom.

When the children came running into the room, an automatic cease-fire went into effect. Rose wore her happy-parent mask.

After breakfast, Derrick opened the garage door and changed the oil on the Mazda, while Rose scrubbed the master bathroom harder than necessary. She fumed about their tiff, her mind replaying the argument. It seemed the more questions she asked, the less her husband talked. Although the frightening dreams about Billie Ray and Derrick had subsided, they'd been replaced by a dreadful feeling of impending loss.

"Damn it," Rose muttered, applying more cleanser to the tub. She was startled when Derrick placed his hands on her lower back and drew her close.

"Rose, I'm sorry that I yelled at you. You know I love you. I'm not trying to shut you out. At the moment, I have more than a few things on my plate. Things that aren't important inside the family. They'd only make our private lives crazy and cut into what small amount of time we have. Do you understand?"

"Yes, but the dreams scare me. Please—"

"You must trust me, dear."

"I do, but I can sense when something is wrong with you or the children. So if you would confide in me, I would relax."

As Rose pulled off her plastic gloves, Derrick took a deep breath and paced. "Okay, we're slightly behind in the polls and Henry panicked. As campaign managers go, he's all right, but I pay him to be the calm in the storm—not be the storm. And he's been a pain about deadlines and personal appearances."

"And?"

"And right now our philosophies are different on where the campaign should be headed. I reeled him in last week, but he spun out of control anyway. Without consulting me, he made a smear commercial about Compton. Unfortunately, that leaves me with two unpleasant choices—use a commercial I don't like, or lose a big chunk of my television budget."

Derrick caressed Rose's concerned face. "See, it's boring stuff. There's nothing you can do."

Before Rose could answer, Derrick kissed her.

When it ended, Rose said, "You're the most irritating, pig-headed man."

"Uh, huh," Derrick said. In one smooth motion, like a dancer, he placed Rose's arms around his neck and lifted her. Carrying her into the bedroom, he whispered, "Let me make love to you."

Rose inhaled Derrick's earthy scent as he lowered her into bed.

Within seconds they were enjoying the rhythm that only their bodies could make. Derrick was being gentle and patient. But Rose dug her fingernails into Derrick's back, urging him with her hands and pelvis to push harder.

Chapter 17

Seated in the only chair near Miss Stalch's desk, Rose waited for Derrick.

Even though the secretary's back was board straight and eye contact impossible, Rose decided to begin saying her rehearsed lines. Her agenda was twofold: she needed the company of a clearheaded woman, and she wanted to pump Derrick's secretary for any information that would eliminate her fears about her nightmares.

"Miss Stalch, I know you're terribly busy, but could we talk for a moment? It's about Derrick's welfare."

Miss Stalch put her file folder down on the desk, swiveled around, and let her half-glasses dangle from a chain around her neck.

"I hope you won't find this crazy, Miss Stalch, but recently, over the last few weeks, I've had some dreams involving my husband and Billie Ray Cofer. The dreams are frightening. Something to do with Derrick's campaign and a gun. But, thank God, they're not associated in any way with the campaign. That I know of. Probably silly meaningless nightmares."

Miss Stalch sat stone-faced.

Rose cleared her throat. "You see. Derrick won't talk about the details of his work with me, and generally, I don't need to know, but I'm afraid that he might be in over his head—"

"Mrs. Grey, I can assure you that Derrick isn't losing control of his business affairs, including the campaign. I would know."

"Okay. But between you and me, is he receiving money for his campaign from that awful man?"

"The source of his funds is a matter of public record. Beyond those facts, I can't help you. You should speak to your husband about your personal fears." The secretary folded her hands in her lap. "Perhaps the campaign's stress is affecting you."

Rose sat back in her chair.

Miss Stalch said, "I only know Mr. Grey as an honorable man who loves his family and city."

"Yes, of course, we know he loves us, and would protect us and the citizens with his life, but the dreams are—" The revulsion on Miss Stalch's face stopped Rose.

"You are stronger than this, Rose. You must put negativity behind you. Your husband counts on your unwavering support at home, just as he counts on mine here. Remember, *we* make him a winner."

Miss Stalch began organizing her desk.

It was Rose's turn to be disgusted. Forcing a smile, she searched for a graceful way out. Finally she said, "You may have a point. I am tired."

"Perhaps a change of scenery might give you a new perspective, a new outlook."

Rose locked eyes with Miss Stalch. *She knows about our domestic squabbles. She is trying to get me to leave town. For Derrick's sake.*

"Don't you have a sister in North Carolina?" Miss Stalch said as she started wiping down her desk.

Reaching for a notepad, Rose said, "Yes. She has been after me to come and see her."

"A perfect solution. I'm sure when you return I'll see the same poised woman Derrick deserves, and I admire."

Standing, Rose checked her watch and handed a note to the secretary. "Be a dear and give him this message. Won't you?"

Miss Stalch nodded.

"Thank you. Sorry I troubled you, Mildred, about this matter. Please excuse me. I can't wait any longer for Derrick; I have an important appointment."

Adjusting her hair over her collar, Rose walked away feeling Miss Stalch's stare. *What a bitch.*

* * *

Elma didn't know what to say to her sister, Martha, on the phone. She hemmed and hawed and then said, "I'll check with Lukin and call you back."

Lukin wouldn't want to go. He'd complain about the drive to Montgomery and he wouldn't trust her to drive alone. The party was Sunday, Elma's only day off.

She hadn't seen her sister in almost a year. "Elma, I love you and I miss you," her sister had pleaded.

After hanging up, Elma built up her courage in front of the bathroom mirror, took a deep breath, and then opened the kitchen door to the garage.

With an open beer by his side, Lukin squatted on the garage floor, sorting through a red toolbox. He said, "Fuck, where's that wrench? Can't change the oil without it." He tossed a pair of pliers aside. The circular wrench lay among the clutter on the cement floor; an anaconda-size extension cord wove through tubes of tile grout, hand dumbbells, and a can of WD-40.

"Are you looking for this?" Elma scooped up the wrench from the floor. In a quick fawn-like leap, she jumped over the debris, landing next to Lukin.

"Thanks, babe," Lukin said, tucking the wrench in a jean pocket.

"Lukin, huh, my sister just called. She's having a party for Susie's tenth birthday and I—"

"Who?"

"My niece, Susie."

"Oh, that brat." Lukin set the parking brake and chocked the rear wheels, securing the truck on the wheel ramps.

"Why would you say that? Susie's a sweet little girl."

Neither she nor Lukin, who was a reluctant and infrequent participant at family gatherings, had seen Susie since the last family reunion picnic.

"I have a right to my opinion, dipstick." Lukin put a tub under the oil pan, allowing it to drain as he asked, "When did you say? I gotta go under the car. Hold up."

"Sunday, about two thirty." Elma fidgeted with her hair, pulling a strand back. "I saw the cutest doll in a shop near the mall and I—"

"Can't go Sunday. Fred's coming over. All I want is a six-pack of beer, the tube, and the Atlanta Braves." Lukin slid from beneath the engine and added, "You don't have any sense of direction. You couldn't find your way to Montgomery without me."

Elma shot back too quickly. "Mom can go with me."

Lukin stood up and smirked as he scanned Elma's body.

"Please Lukin, I haven't been home to see my sister in over a year."

Lukin grunted and gulped his beer. "Thought this was your home. Guess I don't count."

"I meant where I grew up. I didn't mean anything." Elma rubbed a wrist, and then folded her arms over her chest.

He threw the dirty oil filter across the garage, and it dropped a foot from the trashcan.

Without hesitation, Elma walked over to the filter and tossed it into the receptacle. She focused on Lukin's back. "I told Martha you would probably have other things to do, so she wouldn't expect both of us, necessarily."

Lukin plopped his back onto the creeper and looked up at her. "So, you already told her you were coming and I wasn't. Right, shithead?"

"No, it wasn't like that. You're twisting what I said." Elma slumped, making herself smaller.

Lukin sat up. He took a drink before he swept the air with his empty beer can. "Oh, yeah, make me out the mean drunk," he said. "I know what your family thinks."

"That's not true. Mom thinks you're great and Martha likes—"

"Martha thinks I'm a loser. But her dickhead, yuppie husband couldn't fight his way out of a paper bag. Too busy kissing her ass."

"Maybe you're right." She crept toward Lukin. "I'll be home before dark, around six. I can leave you a dinner in the fridge to heat in the microwave." Folding a shop rag and smoothing it, she added, "Or I can cook when I get home. Okay?"

"Can't say about Sunday," Lukin said, lying back down on the creeper. "But for now, don't go anywhere. Might need you to rub my back or my pecker after this job's done." He grinned and shoved himself under the truck's engine block. "Yeah, depends on how well you do, missy."

Elma gazed down at her feet. He was demanding another test of her loyalty. However, unless Lukin got drunk on Sunday, he'd probably let her go. Elma sighed and her breasts heaved under her white shirt.

When Elma looked up, Lukin was standing near her with lust in his eyes. "Come here, girl. Unbutton your shirt."

Elma knew what was coming—sex in this dirty garage.

"Unclasp your bra. That's it. Let those puppies go." Placing his greasy hands on her breast and leaving black goo tattooed on her skin, he lowered his head and pulled a nipple into his mouth.

He bit her nipple.

Elma cried out. "Ouch, you're hurting me."

Lukin spun Elma around and shoved her against the front of the truck, pushing the front of her upper body into the engine. Her knees hit the bumper and her breast smashed into the battery posts. She could hear him unzip his jeans.

Lukin grabbed her hair, pulling her chin back, as Elma fought for breath.

He lost his grip long enough for her to gasp, "Let go."

"Shut up, cunt!" he said as he spun her around and punched her in the face. Before Elma could recover, Lukin forced her denims off her hips and stuck his penis into her dry vagina, tearing the lining.

"Tell me you like it."

Dazed, Elma said, "Huh."

"I'll fuck you 'til you tell me."

Elma tried to kick Lukin, but he grabbed her around the throat. "Big mistake," he said, and then squeezed until Elma lost consciousness.

* * *

When she went limp, Lukin propped his wife against the truck and finished. Lukin felt like a God and thought about killing Elma as his semen exploded inside her. Satisfied that his sperm completely filled her, Lukin let go of her throat.

He carried Elma into the living room, laid her half-nude body on the couch, and smiled when he saw a droplet of blood on her nipple.

Elma moaned. Her eyes flew open, wild with fear.

Towering over her with his legs spread apart, Lukin laughed like a maniac.

Elma recoiled into a fetal position and covered her ears.

Still laughing, Lukin said, "Okay. I guess you can go."

* * *

"When is the last time you visited Harrington Hills?" Carly said, opening the door to the facility for Marci.

"Oh, I don't know. Sometime last year, I wrote a fluff column about a middle-aged businessman, "good Samaritan" type, who played the guitar here. The consummate volunteer brought joy to all you survey."

As they walked down the hallway, Carly could see several patients in wheelchairs using the wall railings to pull themselves along. One octogenarian maneuvered his walker down the hall juggling an IV bag on a stand.

"Jeez, I hate the smell of this place," Marci said.

"Why? It's spotless...smells like flowers. Maybe, Lily of the Valley talcum powder."

"Exactly. It masks the less-than-pleasant aspects of *dying*."

"Marci, you always point out the grim side."

Marci shrugged.

"Not to worry, in a weird way, it's helpful." Carly grinned. "It keeps me grounded.

But—."

"Whatever," Marci said. "Now, where's Constance's room?"

"Number 316, right?"

"If I remember correctly, it should be down this hallway. By the way, how was sweet Mary Williams?"

"She's already contacted The Southern Poverty Law Center and probably the NAACP. We're considered bumbling idiots. And in her shoes, I can't say I wouldn't feel the same."

Marci only grunted.

When they arrived, the room was empty.

"So," Marci said, "what do you think—sundeck or television room?"

"I vote for the sundeck, but getting back to—"

"Follow me, Miss Sunshine."

"Not until you tell me what really bothered you about the man with the guitar?"

"Come on, "Marci said, entering the hallway. "The guy was too perfect." She peered around a Polo-shirted staff member dragging a mobile laptop desk down the hall. "He grated on my last nerves."

"Faking it, huh?"

"Yeah, I guess we all are to some degree, but this rich guy was off the charts. A Ken doll orthodontist."

Carly laughed. "I admit I have trouble dealing with wealthy folks myself. As my mother would say, 'We're all prejudiced, so we're all the same.' I could never decide if she meant that as a positive or negative comment about mankind."

"Well, get ready for your first interview with the filthy rich. There's Constance," Marci said, pointing toward a group of elderly men and women playing cards on the deck. A woman in a pink dress suit with black trim waved at one of the attendants. "That's her," Marci said, "the one that just flagged down a staff member."

"Oh, my God," Carly whispered. "She isn't wearing a designer suit to play cards?"

"Yes. You got to admit it makes her stand out from the crowd."

They walked through a maze of tables and flower urns and approached the lady in pink. "Mrs. Deeter, I'm Carly Redmund. This is Marci Eplund. I hope we aren't disturbing you. Did Harold Dexter tell you we were coming today?"

"Oh, yes, how wonderful to meet you." She nodded. "Of course, a pleasure to meet you both." She took both of the young women by the hand. "Harold is such a dear friend. And he thinks Carly is exceptional. "

She introduced the women at her table, and then patted the forearm of the spry gentleman in the group. "This is Alfred Jennings, my current beau," she said smiling. "Isn't he adorable?"

"Well, I ... ." Carly stammered.

"Take my word, dearie," Constance said. "He's a keeper."

Carly and Marci exchanged glances.

After a dramatic sigh, Constance waved to her elderly friends. "You must excuse me. I need to take these ladies back to my room for a gossip session. You aren't invited. Goodbye."

Constance tiptoed down the hall with short bursts of energy like she was remotely controlled. The petite woman in heels occasionally paused, rocking forward slightly and gesturing—showing off her gold-and-diamond bracelet. She explained the social life at the center including the sexual affairs. Her mischievous grin made Carly wonder what secrets Constance was withholding.

As they entered Constance's room, she offered them some tea. The room was like a Hilton Inn suite with a sitting room and small balcony overlooking the golf course.

"Please, be comfortable," Constance said, directing them to a pair of striped-silk arm chairs. "We should get old business out of the way before tea," she said sitting on her white couch. "First, would you like to know why I agreed to speak with you?"

Carly nodded.

"I thought you would. Besides the fact that I wish to clear my son's name, I wish to ... . Yes, on several occasion through the years I've unburdened myself to Harold about my indiscretions. He has proven to be a trustworthy friend."

Hoping her poker face was in place, Carly said, "Of course, Mrs. Deeter, go on."

Marci coughed in her hand, covering a grin.

Constance shifted her shoulders, shot Marci a look, and then addressed Carly. "Please, call me Constance." Smiling she asked, "Who is that woman sitting over there?"

"That's Marci, my friend. The reporter. Remember?" When Constance didn't answer, Carly continued. "What we need to know is what Jack told you about the night of the fight on school grounds? Marci tried to talk to Jack, but he wasn't forthcoming."

"I see," Constance said, swinging her gaze from Marci, and then back to Carly. "Is she recording this conversation?"

"No. Marci wouldn't do that without your permission."

"Now what was the question? Oh, yes, now I remember," the elderly woman said. "No doubt, Jack was remaining loyal to Derrick, but my concerns rested solely with my son. He did nothing wrong. Derrick, on the other hand, was and is a scoundrel."

"Is that why you changed Jack's school in his senior year?" Carly said.

"Yes, Jack's future was at stake with West Point on his horizon; I simply separated him from Derrick." She crossed her legs for emphasis. "I never did like that boy."

Carly exchanged glances with Marci. West Point hadn't been in Jack's bio information.

Before Carly could ask another question, Constance said, "Do you know why Jack joined the Air Force?"

Carly shook her head.

"His grandfather was in the Air Force in WWI, and Jack loved his war stories. But...Jack's father, Jack Sr., bless his soul, in his last months, toured Europe with me—carrying an oxygen tank. He'd had several heart attacks." For a moment Constance looked lost.

"I've heard good things about your late husband," Carly said. "But you were speaking about Jack's grandfather being in the Air Force and—"

"Yes, about my Jackie boy. He couldn't stand the sight of blood. Even hunting and killing animals sickened him. He couldn't have killed a man face to face."

"Uh huh," Marci said. "But did Jack own a pistol?"

"No, why?"

Carly caught Marci's gaze and interceded. "It's complicated, but we're trying to fit the puzzle pieces together."

"In other words, you won't tell me," Constance said. "It doesn't matter." Rubbing her fingers over a suede throw pillow, she added. "He told me once he always felt guilty flying above the troops fighting on the ground—no matter how many lives he saved through air support."

"Excuse me, Constance, but Marci has a point. Jack was in ROTC, knew a lot about weapons, and had access to other guns. It was possible—"

"My husband never owned any weapon, except a Remington shotgun. Jack used the shotgun the few times he went hunting as a kid."

"But Jack was involved in the fight?"

"Of course, he was there, but he didn't kill Terence. Derrick did. Jack came home early that afternoon to be with me as his father had requested. You see Jack Sr. was out of town a lot. Ask Derrick's other friends why they threw Terence down that well."

"Did Jack resent Terence's presence at their high school?"

"*Their* high school?" Constance huffed. "Who do you think paid for that school? White property owners. If you're implying Jack hated Negroes, none of us true Southerners were thrilled when integration was forced down our throats, threatening our way of life. But we're not beasts. In my family, our servants were always treated as part of our family, and my Jack loved his nanny."

"So, words like servant and nanny don't suggest less than family to you?" Carly said.

Constance stood and straightened her skirt. "Yes, he surely did love his nanny." She paused, looking toward the patio glass doors. "Oh, my, it's dusk already. Too late in the day for tea. What a shame."

Constance ushered Carly and Marci to the door.

Smiling, Constance said, "Next time, I hope we can speak about more pleasant matters."

Neither Carly or Marci spoke until they reached the atrium.

"Well, that was bizarre. What do you think, Marci?"

"Yeah. If she remembers the past accurately, Jack probably wasn't the shooter."

"Maybe. Hold up. I see someone over there. Carly stepped toward an aide pushing a mop bucket. "Elma, is that you?"

"Hello, Officer," Elma said, fidgeting with her hair. "I work here part-time. Clean and stuff. Every little bit helps." She turned to leave, but Carly stopped her and introduced Marci.

Elma nodded and looked down at her scrubs.

"What a shiner. Are you all right?" Carly asked.

"It wasn't Lukin. Really. Doing laundry in the basement, the light burnt out, and I hit my head on a stud. Clumsy me."

Carly scribbled on her notepad, tore off the sheet, and handed it to Elma. "Look hon, if you ever want to talk, here's my number. You take care."

Chapter 18

"What's up, Stewart?" The computer screen flipped back to the menu page as he jerked in his chair and whipped his chair around facing Marci's large bosom.

"What's the big deal? Sending secret intel to Moscow?" Marci said.

Stewart blinked a couple of times. "No. I'm talking to my mother, huh, about her birthday."

"Right. Let's substitute girlfriend for mother and sex for birthday, and then we might be close to the truth."

Stewart's face flushed to a bright red.

"Look Stewey, we all gotta have a personal life. Even you, Mister Brilliant." She kissed the top of his head, which produced a smile from him.

"But, dear Stewey, I need that information you promised me days ago, the stuff on the executive board members of MSU Corporation. If you can tear yourself away from your *mom* long enough to give it to me, I'd appreciate it." When Stewart didn't respond, Marci said, "Don't tell me you don't have it."

"I got it. Give me a couple minutes, while I, huh … . Would you bring me some paper from the supply closet near the copy machine? The one in the hallway."

"Yeah, sure. I can see you are totally out of paper," Marci said, pointing to the ream of paper in the printer. "Say goodbye to your mother for me while I make myself scarce, grab a cola, and fetch the paper you don't need."

Stewart shrugged and began tapping on the keyboard as Marci left with a warning. "Hear me, lover boy. Just produce my stuff, el pronto, or I'll hack off your motherboard."

Stewart double checked the hallway. Marci was gone. Bringing up his instant message window, he sent a message to Noreen.

* * *

Lukin tucked the .38 Smith & Wesson revolver in the back of his waistband, still pumped from fucking Elma in the garage. Carly lived about five miles away. When he thought about breaking into her apartment, his pulse raced. He'd fantasized about killing a few people who'd stood in his way, but this was going to be the real thing. He felt a little out of control.

* * *

Across town, a spring storm beat against Carly's bedroom window as lightning lit up the late evening sky, followed by a sharp crackling sound, and then something heavy dropped on the roof. Hail pelted the metal siding.

She snuggled with a pillow and thought about her recurring dream of Mitch. Parts of the dream were disturbing, but the silhouette in the window, which gave her permission to borrow the 1954 Chevrolet, seemed like an old friend.

Pulling a blue afghan around her shoulders, she watched the storm through the roof skylights. Peace engulfed her, and she drifted to sleep.

* * *

Taking a hit of the cocaine, Lukin enjoyed the numbness flooding his senses. He had bought the stuff at a neighborhood barbershop thinking it would fast track out of the body. The probation officer never bothered to ask the lab to test for it. Heavy caseloads made for slipshod work habits. The White Lady fooled them all.

Lukin lit a cigarette, brushed the white powder from the end of his nose, packing his stash inside a cd case, and headed outside.

Running to the truck, the rain drenched him before he dove into the truck cab and kicked at a sack in the floorboard. It stuck to his work boots as he adjusted a plastic tarp over the missing driver-side window.

The white Dodge was a standard-shift pickup. Lukin had run it off the road a few years back, drunk. He'd cracked the front windshield with his head, and had mangled the right-front quarter panel against a tree. The heap still produced squealing noises rounding a corner.

He pushed his leather gloves and ski mask across the seat and pumped the gas.

"What a piece of crap," Lukin said, thinking that pretty much summed up his life.

As the wipers scraped the windshield, a shiver went up Lukin's spine. *Hell, the break-in should be a piece of cake.*

He could use the storm to cover his entry from the back deck, and if jimmying the sliding glass door from the frame didn't work, just in case, he would bring a glass punch.

At the first red light, he pulled out a miniature zip-lock baggy and put white powder on his long pinky fingernail before sniffing the substance up one nostril, and then the other. Savoring the numbness, his head cleared and euphoria overtook him. At first, he felt invincible, but then he began to sweat. Droplets rolling down his back.

Shit, I wished I'd had a partner for this one. But the hard-nosed guy who had hired him had made it clear—no witnesses. Lukin wanted another hit of cocaine, but he didn't want to be too wired.

Spotting Carly's house, he circled the block twice, casing the loft apartment above the downstairs duplex, once a fine nineteeth century home. Lukin was in luck. Harold and the old bag, Dotty—now fussing at each other—were loading a suitcase into a minivan. They backed down the driveway leaving the garage doors open as Lukin spied Carly's vehicle, parked in its usual spot near the side entrance. Even better, the loft was dark.

Last night Ned had phoned Lukin on the throwaway cell and had told him Carly's assignment for the next day would be an early-morning traffic detail. No doubt, Ned's doing.

Lukin considered ditching his plan and kicking in the downstairs door in the garage, but he wasn't sure if the two floors still connected. Years ago, Lukin had played inside the house with the Longino kids. The parents had kept an eye on their brood's shenanigans by climbing the narrow staircase off the kitchen to the upstairs bedrooms.

Lukin shook his head. *No improvising. Stick to his plan, less likely to fuck up.*

He parked on a side street and walked behind two houses before reaching the back of the apartment. He pulled on the gloves and ski mask, and then climbed the stairs to the upper deck. Dressed in black, he faded into the darkness.

A crack of thunder and a lightning bolt made him jump.

Lukin took a deep breath, felt for the screwdriver and glass punch in his sweatshirt pouch, and flashed a mini flashlight at the lock. A standard flip lock. An easy entry. Holding the flashlight with his teeth, he was thankful that the cheap lock eliminated the necessity of pulling the door off the track.

As the rain eased, Lukin froze, waiting for the lightning that never came.

The winds increased and moved the rain in sheets away from the deck and then back at him, making it difficult to see. He grabbed the screwdriver to push the lock tongue down, when he noticed a bar jammed in the door track. Without hesitation he punched the corner of a pane. The safety glass marbleized into a pattern of small granules but stayed intact. Agitated that the glass didn't shatter, he scooped up a potted plant, and threw it at the center of the pane. The shattered glass pane cascaded on to the carpet, making a sound similar to the icy rain.

He stepped inside the darkness and listened. Trying to separate the roar of the storm from the silence inside the house, he surveyed the room. He walked through the living room that led to an open kitchen area and the main entrance. Instead of a ceiling, high wood beams and pipes hung overhead.

Lukin moved through the kitchen checking for any signs of a dog. A related bowl or bed. Nothing. A huge bookcase created a type of hallway leading to the bedroom. Across from the bookcase, a pod structure served as a bathroom. On the door hung classic car signage that Lukin noticed too late. Shouldering a sign loose, he caught it, but dropped his flashlight. The sound reverberated around the loft.

With his heartbeat pounding in his ears, he scooped up the flashlight, and edged into the bedroom. Lucky for him, a radio near Carly's bed played a bluesy song covering any noise.

Carly turned over in bed. Her curly hair fanned across the pillow giving her a little girl appearance.

Stepping closer, his eyes followed the curve of her neck to her small breasts cupped under her gray, spaghetti-strapped T-shirt. Her long legs curled in a fetal position around an afghan. Her cotton panties were barley visible.

WELL OF RAGE

Turned on by this childlike image, Lukin dumped his plan for a quick kill and pushed Carly over on her back, pinning her shoulders.

Her eyes flew open. Grunting, she raised her arms and pushed Lukin's elbows outward. As he collapsed on the recruit, she struck him in the face with her forearm and rolled out of bed.

Lukin lunged and caught the end of her T-shirt. A shoulder strap tore and Lukin shouted, "Come here, cunt," but she elbowed his ribs before grabbing open the nightstand drawer.

Lukin tackled Carly banging her head into a brass lamp. Holding Carly's neck down on the top of the table and watching her struggle to breathe, Lukin smiled. "Now little missy, I'm going to fuck you for free before offing you for the man."

* * *

Somehow, Carly didn't black out. Yellow flashes of pain radiated inside her brain as she frantically searched the drawer for a gun that wasn't there. As the masked stranger tore at Carly's panties, loosening his grip on the back of her neck, she head-butted him.

"Goddamn it. That's gonna cost you," he bellowed, wiping his bloody nose on his sleeve.

Carly circled the bed toward the doorway. Estimating how far it was to her police gear in the corner, she baited the guy. "Come and get me, you lowlife son-of-a-bitch."

He laughed at her. "So you wanna play rough. Happy to oblige."

Carly's mind raced as the man came closer. *Who the hell is this guy?*

The assassin brandished a revolver.

Time slowed as Carly hurled herself to her right. She didn't hear the shots, but felt searing pain in her left shoulder before hitting the hardwood floor. Her field of vision narrowed as everything else went black. Struggling to get up, she bumped against the chair where her duty belt was lying. Blood ran down her left hand as she fumbled for her .9 mm. It was in a safety holster. Her training kicked in: "Push down, lift up, and then forward to clear the holster." No time. Instead, she clutched the Mace clipped to her duty belt and sprayed Lukin in the eyes.

Even blinded, he backhanded her mouth with a powerful blow.

Carly willed herself to stay conscious as her head hit a mounted picture, and then she slid down a wall of glass shards.

A hallucination, Sergeant Dillion appeared saying, "Never give up, Redmund. Keep fighting." While a man with a gun cocked the trigger. "Die, you slut," he said.

Carly bit her assailant's thigh. The gunshot went off. Carly wasn't hit, but her wiry enemy recovered yanking her to a standing position. "Stop squirming. I don't want your blood all over me," he said, sticking the gun in Carly's temple.

She kneed him in the groin, and he doubled over on the floor.

Scrambling to a nearby desk, Carly gripped a brass lamp, slamming it against her attacker's head. He fell backward. Out cold.

Carly collapsed breathing hard. She saw her own blood dripping down her arm.

Her first aid training caused her to tear at her T-shirt using her teeth and her good arm. *Put pressure on the wound.* A strip of cloth wrapped around her injured arm and cinched down stopped the flow of blood. She reached for the phone, punching 911. "Officer down. Officer down. Shot," she said.

Carly dropped the phone.

The asshole was waking up. As he grunted and rolled over, Carly grabbed the assailant's .38. Holding the gun with both hands, she took several deep breaths before she shifted the gun to her weak hand and unsnapped her handcuff.

He attempted to stand.

Adrenaline surged through Carly's body, and she pounced like a wild beast, straddling the man's back. She pushed the predator's face flat against the wooden floor and shoved the revolver into the nape of his neck.

"I want to blow your brains out," Carly said. "If you don't do exactly what I say, I will. Do you hear me?"

He nodded.

From the abandoned receiver on the floor, a dispatch operator kept asking if Carly was okay and repeating that help was in route. *Had Dispatch used caller I.D.?*

Carly handcuffed the man. "Officer shot. Officer down," she said...

She felt cold. Before the gray specks covered her vision and her blood pressure bottomed out, she rolled off the assailant and slid the .38 under the bed. Her brain foggy, something floated through her mind about keeping a shock victim warm. She pulled the tail of the bedspread over her body and passed out.

Chapter 19

As officers arrived at the front of the house, Lukin stumbled down the steps of the back deck with his hands cuffed behind his back and moved like a wobbling duck. The off-centered ski mask blocked his peripheral vision. Curbing his panic, he moaned from pain, scooted his arms under his butt, and climbed out bringing his hands in front of his body. Lukin pulled his mask off and ditched it. Breathing in raspy gulps of rain and air, he dashed toward the woods.

It wasn't supposed to go down like this. He had no plan of escape.

He'd only gone a few feet when he heard pounding feet gaining on him. He turned and saw a uniformed officer, a young white guy, in the beam of his flashlight that was held up over a huge shoulder. A flash of lighting turned the night to day, and for a moment their movements seemed suspended leaving them staring at each other fifteen feet apart.

As darkness returned, the cop yelled, "Stop, police," but Lukin kept running.

Without his .38, Lukin ran counting on the young cop playing by the book, but then the officer stopped and aimed his weapon.

Shit. Lukin reached the woods and jumped over a tree stump, shoving his way through the briars and undergrowth. He bet his life that the cop wouldn't shoot him in the back.

Lukin was right.

* * *

Officer Tharp stopped at the edge of the woods and controlled his urge to follow the cuffed suspect. Without back-up, the young officer knew his sergeant wouldn't approve.

"Radio, I need an ETA on the Canine Unit. I'm 1010 looking for the victim. Stand by for a description of the perp." Tharp congratulated himself on keeping a cool head and not mingling his scent with the perp's, making it impossible for the dogs to track.

A veteran officer ambled around the corner of the building as the young officer broadcast the man's description and flipped to the radio's non-emergency talk-around-channel as requested by his sergeant.

The sergeant ordered a perimeter set up around the woods, and five minutes too late, the area was crawling with cops.

Tharp clicked the button back to the dispatch channel. "Hey, Grey, you think you could help check the house, or was that what you were doing while I was chasing the perpetrator in the rain by myself?"

"Nope. Calm down, rookie. Ain't we still breathing?"

Having three years on the force, Tharp ignored Grey's rookie dig. "Damn, I wonder if the burglarized homeowner's going to appreciate your philosophy," Tharp said.

"Come on. Let's talk to the complainant," The veteran said, adding, "ladies first," as they entered the house.

As Grey stepped through the glass shards on the floor, the radio supervisor informed the officers of a problem. "Be advised the 911 call was placed from an officer's residence. Info not on your monitor. I repeat. Officer needs help."

"Damn it," Tharp said, before keying the mike and running in Grey's general direction. "I copy. Officer down call."

"Back here," Grey yelled.

As Tharp arrived, he saw Grey staring at Carly's half-nude body. "Make that a *she* person down. Meet Recruit Carly Redmund, in the flesh," Grey said.

Gauging the situation, Tharp said, "Jesus, she's been shot. Did you call for an ambulance 1018?"

Perpetually stuck in second gear, Grey said, "I was checking her vitals. Basic first responder stuff. Assessment. Wouldn't want to make any mistakes."

"Radio, I need an ambulance in a hurry. Officer shot in shoulder. I repeat. Officer down. Gunshot to the left shoulder. She's unconscious."

"Just apply pressure to the wound, Tharp. I got everything else," Grey said.

Tharp released Carly's hand and pressed the center of the area with the most blood.

Using the house phone, Grey relayed his veteran-trained version of the situation to the sergeant, whose job was to notify CID and IA.

Grey hung up the phone and turned toward Tharp. "Hey, sarge told me there won't be any aerial support. The helicopter's down because of lightning." He chuckled. "So no infrared or canines. Rain messes up the scent. Good going, Tharp."

He ignored the putdown and continued pressing Carly's shoulder, while repeating, "I'm here. Stay with me."

"Don't take it so hard. If it plays out as usual, the perp will take a nap in the underbrush and strut home after we leave," Grey said. "Don't worry. I've seen my share of gunshot wounds in Nam. She'll be fine."

Tharp glared at Grey. "You're an asshole."

"Okay, knock yourself out. I'll be outside roping off the crime scene."

When Carly moaned, Tharp tugged an afghan from the bed and covered the female officer. "Stay with me," Tharp said. "You're gonna make it. The medics are on the way."

Carly opened her eyes, touched his badge, and blacked out.

* * *

Grey walked out the front door and turned Tharp's siren off. Then digging out a roll of yellow crime scene tape from his trunk, he palmed a .38 from behind his back and dropped it into his duffle bag.

Don Thomas arrived, dangling a cigarette outside the patrol car window. "Hey, Red, how bad and who?"

"Close to low sick. It's none other than my favorite ride-along partner, Carly Redmund."

"You're shitting me? Your recruit?" Thomas said, throwing his cigarette down on the asphalt.

"Yep, it's Miss Carly." Grey tied the end of the crime scene tape to a mailbox and strung it around a large shrub on the opposite side of the walkway, and then he walked to Thomas's patrol car.

Grey elaborated. "Caught a glimpse of the perp running into the woods with my flood light. From maybe thirty feet away." Nodding in the direction of a side street, Grey continued. "Probably come out on Juniper. Got his ski mask from the backyard. Some dried blood, so DNA for sure. You clear he's a white male, dark clothing, approximately five feet ten inches, slim, in his late twenties with light colored hair?"

"Yeah."

"Any questions about who to stop? He'll be the guy wearing Redmund's handcuffs."

"Spunky, damn." Thomas said, not bothering to conceal his admiration.

"For sure. She took a shot to a shoulder and kept fighting, but he stripped her. Good chance she was raped. Life can really fuck you over."

Grey pulled the mask from the front of his trousers. "Yep, if I was in IA and wanted to please the chief, I'd spin it as a domestic gone bad, especially, without this mask and the perp's .38. Think of the bad press."

"Just bad enough to make a recruit resign. Especially since she's already on shaky ground. I like it."

Chapter 20

Carly awoke in the hospital. With painkillers working their magic, she could see only a blurry form beside her bed. She tried to sit up, but the pain radiated down her bandaged arm, and she slid back into the pillows.

"Well, it's about time you woke up. We were beginning to worry." The voice sounded familiar, but it took a few seconds to recognize it.

"Marci?"

"Bingo. The one and only. Your pretty-boy Price just wandered down the hall to buy some coffee. He'll be back momentarily." Marci leaned close to Carly. "Between you and me, he's been mooning over you like a puppy dog. Hasn't left your side. Even lied to the nurses to stay the night. You're engaged."

"Oh," was all Carly could get out. Her tongue felt thick.

"What the hell happened to you?"

"Happened?"

"You're a little slow on the uptake. To be expected. Here. Drink some water," Marci said, sticking a straw in Carly's mouth. "Just nod if I've got it right. A maniac broke into your apartment and tried to rape and kill you. Remember?"

Carly looked up at Marci with tears in her eyes. "Wasn't raped."

Marci took Carly's hand and patted it. "Yeah, your brothers in blue seem relieved. At least the officer standing guard at the door, an Officer Tharp, did." Marci pulled a chair close to the bed as she said, "You fought like a banshee, gal."

The door creaked opened. Marci said, "Voila, your fiancé has returned."

Tim released the metal door and stood transfixed. Grinning. "God, Carly, it's good to see those hazel eyes. How you feeling?"

"Like hell. Better than the alternative."

Tim laughed. "That's my girl, huh, friend I mean." He reddened catching Marci's gaze. "I guess Marci has already told you."

Carly grimaced with pain. She moved around, trying to find a comfortable position in the bed. "Engaged. Be real," she said.

"Okay, I lied but—"

"Right." Carly smiled.

Tim bent over and pecked Carly on the cheek. "Your place's a wreck. Some fight, huh?"

"Yeah." Carly touched Tim's hand and closed her eyes to blot out the pictures replaying in her head. The morphine kicked in. She heard voices from a long way off. With heavy eyelids, she floated into a hazy oblivion hearing Marci and Tim in the background.

"She's out again. I wonder if she knows how serious her injury is," Marci said.

"I doubt it. She was lucky it was a .38 and it just grazed her chest. A matter of a few inches would've hit her heart, or a different caliber bullet would've torn a huge hole in her bicep when it came out."

"Thanks for the gory details, morgue guy."

"Sorry."

"Did you know Carly's requested her mom and dad not be notified in case of emergency? It was in her personnel jacket. Wouldn't give the admin nurse any more information, either. Wonder why?"

"I don't know, but it's none of our business. Leave it alone, Marci."

"Sure. We've got a deal, right after you tell her you ditched the card on the flowers Agent Dugan sent."

* * *

The doctor gave Carly a shot of morphine:

The streetlight leached through Priscilla cross-curtains in the darkened room and backlit Carly's father, Zack Redmund. He grew bigger with each step as his shadow shortened between him and his young daughters.

Ten-year-old Carly perceived his enormous shoulders enlarging as he approached their twin beds.

"You ungrateful brats. You should be seen and not heard," he yelled, and then smashed the wooden bedpost, splintering it inches from Carly's nose.

"I told you to go to bed and be quiet. And that's what I meant." His lips held a thin white line of rage.

Carly froze and darted her eyes at her younger sister, Lizzie, who was tucked in a corner of a twin bed with her eyes peeking over the edge of a sheet.

"If I come back in here, I'm going to whip your behinds until you can't sit down for a week. Are you clear?"

His head lowered and thrashed from side to side, eyeing each girl, like a bull ready to charge in an arena. "I said, are you clear?"

Carly blurted out, "Yes, Daddy."

When he turned and left the room, the terrified girls gaped at each other until Lizzie ran sobbing into Carly's bed. Patting her sister's head, Carly cradled Lizzie until she fell asleep clutching her big sister's nightgown.

Carly crawled over her sister, tiptoed to the other bed, retrieved a stuffed bear, and scurried back. Squatting in the floor, she slipped the bear into Lizzie's five-year-old hands and in the dim light traced the bedpost's six-inch, comma-shaped crack.

Still asleep, Lizzie sucked a thumb, one leg dangling off the side of the bed. Carly jumped across Lizzie, pulled her knees up to her chest, and rocked against the headboard for the remainder of the night.

* * *

The Battle House Hotel ballroom was packed with the rich and famous, but for a moment Derrick only saw Rose. She radiated elegance in her sequined, royal blue gown. Gazing across the room, she caught Derrick's eye. He watched his grandmama's ruby heirloom necklace sparkle on Rosie's neck before returning his attention to Rodrick, a boring little man who loved to pontificate about diversifying his portfolio. Derrick tolerated Rodrick because of his campaign donations.

Rodrick's baldhead reflected the light from the chandelier.

Derrick stifled a laugh as he stole another glance in Rose's direction. Recognizing his raised eyebrow as the high sign to save him from a long-winded patron, Rose excused herself from the governor's wife, a perceptive woman, who nodded in Derrick's general vicinity.

* * *

Rose navigated across the room thinking about how handsome her husband appeared. His square chin and broad shoulders looked magnificent in a tuxedo. As Rose drifted closer, she felt a warm flutter in her lower abdomen that intensified as Derrick drew her close. He hugged her around the waist

In return, she smiled and delivered the rehearsed lines that came more smoothly with each performance. "Dear, I'm sorry, but we must leave. The sitter called. She's worried. Our youngest, Dean, is running a fever."

Without a semblance of sincerity, Rodrick said, "I hope it's not serious."

"Hope not too, but I'd like to check on the little scamp and make sure."

"Of course. It was a pleasure to see you again." Rodrick said, scanning Rose's bosom without pretense.

"You're sweet, Rodrick. Tell your wife, Milly, I said hello."

The men briefly shook hands. "Talk to you later," Derrick said, as Rodrick beelined for the governor's wife.

Derrick said, "Thank God, he's gone. You saved me, Rose."

She laughed. "It's fun playing tag team on that guy. He's such a boring lecher."

"I know."

She gave him a reprimanding look.

"So, I indulged his ego for a few minutes. It's worth it for the check he wrote," Derrick said, patting his breast pocket.

"Okay, just remember you owe me. Now, go get the car from the valet while I visit the lady's room. I need to go home."

He grinned, "Okay, my queen."

As Derrick ducked out to the foyer, Rose rounded the corner of the hallway leading to the gold-leafed powder room. A large tapestry separated the mirrored area from the Italian-tiled lavatory with its black marble countertops.

Smelling smoke, she instantly craved a cigarette and considered giving in, but as she turned from the mirror, she collided with Margaret Pullman, who was exiting a stall.

"Margaret, what a surprise! Are you okay? Did I step on you?"

"No, I'm fine. If I can survive these God-awful soirees, I can survive anything. My only consolation is a cigarette. Sorry about the smoke."

"No problem. I understand. How many fundraisers have we attended?"

"Too many. Henry thinks I've quit smoking, so don't tell. He may be Derrick's savvy campaign manager, but at home he's an old fogy."

Rose nodded. "My lips are sealed."

"Henry is fetching the BMW, because Billie Ray paged. Now, we have to go. Like there's a national emergency."

"Derrick's outside, too," Rose said, blocking Margaret's way to the sinks. "Did you mean Billie Ray Cofer?"

"None other. If he wasn't rich, I doubt Henry would drop everything for that obnoxious SOB."

Rose felt her skin crawl.

"Why would Mr. Cofer call?"

As Margaret washed and dried her hands, she said, "Oh, for everything imaginable. He pages frequently."

"That must be a hassle," Rose said.

"Cofer calls Derrick, too. You must know?" Margaret read Rose's face and shook her head. "Oh dear, you are out of the loop. Billie Ray and Derrick made an agreement weeks ago. He's practically financing the entire campaign."

"Yes, of course, I suspected," Rose stammered. "But Derrick's pager goes off constantly, and I never ask who's buzzing him."

"Let me give you some advice. A wife of a handsome political candidate can't be too careful. Women and powerful men love Derrick."

Margaret applied fresh lip gloss, fluffed her hair, and pulled her strapless dress up over her silicone breasts. "Honey, for more than one reason, I'd pay attention. Look more closely, if I were you."

* * *

Lukin drove around the outskirts of Mobile laying low in rest areas and truck stops. Unable to think straight, he pulled over at a convenience store. The Redmund bitch had cost him some cuts and bruises, but the crazy old man and his .357 were the immediate problems.

Lukin crumbled an empty chip bag and threw it on the floorboard. He needed to finish the job, even the score with Redmund, and make it right before the old man found him. Shifting in his seat, he winced as the pain reminded him of Carly's kick to his groin.

Cunt's gonna pay. The quicker, the better. But first he needed money and a place to regroup.

Lukin threw out the nub of a smoked joint. Lighting another, his hands shook. He smashed his fist against the truck dash leaving a crack over the radio.

"Goddamnit. She made me look bad," he said aloud, and then turned his attention to the radio. The commentator reported that a Warner County officer had survived an off-duty attack, adding a description of the suspect: a white male, five feet and ten inches, in his late twenties. Lukin relaxed.

Shit, a thousand guys could fit that lookout.

He figured the cops weren't geniuses, but at least one officer saw Lukin's face after he ditched the mask. Maybe the police knew who he was and already had traced his truck through DMV records.

Less than twenty-four hours ago, Lukin had waited an hour before coming out of the woods. His truck had been on the street where he'd left it, and no police cars had been in sight. Lukin had jumped into the Dodge and unlocked the cuffs with his stashed handcuff key.

Although there was only one way out of the cul-de-sac, Lukin had skated, despite having to drive in front of Carly's place. He couldn't believe his luck as he drove past the house; the unmarked detective cars were gone and only one uniformed officer stood in the doorway, yawning behind the crime scene tape.

Then he'd felt like a fuck'n invisible man.

Now, he felt like a target was painted on his back. He needed to disappear fast. He couldn't think of anybody that would take him in without question, except, maybe his Uncle Ken in Mississippi. Lukin still had fifty dollars left from the meeting with the hard-ass, "G-Man," but that kind of cash wouldn't bankroll him. His buddy, Fred, couldn't help with the cash because he was on the run from a local bounty hunter.

An uneasy feeling settled over Lukin. He hadn't felt really scared since grade school, but he didn't doubt the threat of the man who hired him. Dumping the truck before leaving the state seemed a good idea. Lukin could borrow Fred's old work van. The doofus kept a front door key under the mat and a spare ignition key hanging on the wall near his kitchen door.

"Remember, if you botch this, I will personally take you out," the old man had said.

When the throwaway cell rang, Lukin urinated on himself.

* * *

"I told you to let this drop, Rose." Derrick said, watching Rose pace in front of his desk.

"Why did you lie to me?"

"To avoid this ridiculous discussion we're having with our kids in the next room."

"But, I know I'm right about Billie Ray." Borrowing time, Rose straightened the fringe of the Aubusson carpet with a toe. "You're tired; I understand. But your platform should stand for something. What will people think?"

The small lines around Rose's eyes softened as she started to walk toward Derrick, but he stopped his wife by pointing an index finger.

"You know nothing about what it takes to run a campaign. I live in the real world. I don't have the luxury of seeing the world through a pink filter. I get ahead by scratching the right back, which in turn, gives me a leg up. In this case, Cofer's the right back."

"But involving yourself with the likes of Billie Ray is a mistake," Rose said, planting herself in front of Derrick's desk. "He hates everyone who's not exactly like him. He scares me. No doubt the man wouldn't flinch at anything—even illegal— to get what he wants. He is *ruthless*." Pausing a moment, Rose continued, "If not for the sake of your career, then think of your family."

"I am thinking of the family. If I lose, we'll have to start over. My career hinges on winning this campaign. After I win this election, we can talk about principles and goodwill toward men."

Rose shook her head. "But association with racist rhetoric will follow you after the campaign. Please rethink this decision."

"I have, and I don't necessarily disagree with everything Billie Ray says."

"What do you mean?"

When Derrick didn't respond, Rose said, "Surely, you don't think that the South will rise again? And all white men will regain their so-called rightful domains?"

Tight-lipped, Derrick said, "I didn't say that. But I do think this country would benefit from more work ethic and less belly-aching liberal 'gimme' shit." He took a deep breath, and then said, "Minorities and women have to realize power isn't gained overnight. Handling crucial decisions without education and experience spells disaster. Right now, the blacks and immigrants, along with your gender, don't have the skills or—"

"For Godsake, Derrick, you're filtering history," Rose snapped. "What about the truth of slavery and discrimination? These issues aren't mere words used to disguise a lazy working class. These people suffered, are suffering. The facts are minorities and women are paid less."

"You're being melodramatic now. Do you think my forefathers had it easy? There's no such thing as a free ride no matter how much the poor want it. Women make less because they're support staff most of the time. They can't possibly do what a man does every day. In my opinion it's physically and psychologically impossible."

Rose dropped her shoulders. "This is an old battle between us." She paused, "Okay, say all that's true. Why Cofer? Why a white supremacy group?"

"Cofer is not different from other men in power, whatever their race. Green is the color of money, and money is the great motivator."

"Then, in the name of money, anything goes?"

"Your last question exemplifies why women shouldn't be in power. You don't understand basic economics."

When Rose turned her back and walked to the window, Derrick softened his tone as he said, "I don't want to talk about politics. I keep our family separate as much as possible. Trust me. Allow this thing to be outside your concerns."

Rose answered him without turning around. "Your work is a part of our lives. It affects us. The way you do your job reflects on your character and sets an example for our sons."

Derrick pounded the desk. "This is none of your business. You're making a problem where none exists. Drop this charade about concern for the family. This is about your stupid bad dreams—your woman's intuition. It's bullshit."

A look of disgust stayed on Rose's face as she backed away saying, "I hope winning is worth it."

Derrick shook his head, returning to his speech notes, and detached from the argument before his wife closed the door.

Chapter 21

On Carly's third morning in the hospital, Detective Sterling and Sergeant Fainey of Internal Affairs arrived. They'd been there before, but Carly had been too sedated to talk.

"We know you're still in some pain, but need to talk to you about the assault," Fainey said.

Carly nodded at the puffy-faced sergeant.

"May we talk alone?" The young detective asked, nodding in Agent George Dugan's direction.

Carly didn't care for the lack of sympathy shown by the IA officers.

"No. He is a friend. I prefer he stay. Anyway, I'm making a victim's statement here. Nothing to hide. Just a formality. Right, guys?"

"I'm George Dugan, here, visiting the sick and injured."

The cops exchanged glances and ignored George.

"Did you recognize the guy that attacked you, Carly?" Fainey said.

"No. He had a mask on."

"What happened?" Sterling asked.

"That's what I'd like to know. He broke into my apartment and tried to kill me." Reading their faces, Carly added, "I think the attempted rape was an afterthought."

"Why?" The baby-faced detective widened his stance. "I mean, are you sure?"

"Yes. To paraphrase what he said: I'm going to rape you for free before I kill you. Something like that."

Both cops were silent as Dugan got up from his chair and stood beside Carly's bed.

In turn, Carly examined the flat line of Detective Sterling's crew-cut and allowed the game to settle down. Finally, she said, "I had the distinct impression someone wanted me dead."

"You mean someone hired him to kill you," Sterling said. "But why?"

Fainey stepped forward. "What possible reason could somebody have for knocking you off?"

"I know I'm just a recruit, but I know too much." Carly reached for the water pitcher and groaned.

George intervened and poured her a glass of water.

The IA investigators exchanged glances again. Then Fainey wrote something down in a notebook.

Marci had gone to the cafeteria before the IA arrived. Carly felt sure George would measure his words, unlike Marci, if he spoke. Though after several minutes of bogus questions, Carly didn't disguise her tone when the suits skirted around the important questions. "By the way, who was the SOB? Carly said.

"What?" Fainey said, never looking up from his notepad.

"The asshole I knocked out with a lamp and handcuffed."

Fainey grunted. "Uniform lost him in the woods behind the house."

"That's crazy. I handcuffed him behind his back before I passed out. Surely—" Carly started to add something derogatory, but George coughed.

"On the night of the break-in," George said, "the police department was short-handed. Manpower was diverted to a

911 call, a murder of a socialite's daughter. The detectives left your place without interviewing the neighbors and rushed to the murder scene at a mansion in Spring Hill, leaving your assailant the opportunity to disappear."

Nodding in Dugan's direction Fainey said, "A little tough on PD, aren't you, George Dugan? Whoever you are? We'll talk later."

Uninvited, the sergeant drew a chair close to the bed, sat, and held Carly's gaze. "Yes, well, we want to ask you how, after being shot, you knocked a man unconscious with a lamp, and then handcuffed him."

"I was just trying like hell to survive. What would you've done?" Carly said.

He leaned closer to Carly. "You must cooperate in an Internal Affairs investigation, Redmund. You have no choice," Fainey paused for effect. "To refuse means termination."

Carly locked eyes with the sergeant.

Sterling sighed. "What the sergeant means, Redmund, is that we want to make this as easy as possible. We have a job to do. We can't catch this guy without your help. You're the victim here, not the suspect."

"Okay, let's start over. You play nice and I will too. By the way, I may be new to street policing, but I'm familiar with my civil rights, as well as the administration's policy."

The sergeant propped one foot on the bed frame, while rummaging through a file folder. He produced photographs of the scene and showed Carly a picture of her duty belt lying on a chair. "Isn't that your gun belt with your loaded .9mm still in the holster?"

"Yes." Carly said nothing else

"Why didn't you use your weapon if your life was in danger?" the sergeant said.

"The thought crossed my mind, but he smashed my head against the wall before I could get it out of the safety holster. In fact—"

"Was there anyone else in the apartment that night?" Sterling asked.

"No. Only one perp." Then she realized what the detective meant. "Let me clarify something. I have no boyfriend or lover."

"What about Tim Price or this man?"

"Tim's a colleague. And this man can talk for himself." She leaned back in her bed. "You know, you guys are a trip."

Carly pressed the button for the nurse. "Unless you guys are really interested in finding the asshole that attempted to murder and rape me, I suggest you leave me alone. I'm in some serious pain here."

Once George flashed his FBI badge, the sergeant and detective started to apologize, but Carly said, "You know, I'm thinking that I haven't been treated exactly swell by you guys."

As Marci entered the room, Carly added, "I've been rude. Let me introduce another friend, Marci Eplund, who works for the *Tribune*. Maybe you'd like to spell your names for her before you leave."

Detective Sterling smiled and buttoned his coat.

They started to leave, but the sergeant added, "We'll be back when you're thinking more clearly, Ms. Redmund."

Carly noticed the distended veins in his neck and temple.

As the investigators walked through the doorway, Carly blurted out, "In case you guys really are interested in catching the perp, it's tied to the bones found on the Deeter farm."

The IA detectives didn't look back.

After the suits left, Marci did her cop impression: "Redmund, you have no choice but to cooperate. You're a peon."

They laughed.

"Okay, I admit I eavesdropped before I made my entrance," Marci said.

Carly shook her head. "They've already decided it was a domestic, Marci. They're not going to investigate."

"Nothing like going through the motions. Major egos just walked out of here," Marci said. "I loved it when you told them to spell their names for me."

Carly grinned at George. "Did you see their faces when I reminded them I could refuse to talk to them if they treated me like a suspect?"

"Yeah, but I didn't get it," Marci said.

George turned toward Marci. "See, under the guise of an administrative investigation, there're no Fifth Amendment rights. So they can gather their probable cause to arrest during a routine interview, and you're toast. It's a "catch-22." If you don't answer their questions, they fire you."

"So basically your civil rights are limited, if not defunct, when you put on the badge."

"Pretty much," Carly interjected. "The veterans say a shooting on duty can bring out the Monday morning quarterbacks. Big time."

"That stinks," Marci said.

"Even more than you know." George stretched.

"Do I sense a firsthand experience lurking in your past?" Marci said, rifling through her bag.

George shrugged.

"Later, big guy. I want the dirty details." Grinning, Marci withdrew a printout from her bag.

"Getting back to the real matter at hand, I have a copy of the call from communications. Apparently, the men in blue didn't come inside your loft right away because the bad guy was running out the back as they rounded the corner of the house. The police report stated the cuffs were in front of him and his mask was ditched, but never found."

"They didn't find the mask, that doesn't make any sense. I handcuffed him in back."

"I'm sure you did, Carly," George said, touching her arm. "He just stepped through his arms. It happens."

"Okay," Marci said browsing the printout. "Responding officers weren't informed that an officer was down until seven minutes into the fiasco."

"Great! After I dialed 911, I dropped the phone. When radio finally answered, I was a little busy handcuffing a perp, and then I blacked out. What happened to the .38 I ditched under the bed?"

"I don't know." Marci said offering the call-log printout to Carly.

"Not right now. Maybe later," Carly replied. Tears swelled in her eyes for a moment. "The gory details will be safe in your hands until then."

A knock on the door interrupted them, and a black female technician entered and checked Carly's blood pressure. "Miss, how are you today?" the tech asked.

"Being honest, I could use some good news."

* * *

Ned quietly opened the heavy metal doors of the morgue and watched Tim scour the stainless steel sinks with bleach.

Without looking up, Tim said, "How was lunch, Gordie?"

"I wouldn't know. How do you stand that bleach smell mixed in with ripe organs?"

The unfamiliar voice made Tim wheel around grazing the sink edge.

"I can't say I notice it any longer," Tim said addressing a gentleman dressed in a raincoat worn over starched khakis and a dress shirt. When the man walked closer, Tim noticed the raincoat was dry, and the man's scraggly salt-and-pepper beard seemed out of whack with his otherwise neat appearance. "May I help you?" Tim said, smiling.

"Well, that depends. Are you Tim Price, the assistant coroner?"

"Yes. The coroner is at lunch. He'll be back shortly. But usually we meet people out—"

"I want to talk to you."

"Okay. What was the name of your loved one? The one you've come to see?" Tim pulled his plastic gloves off and threw them in a hazardous-waste disposal can.

"This isn't a personal matter."

Tim discarded his surgical gown as he said, "Surely, you'd prefer to come inside to the office? Please."

"No, thank you. I think this room will do."

"Excuse me." Tim laughed. "That's a first."

The intruder stared.

Tim cleared his throat. "So, how can I help you?"

"It's more like, what I can do for you."

"For me? I don't understand."

"Wouldn't you like to be coroner?"

Tim retrieved a clipboard with an autopsy report. "You mean, when the present coroner dies of old age?"

As the man moved closer, he swung a knife on a chain.

Tim backed up shielding his chest with his clipboard.

"No. Opportunity knocks," the man said. "I can help you develop your questionable potential and remedy your current shortage of funds concerning your mother's health care. Isn't she at Mount Sinai nursing home?"

"How do you know about my mother?"

Ned dropped the knife on a tray and stuffed his leather gloves inside his coat pockets. "Relax, Mr. Price—no need for paranoia. It's widely known. Employee gossip. I'm sorry about your mother."

"My mother isn't your concern. Who are you?"

"Tim. May I call you Tim?"

"No."

"Tim, this is a win-win situation. You back off on your ill-advised investigation concerning the death of Terence Washington Williams, and all your financial problems will be solved."

Tim put his clipboard down on the sink ledge. "Who's attempting to bribe me?"

"You disappoint me. This is a gentlemen's agreement." The man invaded Tim's body space.

Again, Tim stepped back. "Come on. You can't be serious."

Ned stretched, retrieved his knife from the tray, and then began to clean his nails with the half-opened knife.

Tim stared on the knife. "Okay, who are you?"

"My name isn't important. However, the people I represent are powerful. They can make or break a county employee's career."

"But, as you have pointed out already, I'm insignificant with questionable potential. Why bother with me?"

"My friends prefer persuasion to force. However, if you refuse their offer, you and your girlfriend, Ms. Redmund, could be at risk."

Ned crossed in front of Tim. "I understand Ms. Redmund was attacked recently—an awful thing to go through. Probably some scumbag. Please send her my wishes for a speedy recovery."

Tim clenched his fists.

Ned made eye contact. "Let's be reasonable. Another facet of our problem is the press or Ms. Eplund. I know you're curious, as any investigator would be, but a cover-up conspiracy isn't afoot. You and your friends' unauthorized meddling could cause unnecessary embarrassment." He walked to Tim's side and gripped his arm. "Believe me. There's no foul play hidden within the big, bad system. Terence committed suicide, because his grades had plummeted and his college scholarship had been rescinded."

"Really," Tim said, almost nose to nose with the man. "What a convenient spin you put on Terence's death. But I doubt your version will be supported by the physical evidence."

"Please consider my offer carefully." The man paused, and then added, "'Forsake the foolish and live,' Proverbs 9:6. What would your Jewish mother advise you to do?"

Tim opened his mouth to tell the man to go to hell, but Ned flicked his wrist and locked the blade of the knife into place. As he walked away, he scraped the side of the metal gurney with the glistening blade, leaving a deep groove down its entire length. With a contemptuous smile, he stopped and blew the metal shavings away. Holding the switchblade out from his body like a priest with an incense thurible, he flicked the blade closed one-handed. The ritual completed, he left without another word.

Tim couldn't move.

* * *

Lukin changed jeans and threw a change of clothes into a plastic bag. Then he searched Elma's underwear drawer, old purses in the closet, and under the mattress for cash. Nothing. Lukin was sure his old lady squirreled money away. If he went to the hotel, at least he could take what money she had. When a shadow crossed the blind outside the bedroom window. Lukin ran toward the door.

* * *

Lukin slapped the hotel counter and blurted, "Hey babe!" making Elma jump.

She fumbled with the registration forms and saved the entered data into the computer. Jerking her head around trying to locate her boss, she said, "What are you doing? The hotel manager can see and hear everything from the office. I thought we agreed … ." She looked down.

"That's no way to treat the man you love," Lukin said. "You know how mad I get when you act all uppity." Lukin lunged across the check-in counter.

Elma gasped and flattened herself against the file cabinet against the back wall.

Draping himself across the counter, Lukin smirked and swung his arm from side to side like a pendulum before he grabbed for Elma and missed.

She stood tall stretching her five feet and five inches "Please leave now. Before my boss comes back, and I get in trouble."

"Relax, goofball." He patted the counter as he prowled back and forth. His eyes darting to the cash register and to the security cameras aimed at the desk. "You wanna go to lunch, hon?" Lukin said sniffing the air. "The smell of money makes me hungry."

"I can see you're not going to leave until you get what you want. How much? I only have a few dollars."

"Babe, you crush me. Can't a guy take his hard-working wife to lunch? I'll just sit here and read a magazine until your ready." Lukin picked up a copy of *People* magazine and slumped into a nearby couch.

Elma answered the ringing phone. After being out all night, her husband had cleaned up before he came to the motel. His hair was even combed, but like a tomcat he sported some new scratches on his face.

Elma told Lukin to meet her outside and scurried to meet Maggie who was heading for the check-in desk. "Can I take an early lunch?" Elma asked. She hoped her boss hadn't heard Lukin in the lobby.

Maggie studied Elma. "Sure. Get out of here. I can see you need a break. I'll cover for you."

As Elma started to leave the area, she saw a police car parked next to the front revolving glass doors. The beat officer usually dropped by mornings for a free coffee. She waved at the officer and walked down the hallway toward the locker room. Entering, she saw her locker pried open and her empty wallet lying on a bench.

She knew without checking the lobby that Lukin was gone.

Chapter 22

Using his twelve-year-old daughter's birthday as the password, J.C. brought up Noreen's email. Acting like a sappy teenager, Noreen's emails to John had increased. The guy wrote in New Age lingo reinforcing his "you're my soul mate" garbage with so-called metaphysical proof. J.C. almost felt sorry for the desperate asshole, but Noreen was his wife. This crap had to stop. Tweedle Dee and Tweedle Dum weren't going to ride off into the sunset together.

Considering Noreen treated him like a kitchen appliance with trash bins full of money, and he was a lousy husband, he hadn't made up his mind how to handle the online affair. He'd resorted to prostitutes a couple of times and a one-night stand with the chief's secretary, which he'd regretted before he shut the motel door. Some days, clarity reigned. He kissed his children, and he forgave himself for being distant. On his worse days, when Noreen withdrew her meager sexual favors, he fantasized about bashing Noreen's head in the elaborate display case full of expensive dolls.

Lately nothing helped. At work the rookie, the ring, the daily grind overloaded him, and at home Noreen's yapping never ceased. Silence replacing his usual one word answers, sometimes, J.C. shut down. In some ways he deserved what he got, but his wife was a rollercoaster of emotions. *Who could keep up?*

Too many days, Noreen did as little as possible. She stayed in bed and only rallied to clean clothes, buy food, or drive her children to events when they couldn't bum rides. Occasionally, there were mini breakdowns when Noreen faked an illness and kept the children home.

J.C. pretended not to notice. Returning home from duty, he would find the children vegetating in front of the television, eating junk food at midnight.

Manic, Noreen shopped online and at the malls—buying sprees of dolls and household goods, while incessantly lying about it. But she never tried to hide the sleeping pills or wine. At least the self-medication did—at some point—knock her out.

Shutting off the computer in the kitchen, J.C. walked down the hall and saw the master bedroom was dark. Relieved, he left Noreen asleep, and J.C. undressed in the laundry room.

He yanked off his belt, tie, and shirt and hung them on a clothes rack. Ripping back the Velcro straps on his bulletproof vest and flinging the heavy object at a mounted hook on the back door, he watched the vest swing back and forth. It resembled a manikin torso. Emotionless, he poked the vest in the middle of the breastplate. Last year, his old vest had stopped a bullet and had saved his life. Although unable to remember the slug's impact, he relived the paralyzing fear in his nightmares.

Cursing the price of safety, he pulled off his wet T-shirt and exposed the heat rash on his chest. "Damn vest's hot as hell." He squatted, unloaded his duty weapon, and then locked the ammunition clip in a floor safe.

Dressed now in jeans and a T-shirt, he heard his dog start barking in the kitchen. J.C's bulldog ate while J.C. shared the events of his day with the canine. "Russ, the damn civilians screamed all night in my face. Every fucking last one."

Ditching his food on a side table, J.C. flopped down into a vinyl recliner and surfed channels with the television remote. "Shit, my aching back," he said, between gulps of beer. The *Three Stooges* played on the tube, helping him unwind.

Downing three more beers, he watched the slapstick, laughing at the scene depicting an Irish cop extorting money. "Goddamit, we're all crooked sons of bitches," he said aloud. "But you'll call a cop when you're in trouble or scared." He hit his chest. "That's right. I keep you safe. Maintain order." He was a cop twenty-four hours a day. It took its toll.

He wished life were simple like the show he was watching. Life didn't have good guys and bad guys anymore. Everything was gray.

* * *

"What the hell happened, Ned? This is a cluster fuck," Billie Ray said, pacing across the side porch.

The retired agent continued watching three crows on a nearby telephone wire. He exhaled before he said, "Now, hold on. I told you and the others that Lukin wasn't the right man for this job."

"Shit, guess it doesn't matter now," Billie Ray said, glaring at Ned. "What's done is done. But I want the idiot to have an accident. You got me?"

Ned peered in the living room window and saw Gloria walking through the house.

"Keep your voice down. Your wife will hear."

"She can't hear us," Billie Ray said, lowering his voice nevertheless. "I don't want this thing traced back to the militia cell. It has to be a clean kill."

"You ever known me to miss?"

"No. And, by God, you better not this time."

Sipping his coffee, Ned rocked back and forth in the

porch swing. "Dope addicts, like Lukin, die every day. A bad score or a dope deal gone wrong happens," he said holding Billie Ray's gaze.

The militia leader blinked first. "Listen, Ned, I know you can handle this. I'm just worried. I backed Adam when he suggested Lukin, but I knew it was a dumb-ass idea at the time. I should've said something. Damn his friendship with the chief."

Ned smiled as he noticed Billie Ray's eyelid twitch.

"Okay," Billy Ray continued, "We'll just stand tough. Right?"

"Only a glitch, buddy boy."

"You're right. Just a little ripple in the water." Billie Ray took the cigar Ned offered.

"I can take care of Lukin quickly. He's not exactly a brain surgeon," Ned said. "I'll check his old haunts. If all else fails, I'm sure his wife will know where he's hiding."

Billie Ray frowned. "Look. Use kid gloves. Lukin is just out of jail for beating her for the umpteenth time."

"Stop worrying. I'll play the lonely old man who wants to chat and leave Miss Elma smiling. I can see you feel protective of her?"

"Not really. But Elma knows nothing. It's bad business. A man doesn't beat a woman just because he can." Billie Ray smiled slyly. "But—"

"Under extreme circumstances, killing a woman is justified."

* * *

While he washed his hands, J.C. avoided looking in the precinct mirror. He knew what he'd see—the same dead eyes that emanated from the prostitutes and perpetrators on the streets.

They were like kudzu, swallowing him inch by inch.

Fifteen minutes later, J.C. ranted to his fellow officers in the break room: "The system's rigged against the average middle-class guys, like you and me. The rich have their lawyers and shrinks, and the disadvantaged have welfare. We can't win. Just doesn't pay to police." It didn't help. *I get it now. I understand how the thin blue line gets blurry, and why officers crossover, confiscating drugs or money from the street thugs.*

J.C. forgot the epiphany—but he wouldn't any longer follow all the good-guy rules.

* * *

Agent George Dugan whispered in Carly's ear and brushed her cheek with a kiss goodbye.

Marci ogled Dugan's backside until the hospital door closed. "That George. I wish he'd stayed longer," she said with a sigh. "As if he knew I was alive. Must be attracted to damsels in distress."

"Marci, stop it." Carly grinned, adding "He only wants to help us with the case."

A knock on the door interrupted them. A young physician entered carrying a chart. "Ms. Redmund, I'm Doctor Connors. Let's see. This is your fourth day here. How are we feeling?"

"Some pain, but mostly I'm bored."

"That's my cue to leave." Marci nodded at the physician. "Adios, Doc. Later, gal."

"Marci, thanks, I didn't mean—"

"Sure you did, but whatever. Remind me to tell you about something Stewart confirmed." She waved goodbye and mouthed *wow* behind the doctor's back.

Carly looked at the doctor as he studied her chart. "I

wish this dang splint was off my arm. It's cumbersome. Sometimes my fingers go numb."

"How often do you have a lack of sensation? Which fingers?"

Carly waved her pinky and index fingers at him. "Just once in a while."

The physician looked up at his patient and lowered his glasses.

"A couple times a day," Carly said.

"Any numbness before the injury?"

"No."

"It could be minor nerve damage. Sometimes problems occur, but it's too soon to diagnose. In a few weeks, you can start physical therapy. We'll know more then."

Carly sobered. "Hey, Doc, I thought you said this was a clean through shot, nothing but muscle tissue damage. What happened to 'as good as new with a little healing time?'"

The physician laughed. "I told you there were no complications in surgery. But nerves are fragile; they become bruised from the trauma. They may temporarily go on the fritz, and then get better—quickly in most cases, but some do not. It's too early to tell."

"Are you being straight with me?" Carly said, moistening her dry lips. "I can handle about anything if I know the truth."

"I bet you can, Ms. Redmund." The doctor checked his beeper, and then continued, "I have every reason to believe you'll make a full recovery, but no guarantees. If I continue to tell you the real scoop, will you take your pain pills for a couple more days and rest?"

"I don't like the way the meds make me feel."

"That explains why you refused your pain meds today.

However, it will help your body heal faster, speed recovery. You need to tell me when the numbness occurs."

Carly nodded, and they awkwardly shook hands.

Turning her head toward the door, Carly asked, "So, how's my security from the department doing? Is he still there? Haven't heard a peep."

"I believe Officer Tharp likes working this shift."

"He's enamored with the young blond nurse?"

"Uh-huh." The doctor focused upon writing on his clipboard.

"I need to warn her about police officers. Not a sure thing for the long haul."

He smiled. "You're probably too late."

"Just my luck. I get shot and my watchdog meets Goldilocks."

"At least you're alive and everything's mending," the doctor said, snapping the clipboard shut. "We can only put the pieces back together and hope for the best."

"Got ya, Doc. Your job sounds a lot like police work."

* * *

Karl Potter patted his sweaty face with the tail of his jean shirt. Putting the kegs up in the walk-in cooler was a dirty job, and Calpes storeroom smelled musty and dank. The wire shelves surrounding the cooler contained various condiments along with the staples of nuts, chips, and hamburger buns.

As Potter finished, he pushed his glasses up on his thin nose and tried to hear what was going on near the bar where a half-dozen of Billie Ray's men were gathered.

Inside the billiard parlor, a dozen members settled down preparing to come to order for the meeting.

Dave Jordan yelled, "Hey, you cocksuckers, who do we

want to knock off today?"

Billie Ray grimaced as he motioned for Dave to shut up.

Tee whispered, "Birdie's in the back. He hasn't left."

"Damn it, Dave," Billie Ray said shaking his head. "You think you could shout a little louder."

Dave lowered his voice. "Well, hell, just playing around. Everyone thinks we're harmless old farts. Especially me, but—"

"Yeah, I feel sorry for you, Dave," Tee said, "'Cause I heard Sue Jefferson said you were pretty lifeless and harmless when you dropped by to fix her sink."

"Hey, I gave it my best shot. I'm not dead, yet."

Everyone laughed as Billie Ray drank his beer. He missed his friend, Adam, and barely noticed when Potter wandered into the room and laid down a stack of hamburgers.

Potter's words jabbed at the air. "Billie Ray, can you try to leave the place clean when you all leave out...put your trash in the dumpster? I ain't your maid."

"Okay, Birdie. Don't get your panties in a wad."

Dave added, "Did we hurt your feelings, Birdman."

"You ignorant motherfuckers," Potter said. "I'm outta here."

Dave chuckled. "Poor Birdie, he's so sensitive."

After the back door slammed, Billie Ray said, "We have a real mess we need to clean up, and I need your authorization to go ahead."

"You got it," Dave said. "Right guys?"

Before anybody could answer, Tee asked, "Where's Adam?"

"That's just it. His nephew, Lukin, is our problem." Billie Ray took a breath. "Thought it would be better if Adam wasn't here." Everyone knew Carly survived Lukin's attack, but nobody wanted the job of sealing either of their final fates.

Billie Ray let the members squirm, and then said, "I consider this an emergency session. The boy fucked up, and we could be exposed."

Still, nobody brought the vote to the table.

Tee scratched the back of his neck.

"Adam will take it hard," Billie Ray said, "but I recommend the Georgia farmer for clean up."

Finally, Dave took the initiative. "I make the motion that the Georgia farmer finishes the job that Lukin started. Wish I could be there with my shotgun to see it go down."

Silence.

"Look, men," Billie Ray said, "I dislike voting without Adam, but we can't expect him to be impartial."

Tee shrugged. "I'll second the motion."

"All in favor of the motion say, aye." Most of the men gave their consent, prompting Billie Ray to continue, "Any opposed? Good. Nada. I'll see the farmer first thing tomorrow morning."

Tee slapped Billie Ray on the back. "I know this is a tough one for you."

Billie Ray nodded. Ned was already hunting Lukin down, though once Adam found out about Lukin's death, Billie Ray could honestly say all the attending members voted on it.

"Yeah," Billie Ray replied. "I just wish Adam wasn't in the middle of this thing. In hindsight I should've talked him out of it. But he insisted we use Lukin to make the police department happy. They probably wanted patsy material. Now, he's signed his own nephew's death warrant."

Tee leaned closer to Billie Ray and said, "Even if we'd used other options, it might've played out the same with Redmund. Things happen."

"Goddamn it! Adam's gonna be pissed." Billie Ray

shook his head and finished his beer.

"Let me buy you another one," Dave said, grabbing a pitcher and filling Billie Ray's mug. "It will all blow over soon. It always does."

Billie Ray slumped on the barstool. "Maybe. Something just doesn't sit right in my gut about this one."

Chapter 23

Karl Potter shut Calpes' flimsy back door and hurried down the alley to his blue Nova parked behind Sam's Garage.

They had an arrangement. Somewhere between Sam installing Alpine speakers in Potter's Nova and a karaoke sound system inside Calpes, the men had become friends. That's when Karl had dreamed up the idea to videotape the Thursday meetings and asked for a hidden microphone near the cash register.

Although he had fantasized about blackmailing the militant bastard, Karl doubted if he had the guts to confront Billie Ray. When the sound quality of the video turned out to be poor, he didn't bother to fix it and nixed the plan.

But now, he'd overheard the rednecks talking murder. Fumbling with his car keys, he made a decision. With local PD turning a blind eye to the secret cell, he would be better served by mailing the videos to the FBI.

* * *

"Thanks for meeting me again here at the lodge, Derrick. I know it's out of your way."

"Not at all, Billie Ray. I like it here." Both men sat in Adirondack chairs on the wrap-around porch.

"I might as well cut to the chase. This thing's gotten complicated." Derrick remained silent as Billie Ray continued. "So far, nobody has linked you to any of this. Me and the boys will do everything we can to ensure it stays that way and out of the media."

"Yeah, I keep waiting for that Eplund bitch to put my name in a headline insinuating I murdered a black kid. Jesus, it would ruin me."

"She and assistant coroner Price are less of a threat than you think. One of my guys dug up some trash."

"What?"

"Seems Ms. Eplund detoured into an alternate lifestyle before she became a newspaper reporter in our fair city. Her carpet-munching lover might have committed suicide or been helped."

Derrick grimaced and turned his head. If Billie Ray noticed, he didn't mince words as he added, "Mr. Price, the dear lad, has financial problems. Ain't that a belly laugh, a kike—okay, a half Jew—needing money? His mother needs expensive Alzheimer care. So if he feeds us enough information, we may throw him a bone, the coroner's job."

"I see. Everyone has a secret and a price."

"Exactly. At best, we're animals seeking food and shelter. But defective Jews and lesbians are abominations."

Derrick cleared his throat. "Who's protecting our interests otherwise?" he said.

"Let's just say a professional. The less you know, the better."

"I'm not a lawyer," Derrick said, frowning, "but at this stage, I think pleading ignorance is a lame defense."

Billie Ray nodded. "In short, cops have dangerous jobs. And things happen to addicts and thugs like Lukin all the time."

Dust swirled around their legs as Derrick said, "Yes. Things happen."

* * *

Mary Williams paused at the nurses' station to verify Carly's room number. She could have asked the officer in the corridor, but his black skin in the uniform looked like betrayal to Mary. Her brother's brutal arrest during a civil rights march in the 1960s had soured her opinion about law enforcement even before Terence's disappearance. Not for the first time, she questioned her motivation for coming to the hospital with tulips picked from her garden. Mary's late husband would have said, "It was the Christian thing to do."

She wasn't so sure. Although she barely knew this white person and owed her nothing, Mary couldn't shake the feeling that she was somewhat culpable for the policewoman's assault.

Through the years Mary had watched the white community, whether they were directly responsible or not, build their power base on top of Terence and other young black men's bones. She knew they wouldn't just lie down and let an outsider, a Missourian to boot, expose them. Mary had allowed this inexperienced officer to challenge Terence's murderers without a word of caution.

Then, again, neither Carly nor that reporter from the *Tribune* had even bothered to call Mary or warn her about the suicide ruling before the newspaper story broke. No. The assault was probably random or unrelated to Terence's death.

Before Mary could turn away, a man opened the door to Carly's room.

"Hi there. Come on in," he said, stepping aside. "I'm Tim Price." When Mary didn't introduce herself, Tim added, "Beautiful flowers."

Mary gave Tim a cursory glance, thanked him, and crossed the room, depositing the flower vase on the windowsill. As she turned toward the recruit, Mary said, "How's your arm? Is the staff treating you well?"

"Thank you. I'm better today."

"Tim remained in the doorway, waiting for an introduction. "Tim, this is Mary Williams. Mary, this is Tim Price, the assistant coroner," Carly said.

Mary approached Carly's bedside.

"Tim's been helping Marci and me with Terence's case, gathering forensic evidence on the sly," Carly said. "He's really put his career on the line."

Mary's offered her hand. "Sorry. I didn't realize you weren't connected to the coroner's moronic suicide ruling?"

"No, Ma'am."

"That's good. The bastard won't let me bury what's left of my son, because I can't find Terence's birth certificate."

Tim looked at the vase of flower, as he said, "Yes. A real champ."

"He told me to obtain a court order proving I'm Terence's mother. You bet I will, and then I'm going to file a discrimination suit. The spineless bottom feeder is going to wish he'd never heard my name."

* * *

Lukin parked Fred's truck on Oronogo Street in Lacy, Mississippi near Uncle Ken's house. The wood-framed bungalow, nestled in a tranquil neighborhood, displayed the cheerful curb appeal of yellow paint with green shutters.

Aunt Alice had added her touch to the garden with happy statuaries. A painted masonry duck and an elfish gnome welcomed guests to the back pathway.

On the steps to the deck Lukin stopped to survey the yard. The deck overlooked a driveway and a garage with a bay-door workshop. Inside, a fishing boat, his uncle's prize possession, and a huge lounge swing occupied over half the space. Lukin knew the garage door wouldn't be locked.

The summer Lukin had turned eight he'd stayed with his aunt and uncle for two weeks. He remembered how they sat on the swing and waved to the neighbors driving past. They were good people, and Lukin regretted involving them in his predicament. He would stay only a few days, and then head down the road. The law none the wiser.

Before Lukin knocked on the door, he brushed off his clothes and retied his ponytail. A few miles back, he'd bought blue jeans and a T-shirt at a Stuckey's truck stop, but he knew that he still reeked of trouble.

As his uncle opened the kitchen door, a big smile lit up his face. "Well, what do you know? I just told Alice we were overdue for a visitor." He ushered Lukin into the kitchen while saying, "You gotta be careful what you say. Anyone might walk through your back door." He slapped his nephew on the back. "Come on in, Lukin, and take a load off. You look like somethin' the cat drug in. How you been?"

"Fine. But if it's all the same to you, I think I'll stand. My rear end is paralyzed."

"Sure thing. It's a long drive from Alabama. I bet you're beat. Alice, look who's here."

Alice materialized with a basket of folded clothes in her hands. "Oh my, I'm not believing this. Hey, you cute thing."

Dropping the basket on a dining room chair, she scanned the bruises and cuts on her nephew's face. "Come. Give me a hug." On her tiptoes she hugged Lukin.

He broke free, bent over, and stared at the linoleum until the pain from his broken ribs subsided. Patting Alice's shoulder, he said, "I'm good. You should see the other guy." He pointed to his concerned aunt. "But you, you look the same, Aunt Alice. Pretty as a picture."

"Such malarkey, but I love you for saying it."

Uncle Ken plopped into his green recliner marking the entrance to the living room. "Well, she'll do," he said grinning and continued, "What brings you to our neck of the woods?"

"Just wanted a visit with my long-lost Uncle Ken and Aunt Alice." Lukin sat on the sofa. "You know, clear my head. If it's all right, I'd like to stay with you a while. Elma is at her mom's house. We had, a little argument, and she stormed out. I wanted to leave before I did something stupid. I'm working on my temper."

He touched his swollen forehead. "This is from a fight with a buddy of mine, not Elma and me. I haven't hit her since before I was placed on … . I agreed to go to anger management classes."

"You're always welcome here. You know that." Ken rubbed the arms of the recliner. "Problems again?" he said.

Alice flashed Ken a warning glance.

Lukin knew his aunt's philosophy whenever family was in trouble with the law: It was private business. Hailing from poor Ozark mountain kin, moonshiners, who always ran one step ahead of the state troopers and ATF, she didn't trust the government.

Alice smiled at Lukin. "We're so proud of you, taking those classes. Aren't we, Kenneth?"

"Right proud, son. Takes a real man to admit when he's wrong."

"Thank you, both. I'm really trying to clean up my act, but I want to have a baby so bad and sometimes I feel like Elma doesn't want children." He faked a pained expression and stood. "Can I use your bathroom?"

Alice used a soft tone, "Sure, hon, it's down the hall. You remember?"

After Lukin stepped into the hall, he stopped short to eavesdrop.

"Now, Ken, the boy needs a place to stay for a few days. For whatever reason, it can't be made worse if he stays and rests here. What we don't know can't hurt us."

"Guess you're right, but I swear that boy'd rather die than tell the truth. There's no telling what he's mixed up in. Could be drugs, guns. I'm serious, Alice. Drag us—"

"That boy ain't an idiot. He's just having personal problems. He wouldn't do that to us."

"I hope you're right." Ken gazed at the female newscaster on the television. "You think Elma's okay?"

"She is, or that gossipy sister of mine would've called. Claire only calls with bad news. Besides, I'm not so sure that Elma's doing right by Lukin. Having a baby might make things get better."

Lukin shifted his weight and a floorboard squeaked.

Alice whispered, "Hush now, he's coming back."

"But I didn't hear any water—"

Lukin rejoined the couple, which was trying to appear as if they'd been watching the news. As Alice tucked strands of salt-and-pepper hair behind her ears, she said, "Lukin, would you like a cinnamon roll? Homemade."

"I'd love one. You're the best."

"You sweet thing," she said, wiping her hands across her apron. "You'll see. One of my rolls and coffee will fix you right up."

* * *

"Recruit Redmund, may I come in? I should have called first, but—"

"No, please, must've dozed off from boredom. This hospital bed sucks."

The lanky man stood, balancing a plant and card, and shifting his weight back and forth between boots.

"Aren't you an officer?" Carly asked.

"Yes. I should introduce myself being out of uniform and all. I'm Officer Doug Tharp. I was with you until the paramedics arrived."

"You're badge number 276. You held my hand and told me I would make it. Thank you. You'll never know how reassuring your voice was to me. I appreciate what you did."

The young officer took a second to met Carly's eyes. "I'm not so sure you need to be thanking me. The call got messed up."

"I know it's—"

"The perp got away. We. I didn't come inside the house straight away because …. Look. My only shot was at the guy's back."

"Radio was rattled. She didn't tell you that an officer was down. Just a burglary in progress." Remembering the perp's mask wasn't found, Carly's instincts told her Grey, not Tharp, was the culprit. "You followed procedure," Carly said. "It happens. Forget it."

"How'd you know about communication's glitch?"

"Let's just say I have a friend, who has connections and obtained a copy of the tape from radio."

Tharp nodded. "I brought you a houseplant," he said, unloading the gift on a side table.

"Thanks. Please, sit down. Company's a welcome diversion from the nurses and doctors."

Tharp grabbed a chair, as Carly said, "A few officers dropped by from my academy class on the second day, but only one or two. I don't count the two IA jerks."

"Speaking of IA, I need to get something off my chest." Tharp popped his knuckles. "When they took my statement, they kept twisting what I said. I tried, but they didn't want to hear it."

Carly sat up straighter. "Yes, go on."

"After the third degree, they told me not to talk to anyone about the call, including you. Like you're being investigated for doing something wrong. I just didn't like the way it all went down."

"Yeah, freedom of speech isn't IA's forte. Besides, they're blowing this off as a domestic fight, despite the fact that I have no boyfriend, and the guy wore a ski mask."

"Weird."

"Not really. A couple of weeks back, my training officer pinned a neglect-of-duty charge on me after he took some evidence. I'd say the "powers that be" want me gone."

"Officer Grey? You kidding?"

"Nope."

The officer looked to and from the door. "I never told you this. I was warned not to get involved, but rumors are floating around that you're trouble, an accident waiting to happen. And fragging might be in your future."

"They want me dead, not just gone. Are you sure?"

Tharp nodded. "A few loudmouths speculating about a not-so friendly fire incident. Who knows? But I don't think they had anything to do with your aggravated assault. When I heard the brass was pulling your security, I decided to catch you before you went home.

"I'm still considered a rookie by most veterans, so I can't do much. But I wanted to give you a heads up, do the right thing."

Carly locked eyes with Tharp. "You're a stand-up guy. I understand. Maintaining a low profile's a good idea. It wasn't my intention to rattle any cages. I'll keep our visit on the QT. You better go."

"I hate this whole thing. They don't train you about this kind of thing in the academy."

"No, they don't."

Tharp extended his hand to Carly.

When she released her firm grip, she said, "You did your best. All you can do. I'll be fine." Carly smiled. "Now, if you'll excuse me, I need to make a phone call to my sister."

The well-meaning officer turned to leave.

As Carly picked up the phone, she said, "Keep it in the middle of the road, Tharp."

The officer almost smiled and left.

After the door shut, Carly quit pushing random buttons and replaced the phone on the side table. Looking out the window, she ruminated. "They don't know us Missouri gals. We're survivors. I'll die when I'm ready or when God chooses, not before."

Chapter 24

Searching for cheese, Carly poked her head inside in the refrigerator and let Agent Dugan wait. "Last time you dropped by, V had twisted your arm and had made you visit me. Right?"

George Dugan laughed. "No. By the way, I like your place."

"Thanks. It's good to be home."

"I confess. That was my cover story for your friend Tim's benefit. I just felt like seeing you. But now, I have some helpful information."

Shielding her injured arm, Carly slammed the refrigerator door with her backside. "Tell me."

"Now, this is off the record. Do you need some help?"

"Naw," Carly said, putting the cream cheese and bagel on a paper towel.

"I'm not even assigned the case, but an anonymous citizen sent us a video of our local militia having a meeting. They were discussing the elimination of a certain problem named Lukin. The Bureau thinks the guy that owns Calpes' billiard parlor, a Karl Potter, mailed it.

"The problem is the video may've been edited. I cruised by the place yesterday, drank a beer, and I'd say the background shots on the video match the inside of the joint."

"Gosh, I know a Lukin Hall from a domestic J.C. and I worked. We arrested the guy. Would you mind spreading the cream cheese on the bagel for me?"

Dugan obliged. "How close is Lukin's build compared to the perp who assaulted you?"

"Close." Carly sat down and tucked a hospital pamphlet about counseling for trauma victims under a stack of bills.

"Adam Hall is Cofer's best friend, Lukin's uncle, and a member of the militia," Dugan said. "It can't be a coincidence. I believe the group hired Lukin to rough you up, warn you to leave town, or possibly kill you." He shrugged. "The members have referred the matter to an unknown bad guy for clean up—meaning Lukin's a dead man walking and you're at risk."

"The list grows long. If the militia's hired help doesn't complete the job first, my training officer and his buddies may finish me off when I return to work."

"Holy Christ," George said. "You need to be—"

"Probably just testosterone talking," Carly said. "But I'm not totally paranoid to be concerned, because my precinct welcome mat—so to speak—has been lost."

"What do you mean?"

"Just a gut reaction. On my way home from the hospital, I had Tim wait in the car while I went inside the precinct to get my paycheck. Not a soul asked about my arm." Carly shrugged. "Anyway, what proof do you have Cofer's the head of the militia?"

"No direct link other than the video. Minus T-shirts with their logo, it's circumstantial. Cofer's good at what he does. Keeps himself insulated from direct connection to the cell on the internet, but they recruit members through website propaganda. I've been tracking their activities through Klanwatch."

"Should I Google Klanwatch?"

"Not a bad idea. Although it won't tell you much you don't already know from your academy classes on white supremacy groups."

"Small groups of resistance?" Carly asked.

"Exactly. Technically, the militia is an offshoot of the Klan."

Carly nodded. "No cross burning. Just hate crimes, collusion, and hired assassins."

"Something like that," George said.

Carly took a bite of her bagel, washed it down with coffee, and then said, "I wanna be there when you take them down."

"I told you it's not my case." They locked gazes. "Maybe, I can maneuver an assignment on the team. Jeez. You're not even official PD, and my boss and your chief barely speak. It will be a hard sell."

"I get it. So don't ask."

George's dimples flickered. "Redmund, you're thinking like a veteran-rogue cop now. I like it. I'll see what I can do."

* * *

When Ned arrived in Lacy, Mississippi, he staked out the house where Lukin was staying and followed Ken and Alice Hall to Mount Zion Baptist Church. After they went inside, Ned returned to Oronogo Drive.

If Ned judged Lukin accurately, he was inside without any weapons. Lukin felt safe and at home, a dangerous mindset for a man on the run. Just in case, Ned stuck a .45 with a silencer in the side pocket of his overalls before he knocked on the back door.

Waiting for Lukin to answer the door, Ned pulled down a ball cap over his freshly shaved face. Lukin opened the door a crack as Ned said, "My car broke down. Can I use your phone?" Lukin didn't recognize Ned until it was too late. He forced Lukin back into the kitchen with a jab to his chest.

"You're not glad to see me?" Ned said, taking off his hat and glasses. "I'm hurt. You think I meant what I said the last time we spoke?"

Lukin kept backing up until he reached the living room.

Ned paused to savor Lukin's hands up in the air before pushing him down into a chair next to a desk. "You pathetic piece of shit."

Lukin struggled to breathe as he said, "Please, don't. I can explain. I can fix this."

"No, you can't, boy. It's over. Your stay on this earth has been cut short by your own stupidity."

"My wife's pregnant; I swear I can make this right. Just don't kill me." With wild eyes Lukin searched the room for an escape and sprinted from the chair, but he tripped and sprawled on the floor.

"Get up, you dumbass," Ned said. Lukin crawled to the chair and pulled himself up into the seat.

"You try to run again, I'll torture you before I kill you."

The blood drained from Lukin's face. "You know Elma? She's my wife."

Methodically, Ned took out plastic gloves from his overall pocket and put them on. Then he took his .45 and put the end of the barrel between Lukin's eyes. Retrieving a baggy containing a lighter, a spoon, and a speedball of heroin and crack, he threw the stuff on the desk and instructed Lukin to heat the lethal combination.

Ned watched the mixture liquefy. He had bought the drugs at a truck stop near the state line using an old test kit to verify the purity. Lukin would be going out with the premium high of his life. *Too good for a man who beats his wife.*

Sweat dripped down Lukin's temple as he pleaded. "Look man, it doesn't have to go down like this."

"An overdose or a bullet in the head. Your choice. Besides, who knows, you might survive. If you do, all is forgiven."

Lukin closed his eyes and swallowed hard. "But I'll never say a word. Swear to God." He bowed his head. "Elma's got nobody but me."

"That's not giving the gal much credit." He handed Lukin a rubber tourniquet, and then smashed the gun into the side of Lukin's skull, cocking the weapon.

Lukin howled and wrapped the tourniquet around his upper arm, pulling it tight with his teeth. Dewy-eyed, he said, "I'm begging. I love my wife."

"Lying asshole. You've never cared about anybody but yourself. Now it's too late."

Lukin shrank in the chair as he inserted the needle in a vein. When the drug flooded his blood stream, he dropped the syringe and slouched against the back of the chair. His eyes rolled back in his head. Gasping, he convulsed and exhaled a death rattle. Spittle ran from his mouth.

Ned took a set of car keys from Lukin's pocket, and surveyed the room. He left the scattered residue of crack and heroin on the desk for the police to find, took off his gloves, and with a paper towel wiped the kitchen door.

Walking with purpose to Lukin's ride, a beat up van, he put on a pair of work gloves, found a toolbox inside, and pocketed a screwdriver. He rummaged in the center console, saw a .38 special, and left it. The only .38 that interested Ned was the one used to shoot Carly. The gun Officer Grey had disposed of it. As expected, Ned found the paper and photograph that he'd given Lukin stashed underneath the front driver's seat.

Another loose end tied up.

Before exiting the van, he stuck the note and his gloves in a pocket. Flipping the screwdriver over in his hand, he walked to his car. He poked his head under the hood for a minute or two, as if he was fixing his car. For the benefit of the neighbors, he exaggerated wiping his greasy hands and the screwdriver with a shop rag on the porch before he returned the borrowed tool and the keys to Lukin's pocket. He was careful not to touch anything without the rag. After he slammed the back door of the house, he waved to a nonexistent figure in the kitchen window, yelled, "Thanks a bunch," and then walked back to his rental car.

He took off his overalls and folded them with the .45 still in the pocket and laid the parcel in a briefcase. Locking the case, he set it on the floorboard. As he slid behind the wheel, the dash clock read nine-fifteen.

Lukin's body was still warm when Ned discarded the gloves at the first rest stop and set off for Mobile and dinner with the wife. Carly could wait for another day.

* * *

As Tim entered the kitchen, Carly swallowed a pain pill and washed it down with water.

"How was your day at work, hon?" Tim said.

"Light duty is awful," Carly said. "My arm hurt all day while I answered a million questions from unhappy citizens and took their reports over the phone. They wanted a cop to show up at their door about little Johnnie's stolen bike. And when the throbbing in my arm escalated to can't-stand-it status, just for laughs and giggles, I went to physical therapy. Kicked the pain up a couple of notches. Does that answer your question?"

"Wow, testy. I get it. You're in pain and desk work drives you crazy."

"Let me put it this way. Physical therapy wasn't a picnic, but at least there was a point. Taking personal phone messages from four women for the "Rev" or Officer Brown was a waste. Now, I know why he volunteers to work the desk."

"Jeez, four women. How's he keep up?"

"Don't know. Don't care."

"So, you went to therapy on duty?" Tim said.

"They docked me sick time because they said it's not a job-related injury. I guess the fact that somebody tried to kill me isn't enough. Classified as an off-duty injury."

"What happens when your sick time runs out?"

"I lose pay." Carly leaned on the counter and grimaced from the pain.

"That's tough. I guess this is a bad time to talk?" Tim turned to go.

"Oh, no, I stayed awake instead of crashing. Talk."

"I do need to explain something." He hesitated squirming. "I should've told you the last time Marci was here, but I needed to think. Anyway..." Tim paced.

"Go on."

"Well, I didn't want to worry you with my stuff, but a visitor came to the morgue last week. He was one of Billie Ray's henchmen."

"What the hell?"

"I should've told you. I'm sorry but—"

"You think?"

Tim shrugged.

"What did he say?"

"That I should back off the investigation of Terence's case, and you should lay low."

"Damn it. Was that all?"

"Pretty much. He and his friends offered to sponsor me on my road to success as the next county coroner."

"You told them to drop dead?"

"Not exactly." Tim studied the design in the tile.

"What exactly?" Carly said, raising her voice.

"Hold on. He had a knife and scraped the side of a gurney."

"Shit, a knife."

"Listen, Carly, the guy was intimidating, but nothing happened. He never touched me."

"Tim, you could've been hurt or killed." Carly slumped on the couch. "Why didn't you tell me?"

I don't know. It rattled me at first. I needed to sort it out without your input. I don't think he'll come back. That's why I didn't call the police. The old bruiser made his point."

"Which was, he'll hurt you if you don't cooperate. Right?"

"You weren't there. It's easy to second guess me."

"You could've warned us about this lunatic, made a police report, or something."

"Yes, but I didn't." They locked eyes.

With his stomach in knots, Tim witnessed Carly struggle to hide her disappointment. Finally, she said, "Are there security cameras in the morgue?"

"Outside, not inside."

"Great, so there's no video of him threatening you?"

"Nope."

"What's he look like?"

"Late fifty-something white guy with and, glasses, and a trench coat. He had attitude and a switchblade knife," Tim said. "Looked like a cop, but that doesn't make sense."

"Maybe, maybe not. What if he's PD or retired PD?" Carly paused, considering these ramifications. "Or a "good-old boy" full of himself. Either way, I don't like it.

"I know one thing. Whoever he is, he likes to pontificate about the Bible. Quoted from the book of Proverbs, something about forsake being a fool and stay alive stuff. Gave me the creeps. I bet he knows I'm Jewish."

"Now who's paranoid?" Carly said. "We need an emergency meeting with Marci tonight. To revamp our plan of action."

"I wish you would forget the entire mess and rest. You look exhausted."

Carly flashed a warning look at Tim.

"I'm sensing an uneasy footing between us," Tim said. "I withdraw my objections."

Chapter 25

Drinking iced tea in the kitchen, Carly looked across the table at Marci and Tim, who'd been at odds during their discussion.

"I'm a little punchy from all the pain meds," Carly said. "I need you all to repeat the divide and conquer plan one more time. Please."

Marci groaned. "You're kidding?"

"Nope. I'm serious as any compulsive gal can be," said Carly, who still wasn't convinced their ideas would work.

Marci yawned, balancing on the back legs of her chair, as she said, "I'm going to visit the Pancake House until I spy Officer Grey. I think Sunday is my best bet, but whatever. Then I call Stewart. When he arrives, we sit near the officers and talk loud enough so the words Jack Deeter, militia group, and DA can be heard." She took a deep breath. "Preferably in the same sentence."

Carly nodded. "That's right. You sure you can trust Stewart to hold his tongue at the newspaper?"

"Absolutely. Count him as a fellow outsider, like you and me. Besides, he thinks I'm cute in a big-sister kind of way. Go figure."

Tim and Carly gave each other a knowing look.

"Oh stop it," Marci said. "Nice enough guy. He supplies me information. That's all."

"You're the one making a fuss," Carly replied.

WELL OF RAGE

"Note. This's a comment from the woman who's on her high horse about going-over-the-P-L-A-N. Again!"

Carly turned away from Marci. "Now, Tim, your turn."

Smirking, Tim said, "Do I receive a reward if I'm letter perfect?"

When Carly didn't laugh, Tim attempted a save. "Okay, I go to Derrick's office at the Board of Education and rattle his cage about Cofer financing his campaign. I tell him I don't "take kindly," to people threatening me and obstructing a murder investigation. He'll deny everything, but I'll zing him with, 'Oh, by the way, I saw Jack Deeter in the hallway near Homicide.'"

"That's right," Carly said. "Then I'll play the stupid, well-meaning rookie and go warn Jack that I've overheard J.C. tell his brother about an old friend who's a loose cannon. I fear for his safety. Yadda, yadda.

"Hopefully, make the pot boil over, cause Cofer and the Grey brothers to think Jack has turned state's evidence, and lead Jack to wonder if he's on his buddy's hit list."

Marci crutched chips while she said, "Right into the DA's lap, if we play our cards right."

"Tim, has the ADL set up a meet with the DA?" Carly asked.

"Yes, the physical evidence from my report was enough for ADL to initiate action, but I don't know about this new DA. I hope he'll reopen the case. At least he doesn't appear to be in anybody's pocket, but he is ambitious, smart, and tenacious. A grad from my dear alma mater, Emory."

Carly grunted. "Lordy, how'd he ever win an election?"

"Likely his father's money. His dad is a member of the Million Dollar Club," Tim replied.

"So, he's African American?" Carly asked.

Marci raised her eyebrows. "Beautiful. He's drop-dead gorgeous, not that I voted for him solely based on his physical appearance."

"I'm only interested in what makes him tick," Carly said. "Like, does he have a strong backbone? He'll need it for this one."

Marci nodded.

Carly sipped her tea. "His ethnicity may help us get an airing of the facts, but he'll want an airtight case to issue warrants, and we don't have one."

"However, if the ADL can persuade the DA to notify the Feds," Tim said, "the FBI should pursue the hate crime investigation. Right?"

"Exactly. Man, I'd love to be there when they wiretap Billie Ray and Derrick's houses. And take them down. Wouldn't that be a kick?" Carly mimicked clapping her hands.

"Yep," Marci said.

"No. These guys are dangerous. Trust me," Tim said dropping a cheese cracker.

Feeling her temper rise, Carly said, "Look pals. I'm beat and my arm's killing me, so let's wrap this up. Tim, fess-up time. Tell Marci. Carly struggled to her feet and added, "Now, if you'll excuse me, some major pain meds and my bed are calling my name."

"Wait." Marci said. "Why was I left out of the loop?"

Carly shrugged. "I just found out myself. It happened in the morgue *more* than a few days ago—a man wielding a knife."

"What?" Marci righted herself, making the chair legs bang against the floor. She glared at Tim. "A man threatened you, jerk wad?"

As Carly headed for the bedroom, she heard Tim blathering. "C'mon, Marci, let me explain."

* * *

Officer Brown leaned over the screening desk. "Hey, Redmund, the lieutenant wants you. I'll handle the desk."

"In a minute. I have a live one on hold." After she finished the call, she knocked on the lieutenant's partition.

"Lieutenant Hutchinson, did you want to see me?"

"Come in and have a seat." As the lieutenant placed her paperwork aside, she said, "I have some good news and some so-so news."

"Shoot, LT."

"The good news is that ballistics matched the latent off the shell casing found in your loft to a small-time 42/28 perp. Named, Lukin Hall."

"So, my would–be assassin's creds were he's a burglar and doper, and the other news?"

The lieutenant sat back. "He was found DOA at his uncle's house in Lacy, Mississippi."

"How'd he die?" Carly realized Lukin's death meant a dead-end trail and protected whoever really wanted her out of the picture.

"The coroner called it an accidental overdose, which may or may not be the case. Apparently, he shot up a punch of heroin and crack. He wasn't known for his brilliance, but according to my street sources, he only snorted cocaine when he was flush."

"Convenient. The dead can't talk."

Hutchinson nodded and cleared on a priority one call waiting for the street sergeant at the scene to tell radio the situation was under control. The lieutenant said, "Lacy PD had nothing to add, though I doubt they looked very hard. The accidental death label closed their case."

"That's disappointing, LT, but I guess I expected as much. I'd held out some hope the guy would be caught and questioned."

"Yeah, it would've been nice to find out who hired him."

Carly took a notebook from her uniform shirt pocket. "Anything else about Lukin?"

"The chief's an old fishing buddy of Lukin's uncle, Adam Hall. And Lukin and his wife have had lots of domestics."

"Yeah, I'm familiar. I met the happy couple on a domestic a few weeks ago."

"And there's Lukin's mom, Claire, and her two jailbird brothers, Al and Saul. And, of course, there's Adam's brother, Ken, in Lacy where Lukin died."

"Can you tell me anything about Adam?"

"Never know it by looking that Adam comes from old money. The kind made from slave trading and cotton. In some ways, he's still fighting the Civil War."

"Meaning, he is…?"

The lieutenant leaned forward and said, "Meaning, I have no hard evidence, but he's a white supremacist for sure."

Carly nodded. "Figures. According to my research, Billie Ray Cofer runs the local militia group, so Adam must be a member."

Hutchinson smiled. "You've been busy. How'd you know they're friends?"

"It's a long story. When's the funeral?"

"Excuse me?"

"When's Lukin's funeral?" Carly asked.

"Tomorrow, I think. It was in the obits but…." Hutchinson let her advice go unsaid.

"Thanks, I'll need some vacation time. Can you swing it?"

Hutchinson went to the division computer and brought up a calendar. "Okay, done. Watch your back, girl."

* * *

Carly tuned out most of the funeral service as she scoped the mourners. Her starched linen dress under her arms felt like crushed potato chips as she rose for the last prayer. She hadn't worn a dress in months, and the arm sling was uncomfortable and conspicuous. She was miserable by the time the funeral ended.

The last prayer had been a prolonged Southern Baptist entreaty to lay the dead to rest and to save the living from eternal damnation. She was familiar with the dogma. Her father was a preacher of sorts.

Before the service began, Carly had selected a gray-haired, pillbox-hatted lady to sit beside. The lady pointed to Adam Hall and identified the man next to him as Billie Ray.
"He hasn't been inside a church in years. I know. I go to church with his wife, Gloria. An undeniable saint." The lady giggled. "I hope lightning doesn't strike Billie Ray dead when he steps outside."

After the service, Carly kept her focus on Adam and Billie Ray, who was a large man in his sixties with a rugged face. His flat nose had been broken more than once. The men who walked over to pay their respects to Adam seemed to defer to Billie Ray before leaving. Indeed, the big man dominated the conversations with his voice bouncing off the walls of the church foyer. "I'm tell'n you boys that Lukin was a cute kid. When that pig squealed, little Lukin jumped so high his cowboy boots fell off. That was mighty funny. Yes, sirree, mighty funny."

Adam didn't smile. When Billie Ray patted his friend's back, Adam quickly turned away.

Outside the church, Carly walked closer to Elma. The widow was engulfed in an ill-fitting, black, shift dress, and she acted overwhelmed by the fifty or sixty people milling around. However, if the scuttlebutt was right, Elma didn't cry when notified about Lukin's death, and she wasn't crying now.

In fact, a new strength showed in Elma's eyes as she nodded at Carly and turned to hug a sobbing older woman. A dark-haired woman who'd held Adam's attention during the service. When the pastor had acknowledged the family, he had confirmed Carly's assumption that the woman was Lukin's mother, Claire, and the older couple who had sat nearby were Ken and Alice Hall.

Carly remembered the twentyish-something people, probably Lukin's friends, sitting in the pews with their bleak faces downcast. If Carly's dad was right, if sinning and wild living brought death early, then their lives were almost over. Death seemed random to Carly.

As the family left for the cemetery in the limousine, Carly felt like an intruder. Tim's previous words taunted her. "What are you trying to prove, going alone to Lukin's funeral? Working through your anger is one thing, Carly, but you're sticking your neck out."

Taking action always felt better than waiting. *Although seeing Lukin's coffin was satisfying in a sick kind of way.* Regardless of the reasons, she'd had a chance to study Billie Ray and his posse. She counted twelve men, plus Billie Ray, and couldn't help wondering if there was a Judas among them.

As Adam slipped back into the church, Carly started to follow. Only then, did she notice Billie Ray's piercing gaze convincing her to stop short.

How long has he been staring at me?

Chapter 26

Elma stared at the bucket of fried chicken in the middle of the kitchen table. The funeral-home custom of buying the bereaved chicken, plus Claire's church-lady friends bringing multiple casserole dishes, salads, and desserts, seemed ridiculous to Elma. She only wanted to curl up in her bed and mourn alone.

How long before these well-meaning neighbors leave?

Because everyone routinely used the side-deck entrance near the driveway at Claire's house, Elma grabbed a sweater and headed for the front porch. Finding the door ajar and hearing voices, she lifted a blind and peeked out the kitchen window. Two men stood in the shadows.

Through the screen door, she smelled cigar smoke and heard one of them say, "Damn, Billie Ray, you should've told me. It wasn't right sneaking around behind my back and calling a meeting. I thought we were friends. Still think there was another way."

When Elma realized it was Adam speaking, she shivered and the hairs rose on the nape of her neck.

"No, there wasn't," Billie Ray said, "but I knew you'd say that. Hell, he was your kin. That's why I left you out of the decision. It had to be done."

Stunned, Elma collapsed on the edge of the sofa.

"I still don't know. I can't believe the deal I made with PD wouldn't have saved all our butts. This was too much too soon. You guys overreacted and now my nephew's dead."

Covering a moan, Elma buried her face in.

"No, we didn't. Truth is, Adam, I know this is hard, but he was a worthless piece of shit."

"For Christsake, Billie Ray, he was Claire's son, and I promised that I would watch out for him. I feel like a horse's ass. Was it that SOB Dave Jordan ranting on—shoot first and take names later?"

"Adam, no. You need to get a grip. You know the guys couldn't trust Lukin to keep his mouth shut. He's dead, and there's nothing to be done. You can't change it."

Elma felt nauseated. *How could they talk so nonchalantly about Lukin's death? About his murder?*

She flinched as Adam said, "Do you think Elma will be all right?"

There was a clicking noise, like a lighter being lit, and then Billie Ray said, "I'd bet money on it. She's young." After a pause, Billie Ray continued, "I'd venture to say that both Elma and Claire will be fine. They're better off, really."

Elma's mind was racing. *Oh, God, it was Adam who called Lukin about the big job for Billie Ray's "good old boys."*

Backing up, tears streaming, she raced to her purse to find Carly Redmund's card.

* * *

Marci sat in a booth at the Pancake House listening to the officers' conversation. They couldn't see her because of a plant divider, but she pretended to update her PDA as she sipped coffee. Because the officers sprinkled their conversation with police jargon and codes, Marci became a little concerned and wondered if they were talking about her.

As usual, Stewart was late. Irritated, she spied the waitress approaching for the third time.

"Would you like to order now?"

Marci gave the waitress a go-to-hell smile, but said, "Thanks, I'll take some wheat toast."

When Stewart finally slid into the opposite side of the booth, Marci registered Stewart's gelled hair. "About time, Stewey. What's up with the hair? A hot date with your emailer?"

"So, I didn't rush over here on my Sunday, my day off. I woke up first. Sue me." As he turned over a cup, he said, "God, I need some coffee."

Marci raised the carafe and poured.

"Thanks," Stewart said.

"You're welcome. By the way, your new haircut is, huh, spiffy."

"Please, can we move on? Did you order?"

"About twenty minutes ago."

Stewart caught a passing waitress's attention, ordered pancakes and eggs, and then rubbed his hands together, as he said, "Jeez, it's a meat locker in here. Could you turn up the thermostat a couple of degrees?"

"I like it cold," Marci said. "I think better in a cool environment.

The waitress shrugged and left.

"All I want to do is eat in comfort."

"Can we move on, wimp? We need to talk. Did you bring the information?"

"Yep, here," he said, handing Marci a manila envelope filled with scrap paper. Stewart thought this part of the plan was stupid, but Marci had insisted—just in case the cops hadn't sat where they usually did and saw the exchange.

Marci leaned forward. Despite the concocted plot, her eyes glistened with enthusiasm. "A reliable source of mine says Jack Deeter's name has been floating around the DA's office. Everyone knows he's connected with the local militia—our local hate group here in Mobile."

"Really," Stewart acted confused. "What do you want from me?"

For J.C.'s benefit Marci asked Stewart for information she already knew. "One, I need you to search the Web for confirmation that Billie Ray Cofer's the group's leader. Also, see if he's involved in sponsoring local politicians and find out who owns MSU Corporation."

They halted their conversation when the waitress arrived with their food.

Stewart studied Marci. She bit into her toast. "This toast is cold. The witch."

"All righty, then," Stewart said, checking to see where the waitress was in the room before reciting his memorized lines. "I'll check the financial data on Cofer, but how do you know local PD is after Cofer?"

He'd repeated Cofer's name twice in one sentence making Marci wince, but she replied, "I know. Okay? You just get me my information so I can write this story, get my glory, and maybe help the DA."

"Yes Ma'am! When do you need it?"

"Yesterday."

"Figures."

Marci raised an eyebrow, an indication for Stewart to keep talking. "I'll browse the white supremacy-related chat rooms. It's amazing what people reveal on the net," he said.

"Great idea."

As the officers passed Marci and Stewart, they overheard J.C.'s conversation with the other officer. "Yeah, Noreen's a pain in the ass lately. Doesn't do a thing except surf the net and use those chat rooms."

Stewart almost dropped his fork. Marci laughed. "You okay, Stewart?"

He nodded in the direction of the officers paying their bills at the register. "That officer and Noreen. Could be a coincidence. Of course, they know who you are, but they wouldn't know me? Shit. You called me by my name."

* * *

Tim walked around the courthouse square for the third time, still having no idea what he was going to say to Derrick. *The bastard probably sanctioned the threats made by trench-coat guy.*

Reliving his confrontation with the mystery man in the morgue and the ghastly sound of the knife cutting into metal, Tim flinched when a garbage truck rattled by him.

He crossed the street and sat under a dogwood tree in front of a bank building. The spring blossoms were luxuriant. He settled on a bench and searched for a few salient questions.

From Stewart's research, Tim expected Derrick to be a slick politician. Although the media hype portrayed him as a humble guy who lucked out, it camouflaged an ambitious man. Nothing about Derrick's career or personal life indicated haphazardness. He had married well and had been groomed in the workings of Mobile's political machine during his tenure as a school principal, and then superintendent.

Derrick had a reputation for verbal sparring, and this meeting would be on his turf. No doubt, Derrick would deflect any innuendo by Tim easily. He reminded himself his goal wasn't to win this round, but plant a seed of uncertainty, goading Derrick to take the bait and to call his cronies.

Even though, the biggest problem was putting aside his feelings about Carly's assault. To center himself. Tim visualized his grandfather Isaac's calm face. *Yeah, Carly would've liked him.* The quiet, unassuming man had fought the Nazis with ingenuity before the war. If Tim prodded his grandfather enough, he reluctantly told the stories of dangerous underground activities, but he refused to talk about Auschwitz. Until his death a decade ago, he carried the burden of survivor's guilt and wore long sleeves to cover his tattooed prisoner number.

His grandfather used to say, "The enemy cannot take away who you are without destroying your faith and hope. Always know who you are, down to your sitting bones. You are a Jew. After you were born, angels marked your birthright above your upper lip, signifying you as special." Then, with an index finger, he would touch the indentation above Timmy's upper lip and bless him. How he loved his grandfather.

Tim got up, ignoring the crosswalk, and trotted across the plaza past the courthouse and eateries. He slowed, unsure which building held the Board of Education before spotting a white historic building with its prominent sign. Once inside, Tim brushed his shoes, tucked in his sports shirt, and surveyed the directory.

"Excuse me, officer. I'm looking for Derrick Grey's office, the Board of Education."

"Third door down the hall, Sir."

Tim thanked the guard and found the office, and then came face to face with his first obstacle. Ms. Stalch. She stopped typing and eyed Tim over her black-rimmed half-glasses.

"Yes, may I help you?"

"I would like to speak with Derrick Grey."

Miss Stalch took her headset off and without checking her schedule book, she said, "You do not have an appointment."

WELL OF RAGE

"No, but this is urgent. I'm the assistant coroner, Tim Price. It's about a case and very important."

"Wait here, Mr. Price. I will confer with Mr. Grey," she said, smiling curtly at Tim. *The gatekeeper in a tailored suit. I wonder if she guessed the color of my underwear.*

When Miss Stalch returned, she said, "Mr. Grey will see you, now."

Tim thanked the stern woman buttoned his jacket before he proceeded past Miss Stalch. Pulling a heavy wooden door, Tim smiled at the forbidding woman before entering Derrick's office.

"Mr. Grey, Tim Price. Thanks for seeing me without an appointment."

"Good afternoon." Derrick stood up, shook hands across the desk, and then sat flattening his red tie against his chest.

Taken aback by Derrick's stature, Tim played it off. "She's an intimidating woman, isn't she?" he said as he pointed to the door.

"Yes, she is. My secretary is, shall we say, territorial. Please, have a seat." A strand of blond hair fell across Derrick's forehead, as he added, "She's worked for me many years, and I don't know what I'd do without her, but sometimes she forgets we are public servants. Our doors are always open."

"That's good."

"Now, tell me what I can do to help the assistant coroner."

Tim took the direct approach. "Frankly, I'm disturbed by a recent visit from a knife-brandishing buddy of Billie Ray Cofer's."

"Excuse me?" Derrick feigned surprise. "How would I know?"

"Don't act naïve, Mr. Grey. I know Cofer's financing your campaign through his militia and his dummy corporation, MSU."

"I'm not hiding anything. Surely, you don't think I'm responsible or knew anything about what happened to you. Were you hurt?" Derrick said.

"No. But I think your relationship with Cofer goes further than candidate and contributor."

"I'm not sure this is within the scope of the coroner's office, but I'm glad to oblige. I need to get my message out there, so people can vote wisely. That's all. It takes money. Cofer and I are not in bed together."

"No, just colluding."

"That's a ridiculous allegation," Derrick said.

"Carly Redmund, Marci Eplund, and I were threatened because of what we know about the murder of Terence Washington Williams. You remember—the kid in Deeter's well."

Derrick didn't visibly react. "I thought that case was closed with the coroner's ruling of suicide."

"Now you're in my purview," Tim said, "but I know you heard about Carly Redmund's attack, her attempted murder."

"Yes, a few weeks ago. Unfortunate, another victim of violence. Terrible, really. How is she?"

Failing to keep a level head, Tim lashed out. "She's blameless and deserves to be left alone to live her life." Tim took a breath. "Isn't it coincidental that the recently, deceased Lukin was Adam Hall's nephew, and Adam is Cofer's buddy? Amazing how everybody seems to know one another in this murderous cycle."

"I fail to see … . My, I have to say you're jumping to judgments and conclusions unworthy of a scientist."

Tim scrutinized Derrick. "I don't think so. You tell your

mongrel militia friends to back off, leave Carly alone. You do that, and I'll forget I know about the gunshot hole in Terence's skull."

Derrick's pupils contracted and the whites grew around his irises.

Tim leaned forward. "I'll even warn you about your compadre, Jack Deeter. He's running scared."

Derrick started to buzz Miss Stalch, but hesitated. "I don't know what you're talking about."

"Remember: Carly remains unharmed. If anyone touches her again, I'll personally see to it that they land in my version of Bible-belt hell."

Derrick hands began to shake as he said, "You're deranged. I'm calling—"

"I'll show myself out," Tim said, standing. "By the way, I saw Jack outside Homicide. Yesterday."

* * *

It was too late to back down. Last night Marci and Tim had recounted their adventures to Carly over grouper sandwiches on the pier, and she'd thought they'd performed superbly. Her friends reminded Carly the three-prong plan needed to be executed within twenty-four hours and her part was to convince Jack Deeter his life was in danger by delivering a packet of incriminating information.

Deeter occupied several suites at the Ritz Carlton outside the perimeter on the upscale side of Mobile. When she entered the hotel lobby, she paused to admire the bustle of patrons surrounded by red and gold drapes and fine wood furniture.

Disguised as a ritzy charity fundraiser, she ducked into the women's lavatory. She hoped a borrowed black power suit and a new pair of Gianni Bravo knock-offs would get her through Jack's office door, but Carly wasn't sure she could pull it off. She preferred the straightforward approach, but Marci and Tim had vetoed honesty as foolhardy.

The restroom matron held out a hot towel for Carly who dug in her clutch bag for her last dollar to tip the matron. Carly thought about the money necessary to live in such a pristine, insulated world. Now, with her purse empty and her Honda's gas gauge sitting on E, she wondered why this part of the plan ever made sense.

The pain in her left arm seemed to radiate to her feet, which were being pinched in the new heels. She'd left the sling at home. A calculated risk. She readied herself in the full-length mirror reflection. A French manicure and brunette wig completed the look. According to the sales clerk, Carly "defined elegance."

It was time. After she wrangled herself into Deeter's office, made her spiel, and left the manila envelope, she would go home and collapse.

Tim had said, "There's no reason Jack needs to know who delivered the warning that his life is supposedly in danger."

Then Marci had added, "Just be Miss Volunteer of Crystal Heights and deliver the envelope when you leave. We're close to our deadline."

Carly straightened her back and pushed open the oak door.

A male assistant swung around in a swivel chair like a child playing on a bar stool. He faced Carly with his hands on his knees and heels lifted. "Hello, may I help you?" he said.

"I am Diana Weatherby from Crystal Heights, and I have an appointment with Mr. Deeter."

"He's expecting you. Please sit down, and I will let him know you've arrived. By the way, love the suit."

"Thank you."

Displaying the finesse of a concierge, the assistant showed Carly to Deeter's office.

"Ms. Diana Weatherby, Sir."

Deeter rose from his chair as the assistant shut the door. "Please be seated, Ms. Weatherby. Would you like a cup of coffee?"

"No, but water would be lovely," she said, sitting on a dark leather chair.

Still standing, Jack poured water from a silver pitcher and returned it to a matching tray on his desk. While he handed Carly the glass, he ogled her crossed legs.

"What's the name of your organization again? I'm sorry. I seem to have drawn a blank."

Carly shifted her legs to one side. "Crystal Heights, but I specifically represent the nonprofit, Bridgewood Haven. We sponsor young women without means who wish to continue their pregnancies. We encourage them to keep their babies by providing a means to independence through educational and technical training. Of course, adoption is an alternative." Carly smiled demurely.

Deeter leaned against his desk.

Carly took in three security cameras as she said, "You have an impeccably furnished suite. A mahogany desk always makes me think of my father."

He returned to his chair and sat down. "The desk is a bit ostentatious for me. Don't you think?"

Carly smiled. "No, it's a fine period piece. Especially, in a hotel suite."

Deeter riveted his dark eyes on Carly. Enjoying the moment, he grinned. "Your charity is a worthy cause, and I intend to contribute. However, I'm due at a meeting, and at the risk of being impolite, how much do you need for next year's budget?"

Carly replied, "We need to supplement the grant monies by a hundred thousand. A tax-deductible contribution of any size would benefit many young women."

Deeter laughed. "You're charming. I can arrange for my accountant to call your organization and write a check today, but I'd rather give it to you. Please have dinner with me tonight. Allow me to give you the check in person and make up for my rude departure."

Stunned, Carly said nothing.

"We can meet at the hotel restaurant downstairs if you wish. Say eight o'clock? My assistant can arrange for my driver to bring you here."

"I...that would be considerate." Remembering the reason for being there, Carly laid the manila envelope on the desk. "Let me leave the corporate mission statement and a list of the board members for your review," she said.

She held Deeter's gaze as she said, "Business first."

"You're quite right," he replied rounding the edge of the desk. He placed his palm against Carly's lower back escorting her toward the door. "Until dinner, lovely lady."

When she drew away and extended her hand, Deeter kissed it. Meeting Carly's surprised look, Deeter whispered, "Good afternoon, Miss Diana. You look so familiar. What a stimulating mystery for me to solve."

Chapter 27

Ignoring the message light on the answering machine, Carly pulled off the wig and threw it onto the coffee table. No talking to Marci and Tim tonight. She beelined for the kitchen. Opening the refrigerator and cabinet doors, she shut them without choosing anything.

Jack is an arrogant bastard. Whether Jack suspected a ruse or not, it didn't matter. Surely, he'd be curious enough to read their doctored documents and emails indicating that PD was watching Cofer and stating Derrick and J.C.'s intention to rid themselves of witnesses. If a granule of mistrust lay between the men, Jack should err on the side of caution. If not, he would have a laugh at Carly's expense.

She randomly moved from one room to the next, yanking off the black suit. Then she stripped down to her cotton underwear and stomped crying down the hallway to the kitchen. There she snatched two boxes of cookies and two bags of chips. Carly dumped the chips in a blue popcorn bowl, and then slumped on the living room couch balancing the bowl on her stomach and drinking from a half liter bottle of cola.

Reaching for the remote, she found a mind-numbing British comedy. After a few minutes, Carly took a pain pill, put the sling back on to relieve the throbbing in her injured arm, and finally laughed at herself.

Cradling the sling at the elbow, she watched the eleven o'clock news and fell asleep with the remote in hand.

The blaring television awoke Carly in midmorning.

Grimacing, she turned off the noise and started gathering the debris: an empty box, stale chips, a candy wrapper, and a wad of used tissues. Her head pounding she thought, *It's a good thing I didn't drink any wine last night. Hate to break two of my rules in one night: Don't drink when you're upset. Don't binge.* As she ditched the last armload of trash, she said, "Okay, the pity party is officially over. Like ole Abe said, '"Success is going from failure to failure without losing your enthusiasm."'"

She was vacuuming in the living room when she saw the red light flashing on her answering machine. She hit the message button. The first message was a cute "miss-you" one from Tim. Carly unplugged the sweeper while the second message played.

A woman's tentative voice said, "Officer, I mean Recuit Redmund, this is Elma Hall. Once you gave me a card, and you came to my husband's funeral. Thank you. I want to talk to you about my husband's death. I eavesdropped on a conversation...after the funeral. My husband didn't kill himself." Elma cleared her throat and her voice quivered as she continued, "But I'll need your help...to prove it. Please call me at the house." She left her phone number and the message ended.

Carly replayed the message. "Yes, finally a break," she said.

Sipping her coffee, Carly called Elma. An old-style answering machine clicked on. Carly hesitated, and then said, "Mrs. Hall, this is Carly Redmund. I'm sorry about Lukin. I think you're right about your suspicions. Call me as soon as possible. At home or my cell." She repeated her request, and then added, "Be careful, okay? I wouldn't tell anyone else about the conversation you overheard 'til we get together."

Carly clicked off and whispered a blessing. "Be safe, Elma."

She took a hot shower and dressed, composing herself before calling Marci and Tim, and then ended up leaving the same succinct voice message on each of their cells. "Hi, this is Carly. Meet me in Generals' Park at noon. I'll update you then."

To her relief, Tim and Marci called back quickly—giving Carly only a minimum amount of grief about her overdue phone call—and agreeing to leave their questions until their face-to-face in the park. Dashing downtown to a sandwich shop, Carly bought three deli sandwiches before heading out. If all went well, she and her friends could laugh about yesterday's misadventure.

Carly's thoughts turned to Elma. It had taken courage for her to telephone. "'It often requires more courage to dare to do right than to fear to do wrong,'" Carly said to herself, quoting Abe Lincoln again. Elma might hold the key to bust the case wide open.

Carly chose a concrete bench behind a large fountain and listened to water splash in the basin. Her friends, walking together, waved at her as they crossed Dauphin Street.

It was a good day to be alive.

* * *

After playing the officer's returned message, Elma stared at the phone. Rollercoaster waves of relief and grief swept over her. Lukin wouldn't be standing over Elma when she awoke. She'd seen him in the casket. Lukin couldn't hurt her anymore.

Elma scrubbed her face with a washcloth. Regret clung to her. Although she longed for a baby to hold in her arms, she hadn't given Lukin a child. Wanting to find some peace, the widow hoped the female officer could uncover the truth about Lukins' murder.

But now, she wasn't sure calling the officer had been the right thing.

Elma bit a cuticle.

The recent conversation with a Georgia farmer in the hotel lobby seemed ominous now. When Elma had complained that her husband didn't want her to go back to school, the nice man, a lay preacher, had said, "Don't you worry, pretty lady. Have faith. God works in mysterious ways."

She'd revealed too much about their personal life, but she couldn't believe that sweet, old man had anything to do with Lukin's death. Still, the talkative gentleman had asked a lot of prying questions. She'd mentioned Lukin was out of town, but... God, she hoped she hadn't mentioned Lacy, Mississippi.

* * *

Carly arrived early at the beach near the Gulf Bay Resort and waited for Elma at the water's edge.

It gave her time to rehash her meeting with Marci and Tim. Tim had tried to console her. "Jack must've seen you on the news. At the Deeter farm. We didn't think about that. It could still work. Let's wait and see."

Marci added, "That's right. Forget about it. Wonder what little Elma's going to tell you."

"I just hope she shows," Carly said. As she gazed at the murky green water in the Gulf, her thoughts shifted to her father. He'd made her feel small and afraid. She understood wanting to fade into the woodwork and fighting the tendency every day. The rookie marveled at the amount of guts it took for Elma to call back and place herself in harm's way to expose her husband's killers. Amazed, Carly realized despite the physical abuse, Elma still loved Lukin.

"Recruit Redmund."

Carly turned to see Elma dressed in a pair of conservative Bermuda shorts and a short-sleeved cotton blouse. Her hair was limp and parted in the middle.

"Yes, but call me Carly," she said, smiling. "I'm glad to see you again. How are you doing?"

"Pretty good, considering." Elma glanced at Carly's sling. "How about you?"

"Oh, I'm much better. I just wear this for sympathy. Mostly."

They laughed.

Carly patted her injured arm. "This will heal. Some things take time." Carly tilted her head toward Elma. "I was afraid you'd changed your mind about meeting me." When Elma said nothing, Carly continued, "I know this is hard, but we can work it out."

Looking away, Elma mumbled, "I hope so. I'm not sleeping much. It's strange. In some ways, I don't miss him." She met Carly's gaze. "He wasn't always kind. Mean sometimes. We had our problems, but I loved him."

"Of course you did. Nobody deserves to be murdered." As the words hung in the air, Carly realized Elma didn't believe her.

A tear ran down Elma's cheek. She wiped it away. "At the funeral—it was you, right?"

"Yes, I was there."

"Afterward, at my house, Adam and Billie Ray were on the front porch. The front door's hard to close. Anyway, it was open a little ways, and I overheard them talking." She paused and took a deep breath.

"Go on," Carly said.

"Something about a vote. Adam was mad because he was left out. Then Billie Ray told him that Lukin couldn't be trusted after he messed up. Billie Ray said something like, 'It had to be done.' Adam disagreed because of some kind of deal with PD. It was very confusing, but I think Billie Ray killed my husband, or had him killed. For what reason, I don't know."

"Do you remember anything else that might be important?"

"Yeah. A few weeks ago Lukin took a phone call in the kitchen. I was washing dishes, and he didn't want me to hear what he was saying. I heard enough to know he was cooking up an important job with big money. But I don't know who with. I was afraid it was a burglary or drugs. I knew better than to ask questions. It would've riled him."

"You didn't want him to hit you."

Elma looked startled. "Usually it was my fault. I always say the wrong thing but—"

"Elma. May I call you by your first name?"

She nodded.

Carly used her warmest tone. "You're not to blame for Lukin's actions. He was a grown man. Responsible for his own actions."

Elma sighed and sank to the sand.

Carly followed Elma's lead and sat alongside her, giving her a minute to regroup. Finally she asked, "Did you know why Lukin left to go to Mississippi?"

"No, he called from Uncle Ken's the day before he... He'd taken my purse from my locker at work a couple of days before the police called me from Lacy." She shrugged. "Said he'd dropped by to take me to lunch. I knew that was a lie.

"Anyway, he was there one minute and gone the next. I'm used to it. He stole my money all the time to gamble and pay for drugs." Elma turned her head away wiping at tears.

"I guess I should've listened to him when he called from the road, but I was mad." Elma paused wringing her hands. "He did a strange thing right before I hung up."

"What was it?"

"He told me he loved me. He never did that...on the phone." She turned her face away, and reached into her purse. "I gotta have a cigarette. Do you mind?"

Elma lit up as Carly said, "Sure, no problem."

"I'm a nervous wreck."

As Carly watched the nicotine kick in, Elma's shoulders relaxed. "This is difficult," Carly said. "But I need to tell you something. The job that Lukin had wasn't a burglary or a drug deal. It was more violent."

Elma's eyes widened. "What do you mean? What did he do?"

"He's the one who tried to kill me."

Elma pressed her purse to her chest. Her eyes darted to Carly's sling. "Oh, my God, I read about a man breaking into your house, the night of the big storm. Lukin never came home that night. I remember being worried, and then he showed up at the hotel the next day. With scratches."

"I got in a few licks, but he probably fell trying to escape in the woods behind my place."

"The man tried to rape you. Lukin tried to rape you?" Elma gasped.

Being afraid that Elma would break down completely, Carly only nodded. They sat looking at the ocean.

Elma ditched her cigarette and leaned toward Carly taking hold of her hand. "That bastard, I'm so sorry."

They hugged each other and cried.

Dusting off the sand half an hour later, they returned to their cars and spoke more light-heartedly. Carly was starving; Elma suggested a burger. Before entering her car, Elma paused. "Why did Billie Ray hire Lukin to kill you?"

"That's a long story. If you're up for it, we can grab some burgers and go to my place. Wash the story down with beers."

* * *

Ned had been watching Carly for days. He liked her spunk. But how did she connect the dots so fast and get Elma to meet at the beach? The abused wife might eventually be a problem, but she could wait. For now Carly was his target. She knew too much. Ned gave her credit on the Jack Deeter scare-tactic scenario. It'd almost worked, but in the middle of packing a bag, Jack had decided to weigh his options more closely. If the Grey brothers were out to get Jack, Billie Ray would know; the nervous businessman called Billie Ray, who in turn informed Ned.

Concerning how much the FBI knew, Ned hooked up with one of his old covert operation buddies, Agent George Dugan. Over pizza and a pitcher of beer at Heroes Bar, they reminisced about a few missions, and then Ned wedged in the real reason for the reunion. "I guess you know about some local boys around here being involved in a militia group?" Ned said.

"Of course, we know about them, but they're pretty harmless. We aren't concerned enough to run any on-going surveillance. They can hate anybody they want, just as long as that's all they do."

"That's what I figured. I'm acquainted with one or two of them. Billie Ray Cofer seems to be the ramrod of the group.

Most days you can hear them shooting the shit and complaining about the government at Calpes." Ned forced a smiled. "I'm a retired geezer, but I'm not brain-dead yet. Thought I'd run it by you."

"We appreciate it. But right now, I think their activities are limited to influencing local politics through their website, not planning hate crimes."

By the third game of pool, Ned was fairly certain that the FBI had bigger fish to fry than Cofer's militia group or Jack Deeter. As for the Grey brothers, they were too busy scrambling to cover their asses to think about plotting to kill Jack.

Though Carly was another matter. He would have to be patient and watch the pawns on the chessboard.

Although Ned found Carly's offensive maneuvers amusing and hoped to wait until she returned to street duty to set up what would appear to be a fragging incident, Billie Ray wanted a brotherhood member to run the recruit down in his truck. "Take her out quick."

Ned talked him out of it. "What if the driver misses or she's just injured? Let's not be foolhardy. I'll handle this. Nice and tidy." For practical reasons, Carly needed to be eliminated before the homestretch of the mayoral election. A scandal wasn't going to happen on Ned's watch if he could help it.

The buzz of the bar filtered back into Ned's consciousness as George Dugan edged his bar stool toward Ned. "So how's retirement?" he said.

An hour later leaving the bar, Ned thought about borrowing the recruit's scheme, but adding a twist. J.C could kill the girl, not Jack.

J.C. was showing severe signs of burnout, and his anger could easily be directed at Carly to ward off the looming complications concerning Derrick's involvement in the Williams' murder. Even Billie Ray didn't know the whole story. An expert at using a person's vulnerability and gaining intelligence info, Ned saw J.C. was in serious trouble. He wouldn't need much coaxing.

Chapter 28

Agent George Dugan left Ned at Heroes Bar near midnight. He chose to walk to his hotel instead of taking the trolley because he needed to clear his head. Seeing Ned rekindled some memories, mostly good ones. The veteran agent had trained Dugan and had helped to hone the young agent's survival skills. They trusted each other. After the unexpected call from the retired agent, Dugan looked forward to reconnecting with Ned. That was before Bureau management got wind of the call. They had made it their business. Applying pressure, they had asked Dugan to use his friendship to convince Ned that nothing was going on, aside from general monitoring of Cofer's group.

While trying to shake the gnawing feeling that Ned's hands weren't completely clean, Dugan stopped to speak to a local cop working security outside The Crescent Theatre, a restored 1930s cinema on Dauphin Street.

The intel hadn't conclusively connected Ned to the militia, only to Cofer. Still, Ned's low-key manner while discussing the group made Dugan uneasy.

Dugan approached his temporary residence, the grand Battleship Hotel. The antebellum lobby made him reflect on Ned's southern charm and the dichotomy of his cutthroat, lay-preacher personality. The bar conversation aside, Dugan was sure of one thing; if Ned had eliminated Lukin Hall, the Bureau wouldn't be able to prosecute. He was that good. The best.

* * *

Socializing with Billie Ray in public broke Ned's no-direct association rule, but he accompanied the top dog to a fish fry at the lodge to evaluate the Grey brothers' relationship and reconfirm his suspicions about the extent of J.C.'s burnout.

Several militia members were present, and it wasn't long before an inebriated knucklehead shouted in Derrick's face, "You're an asshole politician like all the rest. I wouldn't vote for you if you let me fuck your tight-ass wife."

Derrick started to grab the guy, but J.C. stepped between them. Manhandling the rowdy guy outside and several well-placed punches later, J.C. made a phone call to Rose. Derrick's big brother deposited the disheveled mayoral candidate on a bench awaiting the arrival of his furious wife.

Back inside, J.C. dismissed the incident as he poured himself another beer. "Well, guys, I bet he won't be getting any pussy at home for a while," he said.

The obvious key to manipulating J.C. lay in his blind loyalty and protective nature toward his younger brother, his Achilles' heel. This weakness combined with J.C.'s simmering anger was the ideal mixture for Ned to exploit.

During dinner Ned caught a moment alone with J.C. and tested the waters. "So J.C., what avenue do you suggest for keeping your recruit quiet?"

Pursing his lips, J.C. pushed his grease-soaked paper plate away and said, "The quickest route."

"I gather you don't like her."

"Personally, I could care less, but she wants to play by the rule book. Better she goes down than me. She knows too much about my brother's business. He's about the only thing I worry about anymore. Stopping anything in his way has always been my job, J.C. added, dropping his napkin on the tabletop. "Will be 'til the day I die."

* * *

Driving home to the northern outskirts of Mobile, Ned considered various methods for terminating his target. Humming a gospel hymn, "In the Garden," his mind drifted to his garden at his old place in Georgia. He regretted that his new house didn't have native flowers and shrubs. Remembering his Georgia garden, he stopped at the memory of his Rosary Pea bush. It was an interesting plant, and contained poisonous green seedpods. One unripe pod was deadly. The symptoms mimicked the flu. If an autopsy was performed, internal bleeding would be obvious, but Ned weighed this unlikely possibility against the mandatory forensic procedures involved in a shooting investigation. He doubted the brass would request an autopsy in an unsuspicious influenza death.

J.C.'s certainly capable of dropping a pea pod in a plate of food.

Ned felt sure that the problems of Marci and Tim would go away with Carly gone. Plus, her friends had their Achilles heels. Closeted, Marci wouldn't want her lesbian lover's suicide exposed. Tim would be simple. Without Carly's tenacity the assistant coroner's bravado would fade. There wouldn't be any reason to resist the militia's generous offer for money and position. All the contingencies would be cleaned up.

* * *

The receptionist opened the door, and then said, "District Attorney Nelsen will see you now."

Tim exhaled, tossing his magazine.

Madeline Grossman, Mary William's friend and a member of the Anti-Defamation League, flashed him a confident smile. "Relax Timothy. You're going to do splendidly."

As they entered the office, Madeline turned her attention to Jeffery Nelsen "Doesn't he look like Denzel Washington?"

Tim shrugged.

"Mrs. Grossman, it is so nice to meet you. ADL's legal advisor, Edgar James, has nothing but good things to say about you," Nelsen said.

Madeline forced a smile and surveyed the stock governmental desk loaded with files and legal briefs. They shook hands before the DA extended his hand to Tim.

"Mr. Price. Finally, I meet our dedicated assistant coroner."

Tim said, "How did you know—"

Madeline circled a bracelet-adorned wrist in the air, "What a perceptive, charming man. I like you already."

"Thank you, please sit down." The DA motioned to the chairs in front of his desk. "By the way, Mrs. Grossman, I appreciate your organization lobbying to revisie the state's hate crime bill last year. The revisions added needed teeth to the law."

"Yes, I agree."

"Now, what can I do for you two? I have read through the information you sent."

Tim wanted to be articulate, but his mind went blank.

Madeline spoke up. "We need you to reopen this case based on the physical evidence gathered by Mr. Price from the Deeter well. The suicide ruling by the coroner is ludicrous. This whole convoluted disaster is the reason Ms. Carly Redmund was attacked."

"No doubt you're right, but I caution you this case on its face won't be easy to indict, or win." He met Madeline's scrutiny and held eye contact. "However, I am open to discussion. Tim, would you lay out the evidence for me?"

After several minutes, the DA nodded, but said nothing.

Tim took a breath, and then he continued. "Of course, if your office could put pressure on the coroner to send the bones to the state crime lab. Even better."

The DA nodded again.

"CID hasn't been forthright in producing their old case files either."

Nelsen shifted in his chair. "A phone call will remedy that problem. Wasn't that case handled under retired Director Reynolds's régime?"

"Right," Tim said. "I suspect that a missing black teenager wasn't a high priority case for the police in the 1970s."

"That's a given," Nelsen said. "Back then, the Williams's family didn't win any friends because of their strong civil rights stance. My mother and father spoke highly of them. We lived in the same neighborhood."

Nelsen kept clicking his ballpoint pen.

Tim couldn't tell if the DA was truly interested or distracted.

Madeline smiled at Tim.

Clearing his throat, Tim said, "I suppose you know a high school ring was found along with the bones in the Deeter well. The ring was temporarily confiscated by Derrick's brother, Officer J.C. Grey, at the crime scene and returned to property the next morning. He forged Carly Redmund's signature on the property sheet. Blamed her for mishandling of evidence."

The DA rubbed his temples. "A writing expert could eliminate that problem, but it won't do her career any good. His defense will be that he tried to help her by attempting to rectify the situation. It's usually handled in-house."

"Wait a minute—"

"I'm just trying to pick our battles." Nelsen scribbled on a yellow legal pad. "But I need to know everything," he said. "Please continue. Would you like a cup of coffee?"

"No. Carly was subjected to an assault in her apartment a few weeks ago."

"I'm familiar. Is she recovering without permanent injury?"

"I think she'll be all right physically. Emotionally who knows. She's a private person."

"Carly will be a credit to the force," Madeline said, "if she isn't made a scapegoat."

"She must be quite a woman to hold her own in such an attack," Nelsen said.

"Strong as they come." Tim said. "It was this sentiment that had forced Tim to choose Carly over his personal needs and make the recent decision to move in with his infirmed mother instead of paying for expensive private care. Directing his attention back to the DA, Tim said, "By the way, AFIS identified the suspect early on by a fingerprint left on a shell casing. A Lukin Hall."

"Yes, I read about the overdose in some small town in Mississippi. Correct?"

Tim nodded. "Lacy, Mississippi. However, according to Lukin's wife, it wasn't an accident. FYI: Lukin is Adam Hall's nephew. The same man who's Billie Ray Cofer's best friend. I'm sure you're aware they're militia."

"Rumors, yes. No concrete proof. Excuse me, back up to the point about Lukin's wife."

"After the funeral, Lukin's wife, Elma, overheard Billie Ray and Adam arguing about why Lukin had to be killed."

"You realize her unsubstantiated testimony in court would never hold up."

"Maybe, but she has no reason to lie," Tim said. "She was an abused wife, and she should've been happy about Lukin's death."

"Exactly, Mr. Price. Maybe she was involved in Lukin's death."

Tim locked eyes with the DA.

Madeline filled the silence. "Jeffery, we do not presume to understand the nuances of the law. You're the expert. We hope what we know warrants further investigation in this case.

"As I'm sure you're aware, the ADL's ultimate purpose is to obtain justice and fair treatment for all individuals. We're particularly interested in any case involving the militia."

The DA smiled. "Sorry. Just playing devil's advocate. Tim, go ahead."

Tim paused, suspecting the DA would not trust his media source without naming Marci.

"I have a news source who verified that Jack Deeter sold his land for two times what it was worth to the dummy corporation, MSU, which fronts for Cofer's militia group." Tim pulled documents out of his file. "Calpes closes Thursday nights, and the group meets there. Has for years. It shouldn't be hard to prove who's militia. Karl Potter owns the bar."

"Interesting," Nelsen said. "I have recently had other reasons to review Mr. Potter's records. How does this tie the white supremacy group to Derrick Grey?"

"I'm sure you will find that Cofer's money is funding his campaign for mayor."

"I see."

Tim continued. "It's common knowledge that Jack Deeter and his friends dragged Terence from the school grounds in 1974."

"So it's your theory that the Greys and Deeters conspired, decades ago, to kill and conceal the body of Terence Washington Williams, and that the militia group hired Lukin to kill Carly Redmund because she posed a threat to Derrick. While trying to save her job, the recruit uncovered damaging facts about Derrick's involvement in a murder." Nelsen dropped his pen on the desk and leaned back.

"Basically," Tim said.

"And as a result of Lukin's ineptness, he was murdered." Nelsen summarized.

Carly's attempted rape and murder being categorized as Lukin's ineptitude made Tim flinch. He blocked the visualization.

"What about you and this news source?" Nelsen walked around to the front of the desk propping his backside on the edge. "Why aren't you and your source considered obstacles?"

"Actually, I've been warned to back off. A cloak-and-dagger guy left an ugly gouge in one of my gurneys with his knife. Regrettably, the video didn't reveal the guy's face."

"Any prints?"

"No." Tim left out he hadn't called PD.

"Did he mention the militia?"

"No," Tim said. "I'd guess he ex-military or law enforcement."

The DA returned to his chair. "What about your source?"

"She hasn't been threatened so far. We don't know why."

"Could your source be playing both sides?"

"No, Mr. Nelsen. She has proven herself to be reliable."

"Is she a close friend of yours, Mr. Price?"

"Please," Madeline said. "I respect your reservation, but in this instance, it is misplaced. If Mr. Price and Ms. Redmund have verified the source's reliability, then all is well."

"That's okay, Madeline," Tim said. "Yes, she is a friend of mine. We dated years ago."

"It could be a problem later on, but for now, I will concede." Nelsen gave a cursory glance to Tim's documentation and slipped it into a manila folder.

The DA looked up at Madeline. "Mrs. Grossman, please give Edgar my regards."

"Thank you, I will. Can I tell him you are seriously considering reopening the case?"

"Of course, I will call Edgar as soon as I can review all the documentation and facts. Thank you and Mr. Price for advising me on these serious matters."

The DA shook hands. "Tim, thank you for your tenacity."

"The research on MSU," Tim said, as he passed his file folder to the DA

Leaving the DA's office, Tim wondered if Nelsen was a good guy or a bad guy. "Madeline, what do you think about the DA?"

"I think DA Nelsen is an opportunist, and he will find in the near future that our side is the most advantageous place to be."

Chapter 29

J.C. wandered through his father's immaculate house. He headed for the kitchen and then to the next likely spot, the garage.

"Dad, are you there? I came to pick up the kids. Dad?"

Jess was in his garage cleaning and sorting his tools when his J.C. raised the garage door letting daylight flood the workshop. "I'm in here. The children are in the backyard."

"How you doing, son?" Jess said.

"Okay, I guess."

J.C. wondered how long his father had lasted, telling his grandchildren stories and listening to their chatter, before he sent them to play in the backyard.

Jess rested a discerning gaze on his son. "You look tired. Have you been working too many extra jobs? That wife of yours is a slave driver for—"

"No, it's not her. I have a lot on my mind lately. That's all."

"You sure Noreen's not on your back?"

"No, Dad, I told you it's not her." He crossed his arms and shoved his hands in his armpits, a remnant gesture from boyhood. He wasn't about to tell his father about Noreen's online affair. "I don't know. Sometimes life, the job, just doesn't make sense."

"God doesn't always explain, son, but He has a plan." His father winked, as if privy to the universe's grand design.

J.C. walked past his father as tears welled in his eyes. For a moment, he pretended to watch the neighbor mowing the grass. J.C. turned and faked a smile. "Dad, I need to get going. Noreen has a honey-do list for me a mile long, and the kids have soccer and dance class."

Relief swept Jess's face as he said, "Sure. Their overnight bags and such are in the hallway. All ready to go. They're cute, but they wear an old guy out."

"Yeah, they're a handful. Thanks for watching them for us last night."

"I enjoyed it." Jess chuckled. "Well, most of it."

J.C. grunted. "Did they behave at the shop?"

"Yeah, they were fine."

"Seen and not heard," J.C. said without covering his derision.

"Yep."

A metallic taste in J.C.'s mouth brought back the pain of his father's huge hands hitting him. Hatred swept over J.C., and then faded. "Yeah, but you've mellowed through the years. Your grandchildren get away with murder. You've never even spanked them." J.C. surveyed his father's full head of gray hair.

"Guess you're right. Since your mom's passing, I'm a little more patient."

For a moment J.C. wished they were closer. He needed to talk about the darkness growing inside him, consuming him, but didn't. Instead, he gathered the children's bags and filled the awkward lull in the conversation with chitchat about the weather and the new barbecue restaurant that opened near his father's barbershop.

After J.C. loaded the bags in the car, the children hugged their grandpa goodbye.

"Love you, Grandpa," Shelsy yelled from an open car window.

Jess waved to the kids as he walked around to the driver's door. "Remember J.C. God tests one's faith through the tough days, not the easy ones. Hang in there, son. It will get better."

At that moment J.C.'s failure hung on his shoulders like a yoke, but he managed to say, "Thanks, Dad." *Maybe God was with his son at the end, proud, but my dad won't be.* It didn't matter anyway. It wasn't God's job to help all the desperate people in the streets. Cops helped them. Nobody except a cop understood the bleakness of the everyday world.

He drove home with the children arguing in the backseat of the minivan. Their faces were distorted in his rearview mirror. The whole world appeared out of focus.

* * *

In front of J.C.'s house, Carly parallel parked her car and discarded her ugly sling. Her left arm felt almost as good as new. Noticing the neighborhood lawns were manicured, Carly hoped that Shelsy and Devon would be home. Their presence would mean she could focus on them for a few minutes and avoid awkward adult conversations.

Noreen was hard to figure. Carly wondered what kind of woman would stay married to a man like J.C.—the kind of woman who hadn't sent a card or come by to see Carly since the shooting. J.C. hadn't put up a front of concern, either. Truth. They'd been out of sync even before the ring deception.

Carly thought about J.C.'s solid reputation. In a way, she felt sorry for him. A man couldn't help that his brother was a murderer. She could understand being torn between blood and the thin blue line.

Grabbing the brown paper bag that contained a bottle of red wine, she opened the car door sliding across the seat while attempting to keep her blue jean skirt from hiking up. The skirt and blue Polo shirt, dressy by Carly's standards, were pulled from the back of her closet this morning.

As Carly rang the doorbell, she speculated again about the real purpose of the invitation. J.C. couldn't be sure that Carly suspected the ring tied Derrick to Terence's murder. They hadn't worked together in weeks. Perhaps J.C. was going to apologize for the ring fiasco. Was the dinner a ploy to find out what she knew? If that were the case, she would soon turn the tables. Carly put on her best poker face as the door swung open.

Noreen welcomed Carly with oven mittens on both hands. "Hi," she said as her flushed face deepened its color. "Oops, I forgot to take these crazy things off. Please come inside."

"Thanks. Your flowers look beautiful in the front yard." Carly said.

"We enjoy them. Please sit down. J.C. is around here somewhere. Probably on that phone again. Would you like a drink?"

Carly handed her the wine. "I'd be glad to open the wine and pour us a glass. How does that sound?"

"Lovely, thank you," Noreen said. Carly followed her hostess into the kitchen. Carly's first attempts to open the wine failed. Finally, she locked the bottle between her knees and pulled the cork out. Red liquid splashed on Carly's shins. Their laughter broke their initial self-consciousness.

Noreen offered a wet towel to Carly, who wiped at her legs. "I'm not known for my social graces, but the food smells delicious, Carly said. "I haven't had a sit-down, home-cooked meal in a while. This is very nice."

"Thanks. Tell me again where your folks live?"

Pouring a glass of wine, Carly said, "They live in Missouri. I don't see them much. They're not thrilled about my choice of careers."

"I see. Well, they'll get used to it. Give them time."

"I hope you're right. How can I help with the meal?"

Noreen handed Carly matches and a beer and nodded toward the dining room. "You can light the candles on the table and deposit J.C.'s beer out there."

"Okay, will do." After lighting the candles, Carly asked, "Where are the children?"

"Devon and Shelsy are visiting Grandpa Jess at his barbershop, and then spending the night at his house. We're free to discuss whatever we want without interruptions. A rare thing in my house, no rug rats."

"I guess a night away from the kids is a welcomed break for you and J.C."

"Yes, I love them dearly, but this mommy's tired of being a constant tutor and taxi service. Sometimes, I feel like I live behind the steering wheel of a car."

J.C. entered the room and planted a kiss on Noreen's forehead. She almost dropped the roasting pan.

"Like I don't drive eight and a half hours a day in a patrol car to make a living," J.C. said. "Modern life requires mobility."

Noreen said, "I guess so. Boy, you're in a chipper mood." There was a strange light in J.C.'s eyes. Noreen appeared entranced by J.C.'s smile and looked disappointed when he broke away to speak to Carly.

"Carly, how have you been?"

"Much better, thanks." Carly sipped her wine.

"I see the arm is on the mend. Guess you can't wait to hit the streets and be off light duty. That desk work is a bitch."

"In a couple of weeks, I'll be released to full duty."

"We can finish up your field training and get you on out there fighting crime. Just cuff 'em and stuff 'em. Right?"

"Huh, right. I'm looking forward to new experiences."

"Who else gets paid to drive fast and carry a gun, besides the pole-leeces?"

"Exactly." Carly took another sip of her wine and studied J.C. *Who was this guy? Where was her grumpy training officer?*

Noreen placed a cheese ball and crackers in front of Carly, who helped herself. The cheese was laced with walnuts.

Carly called over her shoulder, "Yummy cheese ball, Noreen. Did you make it?"

Noreen yelled back, "Sure did. Glad you like it."

J.C. was standing with his hands in his pockets, watching Carly eat. She tilted a cracker at J.C. "Aren't you going to have some?"

"Nope, I'm not a cheese ball fan, but Noreen and the kids love that girly stuff."

Before Carly knew it, a grunt escaped. This was the opinionated Officer Grey she knew.

Noreen saved her by sticking her head in the doorway of the dining room. "J.C., would you carve the roast?"

"Sure thing. I'll be there in a minute. Carly, you take a chair. Hope you like green beans. It's Noreen's special recipe."

"I do but—"

"Good. That will please her," J.C. said.

"J.C.," Noreen yelled.

"Coming, dear." J.C. rolled his eyes. "If a woman's work is never done, you know her husband's busy."

Carly faked a smile.

Within minutes the table overflowed with food. Carly was impressed with Noreen's formal table setting and savored the candlelight's warm glow and the fresh rosemary and thyme dinner roll aroma.

While Carly waited for Noreen, J.C. reappeared wearing a starched denim shirt with the tails out. "She's still fussing with the gravy," he said. "It'll be a few."

Appearing relaxed and open to conversing, J.C. wasn't any better at small talk than Carly. The room remained quiet except for the low hum of the television. After an uncomfortable lull, J.C. said, "I have a new single action Colt revolver from the 1800s in the back. You want to see it before we eat?"

"Sure, where did you buy it?"

"At the last gun show at the fairgrounds." He ushered Carly down the hall. "I got a great deal on it."

Carly couldn't believe J.C. wanted to share anything remotely personal with her, let alone a novel gun. Complimented, she feigned interest and asked the rote questions she had heard in the academy.

The backroom was obviously J.C.'s domain, a workshop and storage area for his guns. Carly was surprised that the unloaded Colt was already out of the display case lying on the workbench and ready for her viewing.

J.C. insisted Carly hold the antique weapon and dry fire it. "It's a real nice gun," Carly said.

J.C. grinned. "Come on, Noreen will be looking for us. We can't let our dinner get cold."

As the two traveled down the hallway, J.C. pointed to the bathroom. "Guess you'll want to wash up before we sit down."

Carly thought she caught amusement in J.C.'s eyes.

"I guess I should," she said examining her hands. "I won't be a minute."

Inside the bathroom she dried her hands with a towel shaking her head. *He seems too cordial. Am I being paranoid? I guess a gal's got a right after a fricking attempt on her life.*

Entering the dining room, Carly saw J.C. serving roast pork and green beans on the last plate. "We always sit in these chairs. This is your spot, Carly." He pointed to the chair opposite the captain's chair.

A groan drifted from the kitchen. "What's wrong?" Carly said.

J.C. stepped to the doorway and peeked. "Nothing. Noreen's stooped over the oven door taking the pie out. It should be good." Smiling, he rubbed his hands together.

After Noreen sat down, Carly waited for grace. Without fanfare, J.C. delivered a tidy blessing, and then Noreen passed the squash casserole. At her childhood home each person at the table had to pray, followed by a lengthy prayer by Carly's father for the good Christians whom God favored with his many blessings. It never made sense to Carly how a loving God could coldly dismiss so many non-Christians from his mercy.

Carly filled her plate with large portions of squash and mashed potatoes. The yeast rolls tasted similar to her mother's recipe; she devoured two of them with the tender pork roast and gravy, and then nibbled a piece of a green bean. They had been sautéed in olive oil.

When J.C. excused himself and went to the bathroom, Noreen went to the kitchen to retrieve cream and sugar for coffee. Carly took the opportunity to place most of her green beans in a napkin.

She couldn't dispel the vivid memory of a vacation a few years ago when she'd almost asphyxiated. A fruit salad with olive oil dressing had caused Carly's tongue to swell and her throat to close.

When J.C. returned Carly thought she saw the outline of a semi automatic in her host's waistband.

"Carly, you don't like the green beans?" J.C. asked.

She couldn't think of a plausible lie. "I love green beans but …. Truthfully, olive oil and I don't mix."

Noreen placed the creamer on the table as she said, "Oh really, it hurts your stomach?"

"No, I have an allergic reaction to olives…to the oil. It's strange, I know." She rushed into an apology. "I bet I'm the only person on God's green earth you know who's allergic to olives."

"Goodness, you should've said something." Noreen wiped her mouth with a napkin.

J.C. added in a strained voice, "Yes, you should've mentioned that when I told you about Noreen's favorite recipe." J.C.'s face was white and his lips thin. He flattened his hands on the table. "Noreen, I think we're ready for the pie."

Noreen started to get up, but sat back down and picked up her fork again. "But I'm not finished eating."

"Noreen, go into the kitchen."

Noreen spun toward Carly. "I'm sorry. I can't explain this. He's been acting peculiar lately."

"Noreen, shut up and do what I say. Now." J.C. banged his fists on the table, rattling the dishes.

Carly felt defenseless. Her off-duty weapon and Mace were in her purse in the foyer. She held Noreen's gaze before the frightened woman left the room.

Keep him talking. He's losing it. Wonder if he's on any meds?

Wild-eyed, J.C. cocked his head as he said, "Why couldn't you go along with the program for once?"

"I didn't know it would upset you. I didn't mean to insult you, but the oil makes me sick."

"Oh, we wouldn't want to make you sick."

Carly blinked. "I should've told you. My fault."

"Yes," he said turning away from the table.

Carly didn't know what to do.

Noreen reappeared, waiting in the doorway for J.C. to calm down. Raising a hand to her throat, Noreen said, "No harm done. We can still have pie and coffee? Talk for a while."

Revealing the extended veins in his neck, J.C. said, "No. I'm afraid we can't."

"I think J.C.'s angry with me, not you, Noreen." Carly nodded. "Maybe, you should let us talk alone."

Noreen vanished into the kitchen again. Carly hoped Noreen was dialing 911.

J.C. shouted, "Noreen, what are you doing?"

"Cutting the pie."

Carly thought she heard Noreen pushing buttons on the phone.

"Noreen get back in here," J.C. yelled as he pulled out the .22 Colt. "Carly wants to apologize and clean her plate. Finish eating your wonderful green beans."

Carly took a deep breath and tried to clear her mind. Adrenaline rushed through her body, freezing the hand holding a fork. *J.C. is trying to poison me, and he has a gun.*

A smirk spread across J.C.'s face.

The doorbell rang and persisted, followed by a knock on the back door. To Carly's astonishment, J.C. said, "Damn it, Noreen, answer the door."

J.C. slid the revolver back in his waistband, as Noreen

said, "It's Rose dropping off a box of clothes for the church fundraiser.

Chapter 30

Derrick and Billie Ray drank coffee in a back booth at the Battleship Café.

"Billie Ray, I told you I didn't want J.C. involved in this thing."

"I had nothing to do with it. Over a week ago our guy was approached by J.C. insisting he be the one to take out the recruit. Apparently, your brother was worried about the effect of reopening the Williams' case. He heard Tim Price and a Jewish biddy from ADL had gone to see the DA trying to do just that."

"Damn it! J.C.'s always trying to fix things. How'd he know your guy?"

Billie Ray surveyed the room. The restaurant was packed with loud tourists; nobody seemed to notice them. "I don't know. He's law enforcement. Maybe he has connections. But it's not surprising he's concerned. He is your older brother."

"Shit." Derrick emptied his cup. "Last night Rose walked into J.C.'s house, right in the middle of a fracas over green beans. What the hell! When my brother started to lose it, Rose and Redmund hightailed it out of there."

Billie Ray shook his head.

"Now Rose is scared and more suspicious than ever, Derrick said. "She knows I'm mixed up in something. If she backs Redmund's story that J.C. went berserk, it won't be good."

"Calm down, Derrick. Redmund doesn't have any way to prove J.C. added a little something extra to her olive oil. There's no reason for Rose to tie you to any of this or Williams. No harm, no foul."

"Except they aren't stupid, and Rose knows you're my major contributor by way of Henry Pullman's wife."

"Your campaign manager's wife?"

"Yes."

"Still, even if Rose knew everything, she would be a loyal wife. Right?" Billie Ray said, throwing a dollar tip on the table.

Derrick stood up. "Lately, I just don't know."

* * *

"Tim, I have another favor to ask," Carly said sitting cross-legged on her couch with the phone cradled against her ear.

"Okay. For you anything. My computer has booted up."

"Good to know. This requires using your professional contacts."

"All right, I'll pull in a few you-owe-mes."

"I need a cloth napkin analyzed." She knew without forensic testing that the napkin contained poison, but nobody, except her friends, would take Carly seriously. At the Greys' house, the officers had taken J.C.'s word right down the line and attributed the 911 calls to hysterical women.

"A napkin?"

"Yes, from J.C.'s house. It's filled with green beans."

"First, explain why you were at the Greys' house, for Godsake?"

"Because they asked me and because I thought I could pump J.C. for information while I ate a home-cooked meal. Got more than I bargained for."

"Excuse me," he said, "but those reasons sound ridiculous. Crazy."

"In hindsight, I agree. It's a long story." Carly took a deep breath. "You see, I'm allergic to olives and olive oil so I couldn't eat the green beans."

"So you didn't eat the green beans and you're obviously fine. So why do I need to test the contents of the napkin? What am I missing here?"

"Poison."

"Poison?" Tim said, "For the love of God—"

"Yes. Calm down." Carly said. "Of course, J.C. hoped I'd be dead by now but—"

"I'll punch the living hell—"

"Don't, Tim. I'm fine."

"Let's see. I'm a little fuzzy on the details, but you did say dead as in *finito*? When Carly didn't answer, Tim sighed as he said, "Why do you suspect he tried to poison you?"

"Because he made a federal case about me not eating the green beans, plus the way he talked to Noreen. He frightened her. I'm sure Noreen didn't know a thing about J.C.'s plan. She did call 911."

"When?"

Carly changed the phone to the other ear. "After J.C. sent Noreen into the kitchen, or I did." Carly sighed. "It doesn't matter, but Noreen lied for J.C."

Tim exhaled deeply. "This whole thing makes no sense."

"Just bare with me. The sadistic bastard put something in the beans, and he was packing. But Rose rang the doorbell and—"

"Rose?"

"Rose Grey, Derrick's wife—Noreen's sister-in-law—interrupted dinner with a box of clothes for a fundraiser, inadvertently, saving all our skins. Noreen wouldn't leave, but Rose and I got out and called 911 again. When the brothers in blue arrived, Noreen acted like nothing happened, just a misdial on her part.

"The officers took J.C.'s word that everything was okay and left. Now they've got another thing to gossip about. Crazy Carly."

"Fuck that," Tim said, and then added, "Sorry. But I have a right to get pissed when my girl, my friend, almost gets killed. Again."

"Tim, it's all under control for now."

"Why are you so reckless? And I seriously doubt the 'under control' part."

"You're zeroing in on the wrong things."

"Thank God, J.C. didn't do his homework about your allergy."

"Although he was genuinely surprised about it," Carly said. "I'd bet my next paycheck someone else is behind this plan. So, do you have a friend who can discreetly run a toxicology screen on the green beans?"

"Yes, I do."

"I don't know exactly what we're looking for."

"We'll screen it for trace poison."

"Tim, another thing—I can't prove it, but I think someone has been watching me."

"You mean as in following you around? Carly, this is serious."

"You think? Listen. Besides the eerie feeling of being watched, somebody was inside my loft last week. Nothing was taken, but the piece of paper I leave in the door jamb was on the floor when I arrived home from work."

"You leave your doors rigged for intruders?"

"Yeah, stop laughing. I've been doing that since J.C. lied to the brass about the high school ring."

"You cops are too weird. I bet you're not half as scared that someone is watching you or still trying to kill you, as you are about losing your job."

"Listen. One of my throw rugs was also moved. I always keep it lined up with a specific kitchen tile."

"Although I'm glad you're safe, can you say "compulsive disorder?'"

"Not important."

Tim shrugged. "True. Do you think it was J.C. who searched your apartment?"

"No, I think someone a hell of a lot smarter than J.C. is watching me and deliberately left signs to rattle me. Besides, J.C. lost his shit last night. I'm not a shrink, but I'd say he jumped off the deep end, hit bottom, and didn't come up whole."

"Damn, you still haven't told me all of it. Have you?" Tim said.

"Almost. Can you drop by my house to get the napkin? I need to change clothes. Got an appointment I can't miss."

Tim sighed. "I can be there in about twenty, but I don't have to like it."

* * *

Derrick fell asleep unaware of Rose's insomnia. She lay staring into the darkness. The ominous scene at J.C.'s house last night made no sense. Noreen and Carly's stories didn't add up. The women were shaken, frightened, and J.C. was furious. If he harbored resentment over the ring mishap, it was understandable, but to hurt Carly? Extreme. Carly had to be wrong.

Rose repositioned her head on a pillow and listed all the details she could remember. A memory surfaced. She had read about the missing ring in the newspaper. The initials were TWW for Terence Washington Williams, the football star, the same teenager Derrick admitted beating up years ago. Then Terence went missing.

Rose threw back the quilt. J.C. was trying to protect Derrick by hiding the ring. *Carly Redmund hadn't taken the ring after all.* Rose couldn't breathe.

Covering her slip with a robe, she ran downstairs. She needed a cigarette and some strong coffee. Her hands were shaking by the time she opened the French doors to the deck. The warm breeze rippled her robe. She smoked, gazed up at the night sky, and let the tears flow. She'd been so stupid. Too happy to care. She didn't want to face the truth, but there it was.

Derrick hadn't just beaten Terence. He'd killed him. What other inconsistencies had she dismissed? Had he hired Lukin to maul Carly Redmund?

As certainty struck home, she spilled her coffee, lunged for the railing, and vomited her supper.

* * *

Stewart circled Marci's cluttered cubicle. "Where have you been?"

"I took a few days of R&R. You miss me?" Marci said.

"Sure, like my kid sister coming along on my first car date."

"Ouch."

Stewart grinned at Marci. "Your friend, Carly, left a stack of messages. Check with reception. They know better than to leave anything on your desk. The black hole."

She quit typing and looked at him. "Thanks, will do. You know I couldn't function without you, Stewie. Don't be miffed."

He shrugged. "Then where did you go?"

"Can't tell you. As Dugan might say, 'I'd have to kill ya.'"

"In other words, none of my beeswax."

"Correctamundo!" Marci chuckled.

Another computer geek strolled by Marci's cubicle and whispered, "Better get back to work. The boss's in a mean mood today."

Marci yanked on Stewart's shirt sleeve as he started to leave. "Don't mind him. How's your cyberspace romance?"

"Pretty good, except I found out she's married—which is fine. Well, not fine, but I've known all along. Anyway, I can deal with it, but she's married to a cop."

"Don't like the sound of that. Not anybody we know?"

"Huh."

"What do you mean?"

"I mean I'm ninety-nine percent sure my lady friend is married to Officer J.C. Grey."

Pushing back her chair, Marci stood up. "Shitting unbelievable. No way she said."

Stewart turned pale and said, "Freaky, huh? What are the probabilities?"

Now circling Stewart, Marci said, "I can tell you this. It's highly probable he'll cut your balls off." Tortoise-like, Stewart tucked his neck into his shoulders, as Marci added, "How'd you find out?"

"When we were playing *Masterpiece Theater* at Pancake House, I overheard J.C. call his wife by the name, Noreen."

"And."

"I hacked into the county records, and I already knew she lived in Mobile with her husband and two children. Names of the children are Shelsy and Devon. Right?"

"I think Carly mentioned those names." Marci shook her head. "You're in deep doo-doo here."

He tried to smile, but the muscles in his face twitched as he sank in Marci's chair. "To make matters worse, I'm worried about Noreen's safety. She told me her husband flipped out yesterday. Something about a dinner guest refusing to eat something."

Marci leaned over Stewart. "The wife needs to get out while the getting's good."

"Yeah, but she can't visit her artist friend, John, in New York. I'm John."

"You," Marci laughed. "Who would've guessed? Our very own gigolo." She looked Stewart up and down. "You have a Superman body you're hiding, too?"

"No. Some people find my brain sexy."

"Take my advice. Just throw on a pair of tight-ass Levi's if you ever meet her face to face."

"Marci, you're a crude—"

"Only telling it like it is, dearie," she said.

Stewart slumped down in the chair.

"I'm sorry, Stewey. We'll get you out of this thing alive. I promise. Maybe a little maimed, though."

"Thanks."

Marci grabbed the phone. "I need to meet Noreen. I've got an idea how we can protect your friend and use her to help Carly all at the same time."

* * *

"I appreciate your meeting me on such short notice," Rose said.

Carly had barely made the dinner engagement, but she said, "No problem. I'm curious about the urgency of your phone call."

WELL OF RAGE

"I don't know how to say this." Rose put down her menu. "As you know, J.C. is my brother-in-law, and Derrick is my husband."

"Yes, I know." Carly waited.

"What happened at J.C. and Noreen's house focused my attention to some details I'd managed to avoid examining...before."

The waitress interrupted them. The chic trendy restaurant and the high-priced chef's salad made Carly uncomfortable. It seemed odd Rose picked this noisy place to meet. After placing the order, Carly waved at a child at the next table giving Rose time to gather her thoughts.

"My husband and I have always been close, and our marriage has been a happy one. Until recently...." Rose's voice cracked.

Carly finished her sentence, "Until he and Billie Ray Cofer became campaign buddies. Correct?"

"Yes. How did you know?"

"When you're being accused of something you didn't do, you become suspicious and start digging. One thing led to another, and I uncovered your husband's financial arrangement with Cofer."

Rose's face flushed as the waitress placed rolls and house salads on the table. When the waitress departed, Rose said, "You're quite the detective."

"Not really. I had help from a couple of buddies."

"It's always good to have supportive friends." Rose fiddled with her salad and nibbled a leaf.

"Yes, it is. What are you trying to say, Rose?"

"I feel disloyal to my husband, talking like this, but...if what I think is true, then the man I married is not, or never was ...."

"Facing the truth about someone isn't easy," Carly said, forcing a smile. "You know about the ring, don't you?"

Rose slipped her hair behind her ears, and then fumbled in her purse for a Kleenex. "Yes, I know the high school ring belonged to the Williams's boy. Also the bones in Deeter's well." She glanced at her wedding band and blurted out, "You didn't misplace the ring. J.C. took it, didn't he? To protect Derrick."

"That's how I figure it."

Rose hesitated. "It must be true, then, Derrick...Terence's death?"

Carly nodded. "Seems like a solid theory."

Rose shook her head. "This whole thing is disturbing. Maybe, it was accidental." She dabbed her eyes, looked down at the tablecloth. "But the dinner at J.C.'s house doesn't make sense. He tried to poison you?"

Carly nodded. "The green beans contained a Rosary pea, a crab's eye. The green pods are deadly."

Rose gasped. "Are you sure?"

"Yes, the lab report confirmed it. J.C. made a big deal about the green beans. Thank God, I'd hidden most of them in my napkin."

"Was Noreen involved?"

"Judging from her reaction, I don't think so." Carly studied Rose's puzzled expression.

"I still don't get it. Did the green beans taste bad? Why did you put them in your napkin?"

"I'm allergic to olive oil. The beans were sautéed in it. Because J.C. made a big deal about it being Noreen's special dish, I didn't want to hurt her feelings. So, I sneaked the beans into my napkin when they were out of the room."

"You're telling me your allergy saved your life?"

"That and your persistent doorbell ringing. I haven't had a chance to thank you. Your entrance allowed me to escape without further complications."

"Thank Molly Perkins, the church fundraiser coordinator. Talk about persistent." Rose sighed. "Life is absurd."

"And sometimes dangerous," Carly said, watching Rose's smile fade. "I'm sure J.C. intended for me to ingest the poison. He had a gun on him, too."

"What will I do if Derrick is mixed up in all this mess? If he knew about Lukin or J.C.? The attempts on your life? Carly, what will happen to my family?"

Carly reached across the table and patted Rose's hand. "I'm sorry, but I think you already know the answers to your questions or you wouldn't be here."

"God help me. I do."

Chapter 31

From his living room widow, J.C. watched Derrick drive away. *I love you, brother.*

J.C. couldn't bear the thought of being arrested in his house, in front of his children, or being a former cop in jail. He felt nauseated. Walking to the back room, he unlocked his gun cabinet. He methodically oiled his favorite .22 Smith and Wesson. Breaking the gun down and touching the blue steel parts steadied his hands. After reassembling the gun, he shoved the magazine in the butt of the gun. "Locked and loaded," he said as he pulled the action back and chambered a round. "Only, one more thing to do."

Laying the gun on the workbench, he flipped over a practice target on the workbench and wrote:

Dear Derrick,
The next few weeks will be bad. Hang tough, my brother. I'm sorry about the problems caused by the bones being found at the Deeter place. I shot Terence Washington. Why I did dies with me. You aren't to blame for any of this mess. I'm sorry I never told you. Take care of Shelsy and Devon for me. Make them grow strong and proud. I love you. Forgive me.

As J.C. signed and dated the note, the front door slammed followed by Noreen's high heel sandals clomping down the hallway toward the bedroom.

My kids deserve better than Noreen, the whore. Rage

sharpened his focus. He wrapped his fist around the handle of the .22 and walked to the bedroom.

Throwing garments everywhere, Noreen searched through her lingerie drawer.

"You looking for the fifteen hundred you stashed in there?" he said, stepping closer. "I put the cash in the bank for the children. Where are the children?"

"Oh, you surprised me. The children are fine. They're with mom. Where's your truck, hon? It isn't parked in the driveway."

"Very observant for a gal who never knew her husband was checking her emails to lover boy, John."

"Wait a minute. J.C. I never met him. It was a harmless flirtation on the computer." Noreen started to back away.

J.C. cradled the butt of the gun in his left hand in a combat stance, the barrel pointed at Noreen's chest. "Unfaithful slut. Really, I don't give a goddamn. But you fucked with the one rule that a police officer's wife should never break: what occurs in-house, stays in-house. You shared too much information about me, about my brother, with Johnnie boy."

"I don't know what you mean. J.C. You know I love you."

"Bullshit. John better be an artist living in New York."

"J.C. don't hurt him. He has nothing to do with our lives."

J.C. snorted. "Your first concern is *him*, not your children. You really aren't worth a damn, Noreen. You're right about one thing. Dickhead won't be part of our lives 'cause it's all ending—today—in our own cozy bedroom."

"J.C., this is crazy."

He blocked the doorway. Trapped, Noreen ran into the master bath and locked the door. She screamed when J.C.

kicked the door off the hinges and begged before J.C. shot her once in the forehead, once in the heart.

J.C. turned Noreen over and knelt close to her ear. "See you in hell, hon."

He jammed the .22 under his chin and pulled the trigger.

* * *

Doing her best to contain her fears, Carly entered Calpes behind Agent Dugan.

The FBI and Warner County PD joint task force were in full paramilitary gear. To prevent crossfire mishaps, Alpha team did the initial entry, handcuffing Billie Ray and his men at the bar, while Bravo team covered the rear, securing the perimeter.

Carly glanced at Billie Ray, handcuffed and still jawing at an FBI agent, before she moved, heart pounding, with the rest of Bravo team to complete the building sweep. Her attention narrowed as she moved sideways down the hallway, her duty weapon drawn.

Adrenaline and testosterone a volatile combination, Carly heard men behind her shuffling, cussing, and groaning. Someone yelled, "Dirt bag," followed by a cracking sound.

Settle down. Checking herself, Carly controlled her breathing and tried to anticipate where a man would hide in the bathroom.

Dugan broke her concentration. "Redmund, listen to the radio or stand down. One bad guy's still missing."

Carly nodded, surprised that she had blocked out radio traffic completely. Passing Dugan and advancing toward the men's bathroom, she noted the agent enter the kitchen with another officer at his heels. As Carly opened the restroom door with her foot, she swung low from left to right, checking behind the door. The stench of urine hit her nostrils. No sound or movement. She checked the stalls, keeping low, and then doubled back. Nothing appeared out of place. A graffiti-covered palace.

As she kicked the first stall door, Dave Jordan, hiding behind a ceiling panel, dropped down behind Carly. She heard the rack of a shotgun at the same moment Dugan entered the bathroom and yelled, "Gun."

"Not going to prison," Jordan declared as Carly whipped around.

She shot twice without aiming. One bullet hit Jordan's gut; the other took out a lung. For an elongated second they stared at each other. As Jordan tried to make his arm move and swing the shotgun around, Carly pulled the trigger again.

Before Dugan's .9 mm shots registered, Carly had already put a bullet in Jordan's brain.

* * *

Mrs. Williams sat in an antique rocking chair, humming a lullaby her great-grandmother had sung to her. Her sweet Terence could finally be buried in their family plot, and his spirit rest with his ancestors. A newspaper lay in her lap.

Marci Eplund's *Tribune* headline read, "Hate Crime Solved: Local Politician Confesses to Beating an African-American Teenager." Mrs. Williams reread the article for the third time.

On Friday afternoon mayoral candidate Derrick Grey walked into the Warner County Police headquarters in downtown Mobile and confessed. Distraught after local detectives delivered the news of his brother's death, Mr. Grey shocked the community by incriminating himself in the murder of an African-American teenager, Terence Washington Williams.

Grey admitted to beating Terence Washington Williams unconscious, but denied further involvement.

Terence, a local football legend, has been missing since 1974. In early March, his skeletal remains were found in a well outside of town on the Jack Deeter farm. The farm is currently owned by MSU Corporation, a militia stronghold. It is possible that Terence's murder was fueled by the furor over the integration of public schools in the early seventies.

Autopsy results indicated Terence was beaten and shot before being thrown in the well. Major Hadley, of Warner County Homicide Division, declined to speculate whether the DA would charge the Superintendent of Schools with murder or a lesser crime.

The suspect's brother, J.C. Grey, a veteran of the Warner County Police Department, committed suicide after shooting his wife, Noreen, in their home Thursday. Officer Grey, a Vietnam veteran, left a written confession indicating that he shot Terence without his brother's knowledge.

Mary Williams, Terence's mother, told this reporter, "My son's name, Terence Washington Williams, will be heard and remembered. The city's administrators must face their bigotry and be held accountable. One of their chosen officials, Derrick Grey, their Superintendent of Schools, hid behind their protection all these years. He murdered my son in cold blood. Cut him down in the prime of his life. The punishment can't be harsh enough to equal the pain he has caused. The ADL, The Southern Poverty Law Center, and I will be watching closely to see how the DA and the police department handle this white man's prosecution."

Mary smiled. Terence's killer and the main co-conspirator were in jail or dead. The Grey family destroyed.

Justice came in many forms.

* * *

Carly, Tim, and Marci had toasted their triumph with draft beers at Calpes before they drove to Mary Williams's bed and breakfast. As they strolled up the front walk to Mary's house, Carly felt something close to contentment and noticed the breeze making the tree leaves dance.

Mrs. Williams opened the door, smiling. "The crime fighting trio. Please come inside."

"We met at the hospital," Tim said.

"Yes, of course. Welcome, Tim."

Tim scanned the foyer. "Your house is exquisite, Mrs. Williams."

Shaking hands, Mary said, "Thank you, Tim. I've tried to restore the Painted Lady to her original beauty."

"I'd say you've succeeded."

Mary ushered them into the dining room, wherein a crystal chandelier lit the room.

Tim pulled a chair out for Mrs. Williams at the head of the table covered by a white lace tablecloth, a backdrop for a vase of pink roses. While the group chatted, Chef Cato served white wine, vichyssoise, beet and walnut salad, and roasted chicken.

Dinner completed, they adjourned to the screened sitting porch and savored hot mint tea, cheese, and fresh fruit. Tim kept talking about the care of roses, but Carly noticed no one broached the subject of the arrest.

Finally, Mrs. Williams said, "Tim, what can you tell me about my son's murder that Carly and Marci have not?"

"Well, I think you know almost everything. Apparently, J.C. was home on leave from Vietnam at the time of the fight. All these years, nobody, except Jack, knew that J.C. showed up at the Deeter farm. If you believe Jack's story, he left Terence alive with J.C. The .22 was traced back to one of J.C.'s buddies who died in Nam. His wife gave J.C. the gun at the soldier's wake."

Mrs. Williams poured another cup of tea from a Blue Willow tea pot. Her hands were shaking.

Tim cleared his throat. "After Lukin's murder in Mississippi, Carly spoke with his widow, Elma Hall. Did you know she had a weird conversation with a man we suspect was the Georgia farmer? He came to Elma's job, the hotel, a couple of days before Lukin's murder."

Mrs. Williams leaned forward in the wicker chair. "Yes, I have met Elma, a sweet, ambitious young woman. We have spoken about her attending night classes and possibly working here during the day."

Carly wiped her mouth with a linen napkin. "That would be a wonderful opportunity for her. I know she wants to study accounting."

Tim nodded in admiration. "What no one saw coming was J.C. killing himself when he failed to poison Carly. We still don't know the identity of the Georgia farmer who most likely killed Lukin. He left only some drug trace evidence in Mississippi. If he's the guy who entered the morgue and tried to intimidate me, he's retired FBI agent, Ned Caldwell. Who by the way, has disappeared off the face of the earth.

"I guess Carly has bored you with the extensive details of the FBI raid on Calpes, where she put her life and career on the line, for what I don't know."

Carly readjusted her skirt over her knees, and then said, "It wasn't that dangerous. Besides, the department wouldn't have sanctioned my cooperation with the Bureau. And now after the fact, it's no big deal. As they say, 'Better to beg for forgiveness, than ask for permission.' Besides, it may have won me some "atta girl" spunky points with the uniform guys."

"Or maybe with Agent Dugan," Tim added.

Carly looked at Mary. "It was odd, but about the same time we were arresting the bad guys at Calpes, J.C. was killing Noreen and himself. By the way, Tim's autopsy revealed Dave Jordan had terminal bladder cancer. Six months to live. Maybe, he wanted suicide by cop." She shrugged. "Who knows what was in his mind."

Silence fell as the somber events sank in.

Marci broke the lull in the conversation. "Poor Stewart took an extended vacation from the paper. He's devastated." Marci looked at Mary. "Stewart's my research assistant and...the short version is he had an online affair with Noreen."

"Oh, dear," Mary said.

Carly put down her fork. "I should have anticipate, the murder, the suicide. In hindsight, I screwed up."

"No. You're no more responsible than I," said Marci. "I mean I dropped Noreen and the kids off at her mother's. I have no idea why she went back. I shouldn't have played social worker."

"We did what we could under the circumstances," Tim said.

"I agree with this wise young man," Mary said. "All of you did your best."

Carly smiled. "On the bright side, I've been exonerated. Still, the brass hates me. I haven't decided what to do. Stay or leave the department." She looked down before continuing. "Rose made Derrick turn himself in. I'm not sure how. She did mention Derrick left an incriminating paper trail that she found. Of course, Derrick knew that J.C. took the ring. But he still contends that he doesn't know what happened to Terence after everyone left the high school grounds. Jack Deeter has lawyered up. Big-time, expensive lawyer."

Marci said, "More than likely, they'll charge Derrick with first degree manslaughter for Terence's beating—let sleeping dogs lie and accept J.C.'s suicide note as a dying declaration. Case closed."

Mary frowned. "No. It's not over. There will be many emotions unleashed in a trial like this one, but the community will suffer through it and be better off." She sighed and folded her hands in her lap. "Whether Derrick is tried and convicted of murder or not, his life has been ruined by his own past deeds. Already, the community has been forced to acknowledge Terence's death and the hideous remnants of the KKK. Finally, I can start to move on."

She sipped her tea as a dark shadow seemed to pass. "I'll never understand why they had to pick *my* son." Mary gazed outside in the direction of the birch tree.

Carly touched Mary's arm.

"I hope they don't plea bargain the bastard," Marci said.

Mary fought back tears.

"Do you like Conrad Aiken's work?" Carly asked.

Mary nodded.

Carly closed her eyes. "There's a poem in *Time and Rock* about violent death. Let me see:"

> O patience, let us be patient and discern
> In this lost leaf, all that can be discerned;
> and let us learn, from this sad violence learn,
> all that in midst of violence can be learned.

WELL OF RAGE

Carly took a deep breath. "I know I've learned a great deal about myself and human nature," she said, feeling an internal shift as she forgave herself for her past mistakes. "Thank goodness for friends and family."

Marci and Tim exchanged a knowing glance.

Mary smiled and dabbed at her eyes with her napkin. "You'll have to afford me the sympathy I cannot give. I'll never be the same. They robbed me. My son died because of the color of his skin. Forgiveness is simply beyond me."

Carly understood. There it was: some sins were unforgiveable.

* * *

Pensive, the three friends rode in silence back to Carly's loft. As they had left, Carly had noticed Mary's weariness. She would visit Mary soon. From the backseat Carly found comfort in looking at the houses lining her street and at Marci's competent driving. She patted Tim's shoulder as she said, "Even with its sadness, this is a great day to be alive. For healing. Thanks for being there for me. You're both the best."

Marci and Tim smiled.

"No problem, girlfriend," Marci said, parking the car. "I haven't told you I never knew my mom…that can wait."

Stepping from car, Carly asked, "What did you say? What's going on? You guys look like you swallowed canaries."

Tim turned Carly around as Marci said, "That R&R I took. Well… I hope you don't mind I went to Missouri to see your folks."

Carly's heart skipped a beat. Her mother stood on Harold's front porch.

About the author

Lynn Hesse, first-place winner in the 2015 Oak Tree Press Writing Contest, Cop Tales, launched her award-winning debut novel, *Well of Rage*, at the 2016 Decatur Book Festival. The novel is based on her law enforcement experience and centers on how "isms" separate us.

Her short story "Murder: Food For Thought" was published in a 2009 anthology by Wising Up Press and was adapted into the play *We Hunt Our Young*, produced at Core Studio Field Showcase, Emory University, and Core Studio Luncheon Time Series, 2011.

Lynn's short play *Bam, Karma* was produced through Cafe Medusa at Seven Stages Theatre in Atlanta in 2012 and was performed in 2013 in conjunction with *Material Witness*, an art exhibition at Agnes Scott College sponsored by the Georgia chapter of the Women's Caucus for Art.

In 2015, Lynn taught a creative writing course for women at Lee Arrendale Prison in Alto, Georgia. Her fiction and short plays center on reframing traumatic events and exploring the role that forgiveness plays in the healing process. A personal interview focused on Lynn's role as a police officer, as exemplified in the video *Blue Steel*, is available in the Women's Studies Archives, The Second Feminist Movement, at Georgia State University.

Lynn belongs to the following organizations: Atlanta Writers Club, Georgia Writers Association, International Women's Writing Guild, Public Safety Writers Association,

International Association of Women Police, Sacred Dance Guild, Dancing Flowers for Peace, Alternate Roots, Atlanta InterPlay-SoulPrint Players, and Beacon Dance.

Made in the USA
Lexington, KY
16 June 2018